Roses...love...dealing with either exacted a price

Bleeding fingers or bleeding hearts, you paid. Ginna brought the rose to her nose. The dewy softness of the petals caressed her skin, and the sweet tea smell assaulted her nostrils. The pinprick of the thorn was forgotten in her enjoyment of the flower, just as the pain of failure was forgotten in the joy and healing power of love.

She knew then that she had to accept what Ryan offered. She knew that if she went back to Chicago and her stable, uneventful life she would spend the next eight years just as she had the last eight—creating beauty and happiness for others instead of herself. And she knew without a doubt that the shop wouldn't be a panacea for her heartache this time. This time it would only be a place filled with roses and regrets, because she hadn't tried harder to create that happiness and beauty in her own life.

Dear Reader,

Spellbinders! That's what we're striving for. The editors at Silhouette are determined to capture your imagination and win your heart with every single book we publish. Each month, six Special Editions are chosen with *you* in mind.

Our authors are our inspiration. Writers such as Nora Roberts, Tracy Sinclair, Kathleen Eagle, Carole Halston and Linda Howard—to name but a few—are masters at creating endearing characters and heartrending love stories. Their characters are everyday people—just like you and me—whose lives have been touched by love, whose dream and desire suddenly comes true!

So find a cozy, quiet place to read, and create your own special moment with a Silhouette Special Edition.

Sincerely,

Rosalind Noonan
Senior Editor
SILHOUETTE BOOKS

BAY MATTHEWS
Roses and Regrets

Silhouette Special Edition

Published by Silhouette Books New York

America's Publisher of Contemporary Romance

For Sandra—friend, partner,
"sister." Thanks for listening,
sharing, caring and for all the
laughter. My life has been richer
for knowing you. Happy Birthday!!

A special thanks to Shreveport
pilot Terry Rogers, who helped
me get the plane back safely
on the ground.

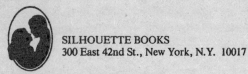

SILHOUETTE BOOKS
300 East 42nd St., New York, N.Y. 10017

Copyright © 1986 by Penny Richards

ISBN: 0-373-09347-0

First Silhouette Books printing November 1986

America's Publisher of Contemporary Romance

Printed in the U.S.A.

BAY MATTHEWS

of Haughton, Louisiana, descibes herself as a dreamer and an incurable romantic. Married at an early age to her high school sweetheart, she claims she grew up with her three children. Now that only the youngest is at home, writing romances adds a new dimension to the already exciting life she leads on her husband's Thoroughbred farm.

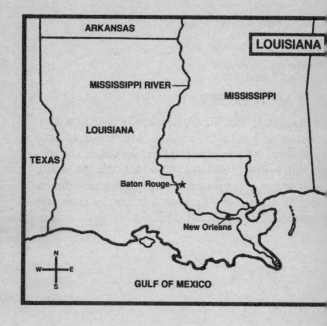

Chapter One

Ginna LeGrand's rose-tipped finger—a finger that trembled only slightly—punched out the long-distance telephone number that came readily to mind even though she seldom called it. She glanced at the clock on the wall and tried to remember if her ex-husband would even be at the barn at this hour. Then all too clearly, she recalled that once he left the house in the morning there was no telling where he would be at any given hour...or when he would return. Let him be there! she thought on a wave of despair. Let me get this over with!

Her silent prayer must have been heard because the phone was answered on the third ring. The man's voice, low and husky, with just a remnant of South Louisiana patois lingering after so many years, fell on her ears with the welcome of ice water to a parched throat. "Catalpa Farm. Ryan LeGrand speaking."

She drew in a deep, fortifying breath. "Ryan? This is Ginna."

The silence at the other end of the hundreds of miles of telephone cable separating her Chicago home from his Louisiana-based thoroughbred farm was almost tangible. When he spoke again his voice lacked the warmth it had held only moments before. "What is it, Ginna? Is Erin all right?"

Erin. The reason for the call. What would he say when she told him... The lapse between his question and her answer must have been longer than she thought, because his voice came impatiently again. "Ginna! Are you there?"

"I—yes, I'm here," she stuttered. She gripped the beige plastic receiver tightly and plunged. "Actually, Erin is the reason I'm calling."

"She's okay, isn't she?"

His voice, so cool only moments before, now held an unmistakable note of anxiety. Whatever else he was, Ginna thought grudgingly, Ryan LeGrand was a good father, and he loved their daughter dearly.

"She's fine," she hastened to assure him.

"Then what is it?"

Her lashes dropped as if by closing her eyes she could block out the whole problem. "She found our wedding certificate."

"So?" he said shortly, uncomprehendingly.

"So?" Ginna snapped, her eyes flying open. "So she's a smart child, Ryan. She can add, and she's had sex education! She figured out we'd only been married seven months when she was born!"

"Since you never bother to call unless there's a problem, I gather she didn't take it too well." Sarcasm and something more laced his voice. It took her a minute to place the tonal qualities. Accusation.

As true as his statement was, it still hurt. A part of her wondered why he should still have this incredible power to hurt her after such a long time. And some inherent knowledge told her that delving into the reasons would only cause more pain. She bristled with indignation that Ryan should accuse her of something he was guilty of himself. Forcing a short, saccharine-sweet laugh, she quipped, "Perceptive, as always, Ryan."

"Sarcasm never did become you, babe," he replied with a sigh of disgust. "Just tell me what the sweet hell is going on."

Her pulse raced at the casual endearment, even though it reeked with insincerity. Where should she begin? With the fact that their once amiable fifteen-year-old was now unruly and defiant? With—

"Look, this is costing you money," he said sharply. "Why don't you stop trying to figure out how to whitewash whatever is going on and just tell me?"

"Fine," she agreed frostily. "You want it straight? I'll give it to you straight. She's trying to destroy me."

Ryan laughed mockingly. "Destroy you? You're as melodramatic as ever, Ginna."

Fury at the insouciance of his attitude raged through her. "Yes, destroy me! Her grades have fallen, she's been cutting class at school and her whole attitude toward me and anything I say is just short of total mutiny."

"That isn't like Erin," he said, a new, more serious note entering his voice at the apparent dismay in hers. "Have you talked to her?"

"Have I talked to her?" Ginna screeched. "Of course I've talked to her!"

"Okay, okay...simmer down," he said in a soothing voice. "Just tell me."

Ginna collapsed into the splitting vinyl chair behind her desk, her posture proof of her defeat. "I've tried to talk to her. She doesn't listen."

"And you want me to have a go at trying to make her see some sense?"

Tears of weariness and self-pity pricked beneath her eyelids. Erin had always listened to Ryan. "Please."

"What do you think I can say that you haven't?"

A disheartened shrug he couldn't see lifted her shoulders. "Explain things to her."

His laughter was soft, almost melodic, yet held an undisguised bitterness. "Explain? What do you want me to explain to her, Ginna? That we made it in the back seat of my Chevy—not just once, but several times?"

The unvarnished truth of his words hit Ginna like the slap of a cold, wet washcloth, rendering her silent except for a sharp gasp of surprise. Ryan had often yelled and cursed during their fights, but she couldn't dredge up one memory of his ever being deliberately hurting and cruel. Obviously the eight years they'd been apart had change them both drastically. She blinked back the tears of humiliation and pain swimming in her amber-colored eyes and struggled to find her voice around the obstruction clogging her throat, praying she could hold a complete breakdown at bay.

"No!" she said in hardly more than an anguished whisper. "You tell her how much we loved each other and how there was no one else in the world for either of us! You tell her we tried to wait. Tell her that her birth was a joy and that we loved and wanted her even though we did have to get married. And you tell her we still love her, even though the love we felt for each other died because we couldn't figure out how to keep it alive!''

Another silence stretched between them. She wasn't even aware that she'd lost her battle with the tears until she found herself wiping at them with trembling fingers.

Finally Ryan spoke, his words low as he apologized. ''I'm sorry. You're right. It was exactly as you said.'' She heard him sigh and could almost see him raking his hand through the thick darkness of his hair. ''She still wants to come for the summer, doesn't she?''

Ginna sniffed. ''I don't know. I think so.''

''Does she know you've told me about all the trouble she's been getting into?''

''She knew I hadn't said anything before, but after yesterday, I think she knew I'd call.''

''What happened yesterday?''

''She got expelled this last week of school for skipping Geometry.''

Ryan swore.

''Oh, Ryan, you've got to help me! I just can't do it by myself anymore,'' she said, her spur-of-the-moment confession surprising them both. ''Don't turn your back on us...please.''

''Did I ever?'' he asked, his words a soft rumble, their meaning causing a crimson blush to stain her already tear-flushed cheeks.

''No,'' she admitted softly. ''You never did.''

''Put her on the plane Wednesday, just as we planned,'' he told her suddenly, brusquely, his voice losing its momentary softness.

"All right."

"And I want you to come with her," he added.

"Come with her! But I can't! I have a business to run."

"So, what's more important, Ginna? Your flower business or our daughter?"

"Erin, of course, but I just can't take off now. It's June and I have twenty weddings..."

"This is something we're in together. She has to hear both sides if we want to make her understand. Get Kay to come and fill in a few days," he ordered in the no-nonsense tone she remembered so clearly. "I'll meet you at the airport."

"Ry-yan!" she cried, furious that he was dictating orders and expected her to go along with them willy-nilly. "I can't..." she began, only to hear the receiver click ever so softly in her ear.

The heat of anger drying her tears, Ginna slammed her receiver down. He hadn't changed. He would never change. She'd be darned if she'd go... Then she remembered the crushing pain and disappointment she'd felt when the principal had called her the day before and explained why Erin was being expelled. She dropped her aching head in her hands, gritting her teeth in fury and frustration. Of course she would be on the plane, and Ryan knew it. It was quite simple, really. She'd used up all her options. She had no other choice.

"What did he say?"

Ginna's head whipped up toward the sound of her daughter's voice. Erin stood in the doorway, a long-stemmed rose clutched in one hand, a paring knife she was using to dethorn it in the other. An anxious look that the belligerent tilt of her chin couldn't hide dulled the usual sparkling blue of her eyes.

"Who?" Ginna asked, being deliberately obtuse in an effort to circumvent another of the head-on collisions they had been indulging in lately.

"Daddy. You were talking to him on the phone, so don't try to deny it!"

Ginna shrugged. "I have no intention of denying it, Erin. After the scrapes you've been getting into, you're bound to have known it was only a matter of time before I told him."

"I don't suppose you ever cut class?" Erin said with a toss of her shoulder-length strawberry-blond hair.

"No," Ginna said, struggling to hold on to her temper and her composure, "I didn't."

"You didn't cut class," Erin began smugly, "but you made out—"

"That's enough!" Ginna said sharply, rising and rounding the corner of the desk.

Prudently, Erin was silent, watching her mother's approach with what Ginna thought was a satisfying amount of trepidation on her usually vivacious features. When she was just a few feet from Erin, she stopped. Her voice shook with anger and suppressed tears as she said in a low voice, "Yes, your father and I *made love* before we were married. But that doesn't make it right, and I only want to keep you from making the same mistakes I did."

Erin stared stolidly back at her mother. There wasn't a bit of softening in her attitude.

Ginna threw up her hands. There wasn't anything else she could say. Sorrow that she was unable to reach Erin at any level filled her. "All right. Fine. Don't listen. I've said it all before so I won't bore you any more by trying to explain my actions. You can think whatever you want of me; you can hate me. But don't you ever, *ever* put those feelings into words. Do you hear me?'' In spite of herself, she couldn't stop the single tear that burst the dam of her lower lashes and trickled down her cheek.

For just a moment, Ginna thought the antagonism on Erin's face faded, thought it was replaced with a look of remorse. Then, with a strangled cry, the girl whirled and left the small room, a beautiful, strong-willed fifteen-year-old, a montage of all the most desirable traits of both parents. Ginna stared at the spot where Erin had stood. Erin, the price Life had demanded for the stolen hours she'd spent with Ryan. Payment for her first and only rebellion that even under the present circumstances, she'd never regretted for a single moment.

Ryan hung up the phone and wiped his sweating palms down the thighs of his faded Levi's. Erin had found the wedding certificate. Even in this day and age it must have been a terrible shock to her. He remembered how he'd felt as a teenager, walking in and finding his parents in a real clinch. He'd been horrified, so he had a pretty good idea of what Erin was feeling. Later, he had realized just how ridiculous his feelings were. After all, he'd always known they didn't get four kids from Sears-Roebuck, but it was still hard to think parents and sex in the same breath. He ran his hand through his hair. It was hard to imagine Erin acting as Ginna said she was. It was harder still to imagine Ginna lying about it.

Ginna. His stomach knotted. She'd been crying. He couldn't see it, but he'd heard the catch in her voice, heard the sniffs as she tried to control the tears. He despised himself for feeling that aching sympathy for her tears after she'd left him as she had, but it was there, nevertheless. He'd felt sympathy and a resurgence of the pain she left behind so long ago. Contrarily, to combat the pain, he'd wanted to hurt her—to make her hurt as he had and did. That's why he'd offered the snide remark about them making it in the back seat of his Chevy.

He shouldn't have mentioned that. Running his hand through his dark hair—fingers splayed wide in the gesture Ginna had imagined only moments before—he heaved a sigh of defeat. He should have left well enough alone. All he'd done was open himself to an assault of achingly erotic memories that whirled through his mind, leaving him fully aware of the depth of his loss, even after all this time.

Ginna's stomach churned; she pressed her knuckles to her lips and fought back the tidal wave of nausea sweeping down on her. She *hated* flying! She would rather have crawled from Chicago to Shreveport. And, as if it weren't bad enough that she was morbidly afraid of flying, they had been plagued with bad weather throughout the trip. They had taken a roundabout course, but even so, the plane had been periodically buffeted by winds that seemed to shake the aircraft like a giant hand shaking a rag doll. She had been so frightened, so sick, she couldn't even be bothered with worrying about her sister, Kay, and how she would handle the busy month coming up, or what she herself would do when she saw Ryan.

Erin, totally unconcerned by the weather, sat in her seat, the earphones to her Walkman looking like a headband against the red-gold of her hair, her vivid blue eyes—Ryan's eyes—focused on the *Seventeen* magazine in her lap. Not that it would have made any difference if she hadn't been otherwise occupied, Ginna thought. Erin was a master at ignoring her these days. Much as Ryan had been all those years ago.

Ginna tried her best not to think of their last meeting four years ago when they'd gone before a judge as Ryan fought for the right to have Erin during summer vacations.

Swamped by the sudden backwash of remembrances, Ginna slumped in her seat, wracked anew with the pain those unwanted memories held. She recalled how Erin had told the judge she wanted to be with her father, how the summers were more fun at the farm than they were in Chicago. She remembered the stunning blow of defeat as Ryan's jubilant eyes meshed with hers across the width of the judge's chambers. She cringed with the recollection of how she'd caved in emotionally, unable to say anything to let him know how badly she was hurting inside, or how badly she had hated him at that moment for taking away her very reason for being.

The plane hit a patch of turbulence, bringing her abruptly and unpleasantly back to the present. Thankfully back to the present. She didn't want to think of the last time she'd seen Ryan. She didn't want to think of him at all.

But fighting the memories was an exercise in futility.

During the pregnancy and the two years following Erin's birth, he hadn't seemed to care what happened to Ginna. He roamed the country, going from one racetrack to the other, never wrote to her and only called on Saturday nights—unless there was some sort of emergency.

She'd tried going with him for about a year, but that hadn't worked either. Ryan left at five in the morning to train his horses and, after coming home to eat and clean up, he went back to the track whether he had anything running in the afternoon or not. She had never really understood why it was necessary to check out the competition or look for a good horse to claim. And truthfully, she hadn't really cared. She just wanted him with her.

When he asked her to go with him to the races she was miserable, tagging after him like a child. Shy and awkward around the worldly people he knew—after all, he was six years older than she was—she usually wound up sitting alone and waiting for him to pay some attention to her. Racing forms might as well have been written in Greek for all the sense she could make of them, and she wasn't even certain how to place a bet. Her mother would have been horrified if she'd known Ginna was even considering betting on a horse race. And so she was condemned to people watching and waiting for the day to end. The only good times, the only times Ryan was really hers, were the nights. The nights when their world was confined to the bed where Ryan, the core of her very existence, forgot the world that claimed him by day and became hers, only hers. There was no stopwatch to time the length of their loving, nothing to compare their past performances to; each time they only got better as they became more in tune with one another's wants and needs.

Still, it wasn't enough.

Tired of moving, tired of being alone, tired of having no one but Erin to talk to, she had asked him to let her wait for him in Chicago where she at least had a friend in her sister. He refused. So she had packed up and returned to Louisiana, taking comfort in the knowledge that there, at least, she could walk the fields and forest when her loneliness became intolerable.

A pinging sound and the statement that they were making their initial approach to Shreveport forced her mind from her memories. The announcement must have penetrated Erin's music, because she closed the magazine and removed the earphones, draping them around the back of her neck. The sight of her mother's obvious fear and the paleness of her face softened the core of her anger and disillusionment. She knew how much her mom hated flying. "We'll be there in just a little while," she said with a grudging sympathy.

Startled yet pleased by the unexpected concern, Ginna lifted her eyes from the catch of her seat belt and attempted a smile. "I know."

Satisfied that she was as protected as she could be, she reasoned that maybe if she stayed busy she wouldn't dwell on the fact that the ground would soon be rushing up to meet them. Drawing her compact from her ivory linen bag, she popped the lid open with hands that shook more than just a little, and for reasons she didn't dare examine too carefully.

A gasp of dismay escaped her lips as she looked into the small, round mirror. Sick or not, she couldn't face Ryan this way! Her eyes looked as if they had been smudged into the whiteness of her face by the careless stroke of a charcoal stick—she couldn't remember when she'd had a decent night's sleep. Her eye makeup was ruined, and her mouth was naked, trembling. She rummaged in her purse for her makeup bag, adding color to her face in a desperate attempt to make herself look like someone who hadn't been sick for a month. The finished result was that she now looked like something from a red-light district, she thought with disgust, snapping the compact shut. She sighed. What did it matter? Hadn't she stopped caring what he thought of her a long time ago?

Within moments, the wheels of the plane touched the tarmac, accompanied by the loud roar of the reversal of the jet engines and a fervent prayer from Ginna. The aircraft coasted to a stop, and the passengers began unfastening their seat belts and gathering their belongings. She wasn't looking forward to her encounter with Ryan and held back until she was almost the last person to disembark, while Erin hurried on ahead, pushing aside the fear of her father's wrath in her eagerness to see him once more.

Dread dogging her footsteps, Ginna made a weak-kneed entry into the waiting room of the terminal. Her eyes found Erin at the exact moment her daughter was released from a hug by a man who stood a head taller than most of the other men in the small, congested area. Even though he held Erin in his arms, Ryan's sweeping gaze roved the crowd, passed over Ginna, then returned. Dark blue eyes met and clung to golden brown as they stared at each other over Erin's head, over the mulling, noisy travelers, over eight long years of separation.

Just as it had when the plane hit an air pocket, Ginna's stomach bottomed out. There he stood, six-feet, three inches of hard-muscled, vibrantly male man. Why wasn't he bald and paunchy? she asked herself, her heart missing a beat as she absorbed his rugged good looks. But he wasn't. His hair was still that raven-wing black that held a touch of blue, and his eyes rivaled the color of the summer sky just peeping through the parting clouds. The short-sleeve knit pull-over he wore accentuated the breadth of his shoulders, and the faded, skin-tight Levi's fit him with the comfort and ease that comes from many washings, clinging to his hips and molding his masculinity with heart-stopping intimacy. From some place deep within her came a sudden recollection of those hard arms holding her tightly, and the bittersweet memory of how well her body fit his ... She stifled a groan and gave herself a mental shake. An aching sense of sadness filled her. Fighting the feeling, she forced her eyes back to his face.

It was the same—yet different. The strong aquiline nose was unchanged, but the grooves scoring his lean, tanned cheeks seemed more deeply etched than she remembered, as did the lines fanning from the corners of his eyes. His mouth—a mouth that had once driven her to the edge of a delicious insanity and beyond—looked harder, more controlled. His mouth. Still beautifully shaped, the upper lip was edged with a heavy black mustache that gave his face a tougher look. She frowned thoughtfully. He'd grown the mustache since she'd seen him last. That was the difference. She wasn't certain she liked it, then reminded herself that it didn't matter if she liked it or not.

Father and daughter stood there watching her approach, Ryan's hands resting easily on Erin's shoulders while he appraised Ginna with a maddening, measuring look. Her spine straightened in an automatic gesture that readied her for battle and she moved forward on legs that trembled and knees that knocked.

''Hello, Ryan,'' she said with what she felt was admirable calmness considering the realization that was slowly chipping away at everything she'd fought for the past eight-plus years.

"Hello, Ginna," he said. The throaty, sexy-sounding salutation sent a shiver of delight scampering through her. She wasn't sure what it was about his voice that was so attractive. Was it the husky timbre, or the lilt of Cajun French that was so much a part of the life in southern Louisiana where he'd grown up? Whatever it was, it still evoked feelings and emotions best left buried in the ashes of their love, which had burned itself out so long ago.

She watched as the outer corners of his mustache climbed upward, revealing even, white teeth in a mockery of a smile as he took in her paleness and the dark circles beneath her eyes that even her heavy hand with her makeup hadn't erased. "You must have had a bad flight. I'd forgotten how terrified of flying you are."

Ginna was reminded of another bone of contention between them. Loving the freedom he felt in flying his own plane, Ryan insisted on flying himself from track to track, even though planes had terrified her ever since she'd witnessed the crashing of a small aircraft in a friend's corn field when she was fourteen. "I don't suppose I'll ever like taking risks the way you do."

His mouth twisted into a wry smile. "No, I don't expect you will."

She wondered if she only imagined the feeling that he was talking about something more than flying. And why, she asked herself a bit desperately, did she still feel the glowing embers of desire curling within her if their love had indeed burned itself out?

Silently, Erin watched and listened to the brief exchange between her parents, gauging every word, weighing every reaction. Noting the apprehension in her eyes, Ryan smiled and said, "Let's go get the luggage."

He wrapped a long arm around her shoulders and grasped Ginna's upper arm in strong fingers, heading them toward the escalator that would take them to the ground level and the baggage claim area.

"Slow down!" Ginna complained. Each step she took set up a pounding in her head, and she was almost running to keep up with him...just as she always had.

Ryan glanced down at her. At five-feet, two inches, her red-gold head barely came to his shoulder. Miraculously and momentarily, the heartache and years melted away. He smiled slowly. "I'd forgotten what a shrimp you are." An answering smile tilted Ginna's mouth upward at the corners. The beauty of her automatic and innocent response sobered him abruptly and he released his hold on her arm.

The downward ride on the escalator was filled with a silence that throbbed with unspoken thoughts. Stepping off the escalator, he urged her toward a bench. "Sit down while we wait for the suitcases. You look like death."

Nodding, too wrung out from her bout of airsickness and the equally upsetting meeting to care about his rude remark, Ginna sank onto the bench, thankful that her legs no longer had to support her, thankful she was spared, at least for the moment, of trying to cope with the crazy feelings his nearness evoked.

But her thoughts were another matter. They refused to surrender to her will. She closed her eyes and leaned her head against the wall. What in the world was the matter with her? She'd left the man! And for what she thought were valid reasons at the time. Anything she might have once felt for him had withered and died long ago. *Then why did your heart start racing when he smiled at you a few minutes ago?* She didn't want to think about that. Not now. She felt too terrible. It would be far safer trying to puzzle out Erin's reaction to her father, Ginna decided, shifting uncomfortably.

How did Erin feel about Ryan? Ginna wondered. She'd accepted his embrace as if nothing was wrong, yet shunned any overture toward affection Ginna made toward her. Erin maintained an air of barely controlled hostility toward her, yet seemed at least ready to meet Ryan halfway. Evidently her daughter had forgotten that it took two to make a baby. Ginna sighed. At the moment it was more than she could figure out.

All too soon Ryan and Erin returned with the suitcases. With a curt, "Wait here. I'll bring the car up," he disappeared into the hot summer day. In less than five minutes, he and Erin had stowed the luggage in a station wagon with Catalpa Thoroughbred Farm, Inc. painted on its gleaming blue and wood-grained sides. Ginna pushed unsteadily to her feet and went outside.

"You ride up front, Erin," Ryan commanded.

Fine, Ginna thought bitterly. He didn't even want to sit beside her. No big deal. Looking up at him with a combination of resignation and defiance, she wrenched open the car door at the same instant he added, "Your mother can stretch out on the back seat and rest."

The unexpected statement which, in a pinch, could be construed as thoughtfulness, threw Ginna both mentally and physically. She stumbled. Instantly, he reached out to steady her.

His hands were so big. Rough. Warm. And gentle.

Aah, Ginna, your skin is so soft. How many times had she heard him breathe the words against her ear? How often had those hands moved exploringly over every inch of her...seeking pleasure points...charting in his mind the secrets of every hill and valley he had discovered?

Her limpid golden gaze climbed from his hands to his eyes. She sank slowly into the fathomless cobalt depths. In that one instant she acknowledged why she remembered his telephone number even though she never called to tell him how Erin was doing, why she was never around when he came to Chicago to see their daughter, and why she had felt so sick with defeat when she'd seen him four years ago. Another feeling of sickness washed over her.

She still wanted him.

In spite of all the arguments, the unpleasant memories and the death of their love, he still had the power to make her ache with wanting. The realization hit her with the impact of a tidal wave. She reeled with the force of it. Her eyes clung to his, and her already pale face drained of every drop of color.

Seeing her literally swaying on her feet, Ryan slipped a steadying arm around her shoulders, opened the back door and murmured softly, "Come on. Ease into the back seat and lie down. You'll be okay in a minute."

She allowed him to help her, uncertain if the dizziness was the aftereffect of the gruesome flight or the result of his touch. He pushed her gently back against the seat, his hands warm on her shoulders. Pressing hot fingertips against her eyes, she tried to force all the feelings erupting inside her head back to the place she'd banished them so long ago. But that, she realized, was impossible...

She felt the car vibrate gently as Ryan started it, heard the powerful engine purring, felt the blessedly cool air blowing against her face. The aftermath of the troublesome flight and the mental turmoil Erin had been putting her through the past few weeks melded with a sobering, staggering knowledge: if Ryan even acted interested in her, she would undoubtedly fall into bed with him ... in spite of all the hurt they'd inflicted on one another the last eight years. She stifled another groan. It was too much at the moment. It spelled OVERLOAD to her troubled mind, forcing her to relinquish the burdens momentarily in the forgetfulness of a troubled sleep...

"Mom! Wake up!"

Jerking awake and pushing herself into a sitting position, Ginna looked out the window at the two-story house where the LeGrand family had resided for forty-odd years. Reputed to be the oldest house in the parish, Catalpa was the ultimate picture of Southern grace and charm. It looked exactly as she remembered. The shutters were the same dark green, and the porch was still painted gray. The multi-trunked crape myrtles that edged the sidewalk were much taller. Ginna was glad to see they hadn't bloomed yet. Their frilly fuchsia-colored blossoms had always been her favorite. The five huge Catalpa trees that gave the house and the farm their names still dominated the yard area, towering over the rooftop, the pristine white of their fragrant petals contrasting against the deep green of their large, heart-shaped leaves. No one knew for certain how old the trees were, but all the old-timers said they had been planted long before the LeGrands had bought the plantation.

The house proper was still imposing, with the enormous double French-style doors opening into the fourteen-foot-wide hallway dividing the house. Still, as beautiful as it was, the house held few pleasant memories for Ginna.

Ryan came from a tightly knit, exuberant family, free with hugs and kisses, who liked to dance and party. His mother, Nora, had been brought up to treat the man as the head of the house. Her husband and her sons were given preferred treatment. If there was a houseful, the men ate first. If an emergency came up and they couldn't be at the table at meal time—something that happened often—they got the best piece of chicken or the most tender cut of meat saved for them. Nora never knew when to have a meal ready, and for some reason Ginna couldn't fathom, it didn't seem to matter. In short, the LeGrand men were catered to and waited on hand and foot and the household was run with a shocking lack of order.

Ginna, on the other hand, was brought up in a strictly regimented household. Meals were always exactly on time, so there was no need to save special pieces of meat. Her father gave her mother a chaste kiss on the cheek every morning when he left for the family-owned department store and again every evening when he came home at exactly five-thirty-five. She didn't remember ever seeing him grab her mother and whirl her around like Lefty and the boys did Nora. Ginna would have fainted to see her father treat her mother with such enthusiasm. She'd never heard them laugh together over a joke and couldn't imagine finding them kissing under the mistletoe at Christmas. She didn't remember ever hearing either of them say the words, "I love you."

Needless to say, her addition to the LeGrand family was met with some skepticism, if not with downright disappointment. Nora and Lefty had always supposed Ryan would marry someone more like them, not someone who didn't know how to laugh and love. Ginna, too inhibited and embarrassed by the open affection to take an active part in the family fun, appeared cold and unapproachable. Although it was never put into so many words, she was left with the feeling that the LeGrands thought she had snared Ryan by the oldest trick in the book. And worse, they couldn't figure out how she'd done it. What they didn't know was that Ryan's virile masculinity, his tender, teasing personality and his kisses and touches had broken through her barriers of coolness, unleashing the inherent need to give and receive love that lay dormant within her.

"Are you going to sit there and stare at the house all day, or are you going to get out and go in?" Ryan asked now. He was half turned in the seat, his arm lying along the back, his brilliant blue eyes staring at her with a hint of irritation.

The irritation caused a flutter of dismay to ripple through her. Her gaze shifted from his. "I guess I'll get out."

She opened the car door and saw that Erin was already making her way toward the group gathering on the front porch of the house. They were all there: Nora, Lefty, Ryan's brothers and several others she couldn't readily identify.

"Come on," he urged. "They won't eat you."

"No . . . I know," she said, rising and smoothing the wrinkles from the pale pink linen skirt she wore. She glanced up at Ryan who was lighting a cigarette. Their eyes locked briefly before he pocketed the lighter and started up the sidewalk with the long-legged, rolling gait generally attributed to a cowboy. She automatically tried and failed to match her stride to his, dreading the moment she would come face to face with her in-laws . . . her ex-in-laws.

They stopped at the bottom step. She stood there, sweeping the faces before her with a blind gaze. Before she could think of anything to say, a wiry bundle of feminine enthusiasm bounded down the stairs and pulled her into a close embrace. She was instantly enveloped in the scent of lilac. Her mother-in-law's voice was warm with welcome and quivering with emotion as she said, "Welcome home, Ginna."

Tears burned beneath Ginna's eyelids; she returned the hug with a fervency that startled her. And suddenly, surprisingly, she felt as if she had indeed come home.

Chapter Two

Thirty minutes later, Ginna collapsed on the bed, exhausted from both the plane ride and the exuberance of the family's welcome. Per usual LeGrand treatment, she and Erin had been hugged and kissed with an enthusiasm that was catching. Ginna couldn't remember touching or being touched so much since... since she'd left Ryan.

Her thoughts returned to pictures of Erin, snuggled in her grandfather's embrace, lifting her face for kisses from her uncles, being enfolded into hugs from aunts and taking her small cousins out to play with their hands tucked securely in hers. She had literally soaked up the love they offered. Ginna couldn't remember seeing her daughter so happy, so content, nor could she recall many instances when she'd offered Erin that touching and closeness.

Guilt settled heavily on her slender shoulders. Her own upbringing—that structured environment where occasional, dutiful pecks were the accepted mode—seemed loveless in comparison to Ryan's. That lack of overtly shown affection had spilled over into her and Erin's life, and she had unknowingly deprived her daughter of the proof of love she so obviously needed.

Groaning and pushing her troublesome thoughts aside, Ginna rolled to the edge of the bed and sat up, her pink skirt a pale splash of color against the bright quilt that doubled as a bedspread. Decorated with dried flowers, baskets, antiques and rag rugs, the room Nora had chosen for her could easily serve as a cover photo of *Country Living*. It was a room Ginna had always liked for the view it afforded from the many-paned windows that faced the east and caught the morning sun. A morning person, she liked that.

She rose and went to view the scene of equine tranquility she knew awaited her. Black board fence delineated the slightly rolling hills of green into large paddocks that held brood mares and their foals. A man-made pond supplied two paddocks with water and gnarled live oaks dotted the pasture, affording some measure of cooling and shade when the horses needed a respite from the heat of the scorching Louisiana sun.

With her hands pressed tightly against the windowsill, she surveyed the pastoral scene, hoping to absorb some of the peace it portrayed. But instead of frolicking foals, she pictured the room across the hall that she and Ryan had shared during their marriage. Did he still sleep there in the massive four-poster bed that dominated the room? Her body sagged against the windowsill as she remembered how his body, heavy—yet not heavy—had pressed her down deeper, deeper into

the bed's softness. She could almost hear his husky
voice whispering French endearments into her ear while
his tongue lazily traced its delicate outline and his
hands, work-roughened and calloused, moved over her
with an expertise that left her breathless and wanting
more of the touching, more of the kissing, more proof
that she was the center of his world.

Hot tears burned suddenly beneath her eyelids.
Where and when had things begun to go so wrong?
And more importantly, why had she allowed it to hap-
pen?

A knock at the door brought her whirling around,
her fingers brushing at the first teardrops that threatened to spill over. "Yes?"

A young-sounding, masculine voice came clearly
through the closed door. "I have your bags, Mrs.
LeGrand."

Feeling a sense of relief at the timely interruption,
Ginna hurried to the door, opening it to a boy who
straddled the fence between youth and manhood. Tall
and muscular, and wearing his faded Lee jeans and
Doug Kershaw T-shirt with the grace and aplomb only
the young can achieve, he stood in the doorway, a
suitcase clutched in either hand. A broad, white slash
of a smile that no doubt sent girls into a frenzy of excitement was now directed at her. "Hi. I'm Kyle Loggins. I work for Mr. LeGrand."

Ginna found herself responding to the smile with one
of her own. "Hello. I'm—"

"Erin's mother. I know," he interrupted. He half
lifted one suitcase and asked, "Where do you want
these?"

She jerked her head in the direction of the spool bed
gracing a far wall. "Just put them on the bed."

Without a word, Kyle easily hoisted the suitcases to rest on the quilt.

"What sort of work do you do for Ryan?" she asked, leaning against the bed's footboard.

"I work mostly with the young horses. I halter break the foals. Let them know people aren't going to hurt them. I get them used to the walking machine, get them ready to break."

"It sounds like a lot of work."

He flashed her another smile. "With a farm this big it keeps me busy."

"Who keeps things going while Ryan is away at the races?" she asked.

"He doesn't go off to race much anymore," Kyle said. "The whole family stays pretty close these days."

A frown drew Ginna's brows together. Always before, the family operation had spread as far eastward as Kentucky and as far west as New Mexico.

"Well," Kyle said, planting his hands on his hips, "I've got to go bring Erin's luggage up. It's been nice meeting you, and I hope you and Mr. LeGrand get everything worked out."

Stunned by his parting remark, Ginna could only stare after him. He hoped she and Ryan worked everything out? Did he know about Erin? No, of course not. Ryan wouldn't spread that sort of thing around. Then what did he mean? Unless... An agonized moan escaped into the quiet of the room. Kyle Loggins thought she was here to try and work a reconciliation with Ryan. That was it. It had to be. Ginna sank onto the bed and covered her face with her hands, wondering how she'd feel if it were the truth. And wondering if she wished it were.

* * *

Hours later, Ginna, a captive of bone-deep exhaustion and a weighty lethargy, forced open her eyes. Dusk had homesteaded the room while she slept, its invisible fingers smudging the lingering light of day into the approaching night. She stared up at the ceiling for a moment, then turned her head to the side. Two parallel lines appeared between her brows when her gaze encountered the sight of a dainty, rosewood chair with a carved back and a tapestry seat. Then she remembered. She wasn't in her Chicago apartment, but at Catalpa. She passed a weary hand over her eyes and raked the hair away from her face before glancing at the gold watch on her wrist. She'd better get a move on it. Nora had stated that tonight dinner would be ready at seven and warned the family that if they wanted to eat, they'd better all be there.

Stifling a yawn with one hand and bolting from the bed, she opened a suitcase and rummaged around for clean under things before hurrying to the bathroom and a much-welcomed shower. Exactly thirty minutes later, she was dressed in pale-yellow cotton slacks and a top Erin teasingly called her "Hi-wy-ian flowerdy shirt"...back in the days when Erin was still talking to her. A last flick of the brush through her stylish chin-length bob, and she headed out the door, filled with mingled feelings about being back in the bosom of Ryan's family.

As she opened the door, the door across the hall opened and Ryan stepped out, his head downbent as he concentrated on tucking the tail of his short-sleeve knit shirt into his freshly starched jeans...his unzipped, freshly starched jeans, she noted with a racing heart.

Rooted to the spot by surprise, she could only stand there staring at him with wide, watchful eyes.

He was still so sinfully handsome. She tried to swallow, but her mouth was too dry. Her palms began to sweat. She didn't need this. Not with the knowledge, fresh in her mind, of how easily he had once led her astray and how easily he could do so again.

Not an ounce of superfluous flesh marred the superb masculinity of his body. His shoulders were wide, his waist narrow, his thighs still rock-hard beneath the sheathing of blue denim. She knew from first-hand experience, experience Ryan used to call "on-the-job training," that the merest touch of her lips to his chest could start his heart to pounding, and one touch of her fingers trailing over the flat musculature of his stomach could set his flesh aquiver. Her eyes glued to his hands, she struggled to control her errant thoughts and her erratic breathing. *This will never do, Ginna Le-Grand. You're here because of Erin, not to lust after a man who no longer cares one whit for you.* Unfortunately the talk with herself didn't help much.

The zipper started its upward movement; Ryan looked up and saw her standing in her doorway staring at him. One eyebrow lifted in mocking question. She had the distinct feeling he knew exactly what she'd been thinking. Mercifully, he didn't mention it. Instead he asked, "Late?"

She nodded and forced her eyes to his, instead of allowing them to remain on his hands as they buckled the gray snakeskin belt that matched the expensive boots on his feet. His eyes smoldered with some emotion she couldn't catalog.

"Some things never change," he offered enigmatically, waving his arm in an elaborate gesture that silently said, "After you."

She preceded him down the stairs, acutely aware of his nearness. He was right. Some things didn't change. She felt the same attraction for him now as she had at seventeen. She didn't like it, but she couldn't deny it, either. All she could hope for was that they get this thing settled with Erin quickly so she could go back to her placid, uneventful life before he began to suspect how she felt.

In honor of Erin and Ginna's arrival, both Ryan's brothers and their families were in attendance for dinner, a casual, buffet meal of fried opelousas catfish and alligator. Ginna was introduced to Brad's wife and paid the required, complimentary comments due his children—three urchins who looked exactly like their father, with the exception of the blond curls they'd inherited from their mother, Cecelia.

Lucas, the middle brother, was there as well, along with his wife, Darlene, a former model from Dallas he had married shortly before Ryan and Ginna's breakup. Wrapped up in her own misery and problems, Ginna had never really made an effort to get to know Darlene before she and Ryan separated. The gorgeous blonde's smooth sophistication had always made Ginna feel like the poor relation.

The room teemed with people and buzzed with conversation, and it wasn't until the plates were filled and everyone was seated that Ryan asked, "Where's Erin?"

All eyes focused on Ginna, who was still so shaken by her unexpected confrontation with Ryan she hadn't even noticed Erin's absence. An uncomfortable feeling at being the center of everyone's attention invaded

her. Where *was* Erin? Couldn't she do what was
expected of her at least once? Just for appearance's
sake? What on earth was everyone thinking? Her eyes
automatically, but reluctantly, found Ryan's. What was
he thinking about his daughter's absence and man-
ners—or lack of them? Did he blame her for the
transgression?

Embarrassment deepened the color of Ginna's eyes
to dark gold. "I don't know where she could be," she
said in a low voice.

Then, as if on cue, Erin bolted into the room clad in
faded jeans and a T-shirt, her dusty feet encased in flip-
flops, her strawberry-blond hair tousled and wind-
blown. All eyes turned from Ginna to the arresting
picture Erin made as she stood poised in the doorway.
She'd obviously come straight from the barn without
making any effort to clean up for the evening meal.
Ginna was torn between a feeling of pride over the pure
beauty of her daughter's wild disarray and anger at the
lateness she knew was deliberate, an attempt to cause
her mother some embarrassment.

Erin's eyes made a sweeping scan of the room's oc-
cupants, ignoring Ginna's accusing look. The look on
her face managed somehow to convey both guilt and
defiance, confirming Ginna's suspicion that she was
seeing just how far she could push her mother. "Sorry
I'm late!" she said breezily, snatching up a plate.

The look and the flip apology tipped Ginna's war-
ring emotions from reluctant pride toward full-fledged
anger. There was simply no excuse for coming to the
table without attempting to clean up, or coming to the
table late when Nora had specifically asked everyone
to be there at seven sharp. Ginna stifled the urge to
shake Erin until her teeth rattled. Without stopping to

consider that she would be creating a family squabble, she said sharply, "Erin, you know better than to come to the table looking like that!"

Erin's eyes took on the angry defiance Ginna had become accustomed to over the past few weeks. She slammed her plate down. "Nothing I do pleases you!" she cried. "If I'd gone ahead and cleaned up, you would have griped because I was late!"

A palpable hush descended over the room; even the children were quiet.

"That's enough, Erin," Ryan said, his stormy eyes narrowing as he razed his daughter's lissome figure.

She stared at him, disbelief in her own eyes.

"Don't let me hear you talking to your mother in that tone of voice again...ever," he said lowly.

Erin could only stare wide-eyed at her father.

"I believe you owe everyone an apology."

The disbelief in her eyes changed to hurt, and her face flushed with humiliation as she looked into Ryan's implacable face. Slowly, she turned to face the waiting people seated at the table. "I'm sorry."

His gaze was unrelenting as he jerked his head toward the door. "Go get cleaned up. And make it snappy."

She left the room at a run. Ginna pushed from the table to go to her. She knew how much it hurt to be the recipient of Ryan's anger.

Hard fingers grasped her wrist, and his voice, sharp with authority, ordered, "Let her go."

Ginna eased back down and turned to him, her eyes questioning—amber probing blue. Realization dawned slowly. The breath she'd been holding in anticipation of his feelings slowly trickled from her under the calmness of his gaze. Ryan was taking her part. "Thank you," she murmured in a low tone.

With the tension of the moment eased at last, the conversation which had ceased so abruptly started up again, and the room gradually took on a festive air once more as Ginna allowed Nora to draw her into a discussion about her business and the traditional flurry of June weddings.

When Erin returned, she was clothed in cotton slacks and a matching crop top. Her appearance as well as her attitude had undergone a considerable change under Ryan's strict tutelage. Ginna sighed silently and in relief, wishing she'd asked for his help sooner, and thankful, for reasons that had nothing to do with Erin, that she finally had.

After dinner, the family trailed en masse to the barn area, where Ryan's father, Lefty, proudly gave Erin and Ginna the grand tour, pointing out his prize stallions and his many stakes-producing mares. Genuinely fascinated, and feeling the warmth of the LeGrand family leeching away the emptiness and hurt of the past weeks, Ginna bombarded her former father-in-law with a barrage of questions that brought a wide smile to his mouth and a speculative gleam she didn't notice to Ryan's eyes.

It was almost fully dark when, shirts sticking to them from the heat and humidity, they trooped back to the house accompanied by the loud, plagiarized medley of song from a mockingbird sitting atop a huge pine tree. Ginna, who felt decidedly grungy after being powdered with dust by a pen full of cavorting foals, said her good-nights and headed to her room, dreams of a shower uppermost on her mind.

Moments later, she stood beneath the cool spray, letting it wash the fine film of grit from her hair and body, her thoughts drawn almost fatalistically to Ryan. Somehow, now that the initial shock had worn off, she wasn't surprised that he sided with her during the confrontation with Erin. Brought up with the security of two parents who stuck by each other through everything, it was only natural that he respond the same way.

She turned off the taps and stepped out of the tub, leaving the shower curtain pulled as a precautionary measure to hinder the mildew that flourished in the semi-tropical climate. She reached for a towel and began to blot the moisture from a heat-flushed cheek, catching sight of her muted form in the steamy mirror. Her actions slowed, then stilled. Reaching out, she wiped the surface of the mirror with the peach-colored towel, for some reason more aware than she'd ever been that she was no longer the young girl Ryan had married.

Her eyes narrowed critically as she surveyed the woman reflected back at her. Her breasts, perhaps too full for her slight body, showed no signs of sagging, and her thighs and buttocks were still smooth and firm, probably because she did aerobics two or three nights a week. Leaning closer to the lighted mirror, she touched a tentative finger to the barely discernible lines radiating from the corner of one large, golden-brown eye. Her skin was clear, lightly tanned and blushed with the glow of good health and a meager dusting of freckles Ryan had once claimed to adore.

Ryan... What was she to do with this new, startling realization that in spite of all the harsh words and accusations, in spite of all the years of separation, she still found him sexually attractive? What could she do?

He'd given no indication that his feelings for her were anything more than a respect given because she was the mother of his daughter. Ginna, more troubled by her thoughts than she cared to admit, sighed and resolutely pushed thoughts of him away while she concentrated on getting ready for bed.

She finished toweling herself dry and combed through the damp tangle of red-gold hair that fell in a short, bobbed pageboy to just below her chin. Naked, she blew it partially dry before donning a frothy ivory and lace gown that plunged almost to her waist. Another quick brushing, a spritz of her favorite perfume and a generous dollop of night cream to her face finished her nighttime ritual.

Flipping off the bathroom light, she entered the darkened bedroom, longing for the comfort of the bed and some respite from the emotional turmoil of the day. Something—she wasn't certain what—halted her progress and started her heart racing beneath the softness of her breasts. Someone was in the room! She started to speak, but before the words could leave her trembling mouth a cigarette lighter flared in the room's darkness, throwing Ryan's features—all silvery masculine angles and planes—momentarily into view against the velvet blackness of the room.

Relief, pungent and sweet, replaced her fear. Her heart continued to race, but for an entirely different reason. Ryan sat in a wing-back chair that afforded him a clear view of the bathroom.

"H...How long have you been sitting there?" The words, disembodied in the darkness, were expelled on a wave of breathlessness.

"Long enough."

She reached out and switched on the bedside lamp, trying her best to ignore the implications of his answer. Blinking at the sudden illumination, she grabbed a matching robe and, shrugging into it, turned her gaze to the chair where he sprawled indolently, one leg hooked over the padded arm while he smoked with a lazy nonchalance.

"What do you want, Ryan?" The question was straight to the point and held a note of challenge totally alien to the woman he'd once been married to. She, too, was surprised not only at the question, but at the tone of voice she'd asked it in. She would never have talked to him like that while they were married.

"I'm not certain I'd ask that if I were you," he told her, his voice, soft and intimate-sounding, holding a note just shades away from insulting.

"Look, Ryan. Stop the innuendo. Can't we act like adults?" she asked, trying to disregard the way her pulse speeded up at his answer. He *had* been watching!

"Since when do you know anything about acting adult?" he quipped sarcastically.

The accusation was true enough, yet she couldn't ignore the ache of pain it brought. "Please," she said on a sigh. "Let's don't fight. Whatever was between us—good and bad—was all a long time ago." She met his gaze squarely, sincerity stamped on her face, which looked strangely young and vulnerable without the mask of her makeup. "I'd like to thank you for what you did at the dinner table."

"What?"

"Siding with me instead of Erin. I appreciate it. I think it's important that we put up a united front if we ever hope to make her understand what happened."

Ryan swung his leg from the arm of the chair, took another long drag from the cigarette and blew a cloud of smoke toward the ceiling. Then he ground out the butt in an ashtray and pinned her with an unwavering look. When he spoke, his voice was low, husky and unknowingly laced with the pain of loving and losing...and not knowing why. "What did happen, Ginna?"

Her heart stopped, then began to pound with slow, sluggish beats. She knew exactly what he was talking about. Without knowing how or why, they had switched from discussing their daughter to discussing *them*. The fact that she made the transition without any trouble told Ginna things about herself and Ryan she'd rather not consider.

"What happened, Ginna?" he repeated, leaning back in the chair with his legs spraddled and his arms folded across his chest.

Her chin lifted; her shoulders squared. She tried not to look at the way the denim splayed tautly across his crotch, and pulled across the muscular thighs she knew were covered with a light sprinkling of fine, dark hair. She forcibly reminded herself that she wasn't the only woman who knew how the hair grew on his legs... Her voice was thick with the remembered pain of betrayal she'd felt when she found her husband kissing another woman. "I found you in the tack room kissing that...that..."

"Her name was Carol," he supplied. "She was my exercise girl."

Her name fell so easily from his lips! And he didn't even deny her accusation! Fury spread through her with the speed of a grass fire, destroying the hurt in its wake. Her eyes darkened with anger as she spat out the words she'd longed to ask eight years ago. "And what kind of exercise did she give you?"

A slow, mocking smile lifted one corner of Ryan's luxuriant black mustache. He ignored her question and observed softly, "You've developed a sharp tongue. Interesting."

"Interesting!" She rounded the bed and crossed her arms, clutching her upper arms to still the shaking of her hands, warming quickly to an anger too long held inside. "What's interesting is that you never explained that little episode to my satisfaction!"

"That little episode, as you call it, was just that. And *she* kissed me. A kiss. One damn kiss and you go tearing out of the racetrack without giving me a chance to explain!" he snarled, levering himself up from the depths of the chair and striding to within a foot of her, a victim of his own rising anger. "And when I got home, what did I find? Nothing. No wife. No child. Like some spoiled brat you ran back to Chicago and filed for a divorce without even giving me the benefit of an explanation. So don't try to put all the blame on me!"

He was right. She had done just what he said. She had put all the blame on him. But she'd seen him kissing that woman. And now he had the gall to deny it was his fault—and after what she'd witnessed! Ginna rode the curl of her anger with her head high and her eyes sparkling. Exhilaration sang through her trembling body. She couldn't remember feeling so alive, unless it was when Ryan made love to her... At that unexpected, singularly sweet thought her anger faded without warning, leaving her feeling strangely vulnerable as it was replaced with more of the haunting memories of Ryan making love to her...

Whirling around, she sought to put distance between herself and the raging awareness suddenly throbbing through her. Before she could take more than the first step she felt hard hands curl around her upper arms and haul her back against an even harder masculine body. A gasp mirrored the shock that held her spine straight and her shoulders stiff. She swallowed low in her throat and struggled to keep from crumbling into a thousand pieces at the feel of his hands on her after so long a time.

Slowly, slowly, Ryan turned her to face him. His jaw was locked into an uncompromising line; his mouth was sternly set. His eyes were cold and bleak as she stared up into them, wondering what he would do next. "Don't run away, again," he gritted out, his fingers digging into the soft flesh of her shoulders.

Ginna whimpered.

His hold on her shoulders eased abruptly. She expected him to release her, but instead his hands began a gentle massage of the abused area. Their eyes met and tangled in a web of confusion at the onslaught of unexpected and varied emotions unleashed in the room. A part of her noted that his fury—so blatant only moments before—was gone now. Nothing remained in his eyes but a heart-wrenching regret. He wouldn't say he was sorry. He never did. Tears burned beneath her eyelids. Ryan... Ryan... Her lashes drifted downward to lie in dark, fanlike arcs against her cheeks.

He released her then. Her lashes fluttered open. The absence of his hands on her shoulders left them feeling cold, left her feeling bereft without the comfort of his touch. She watched as, without another word, he turned and went to the door. Framed in the light streaming in from the hallway, he turned and looked back to where she stood in a puddle of yellow lamplight, her arms crossed before her, her hands covering the places where his had been only moments before.

"Don't ever run from me again."

The door shut behind him. No doubt the words were intended as a threat, but standing there with loneliness washing over her, she could have sworn they held a note of pleading.

An hour later, she was still tossing in her solitary bed. She pushed her hair away from her feverish face, then rested the back of one small hand against her forehead, calling the scene with Ryan to mind for perhaps the dozenth time.

Had he been telling the truth? Had the kiss been as innocent as he claimed? His voice had held an undeniable note of sincerity. *A kiss. One damn kiss and you go tearing out of the racetrack without giving me a chance to explain.*

It had seemed such a big thing at the time. Ryan, her Ryan. Husband, friend, lover and father of her child was kissing another woman. It was a desecration of all she thought was good and perfect. That woman was touching Ryan and he was hers...hers. She was getting kisses that only she, Ginna, and Erin should get...

But in truth, the kiss had only been the final episode in a series of things that'd been accruing for years. He had always been too busy working to spend much time with her. She'd felt pushed aside, unimportant, second string to his career...and his family. Alone, perhaps, the kiss hadn't been so important. But to Ginna, already struggling with a whole string of insecurities, it had been the final weapon of destruction to a marriage already headed for disaster.

But after all this time, one kiss didn't seem so bad. Certainly not enough to end a marriage over, not without explanations, at least. What was it her mother said? Nothing was all ever just one person's fault? She knew she should have tried harder at making their marriage work. She should have had it out with Ryan when she felt lonely and left out ... should have confronted him with the knowledge of Carol and demanded to know what was going on. Why hadn't she?

The answer came slowly, almost as if she were afraid to examine the past too closely. It was her own childhood, so different from Ryan's, that was the culprit. She'd never heard her parents fight. If they'd indulged, they'd done it when their children were gone, or very quietly when everyone was in bed. She supposed she'd grown up thinking fighting just wasn't done. Besides, when things went wrong during her marriage, Ryan had enough temper for two people. He stormed around and yelled, scaring her half to death with his rantings, which usually lasted no more than ten minutes. Then he was over it while she held her feelings inside, letting them fester, adding every transgression he made—large and small—to her storehouse of misdeeds instead of telling him how she felt.

Until tonight.

She didn't know what had gotten into her tonight. She'd surprised herself as well as him when she'd talked back. He hadn't expected that. She still didn't know what had possessed her, but in all honesty, it had felt good. No, it had felt wonderful! She'd never known that a certain feeling of power came with anger. Perhaps that's why all of Ryan's family was in such close association with it. Anger actually made you feel better. It purged and cleansed, however momentarily, and there was little doubt, she thought, that their next meeting would be just as volatile.

Their next meeting. A sudden thought struck her. Why had Ryan come to her room? He'd never said, and it was too much to hope—too farfetched—to entertain the thought that perhaps he'd come to talk about their problems after eight years. No, he'd come to discuss Erin, but because of their argument whatever he'd wanted to say about their daughter had been temporarily shelved. So there would be other talks...and not just about Erin. It was inevitable because Ryan's accusation was too true. She had just up and left, without giving him the benefit of listening to his side of the story. Nor had she answered his letters when he'd tried to explain the circumstances surrounding the stolen kiss. *One damn kiss. She kissed me.*

Uncertainty flooded her suddenly. She'd tossed away her marriage in a fit of pique. Oh, Ryan had been at fault, too, but she was an adult. She should have let him explain. But because she hadn't, she had not only deprived herself of his love, she'd denied Erin that same commodity. Shaking fingers stifled a sob. The tears she'd been fighting ever since he left the room trickled in a steady stream into the hair at her temples.

Like a child in a temper tantrum, she had willfully destroyed something precious to her. Something you couldn't find again. The last one in town. She should have listened. But she hadn't, and like a child, she'd paid for her rashness. Paid for eight long years. All for a kiss. Ginna rolled to her side and swiped at the tears.

It was a lesson learned the hard way; it was a lesson learned eight years too late.

A midnight summer moon hung in the jet blackness of the sky. The darkness of the night was pierced by the mournful song of a whippoorwill. Ryan, long legs crossed ankle to knee, arms resting across the back of the porch swing, pushed back and forth with desultory movements that caused the chains to groan in protest.

Ginna. Back after all this time. Back in his life. Back in his house. Back, not because she still loved him, but because of Erin. He reached into the pocket of his shirt for a cigarette. The lighter flared briefly, and he inhaled a deep draft of nicotine, blowing the smoke out in a long, steady stream.

He hadn't expected to feel that warm rush of pleasure when he'd seen her at the airport, not after the way they'd parted in the judge's chambers. But there it was, that old thrill that had always accompanied his first sight of her, pushing aside the conflicting anger and pain he'd borne ever since she called. Ever since he'd picked her up at the airport he'd wanted to just look at her, wanted to talk to her, wanted to plead with her to listen to him while he explained.

He damned himself and the memories of the good times that had driven him to her room in some sort of foolish effort to set things right between them. He hadn't been prepared for the sight of her just out of the shower, naked and glowingly beautiful. Thank God she'd retaliated at his intrusion in anger, otherwise he'd still be up there fighting the need to love her again and create new memories to haunt him when she went back to Illinois at the end of her short stay—when she left him again.

She had walked out on him. Ryan reminded himself of that fact whenever the missing her and wanting her got so bad he could hardly stand it. She'd walked out on him, but he wasn't without fault, either. That was another thing he reminded himself of whenever he missed and wanted her. He should have seen the cracks in their relationship. They hadn't cropped up overnight. They'd shared a life for eight years, and it had taken that long for the problems to completely chip away the shaky foundation of their marriage. Why was it that he could see it now, with the space and wisdom of another eight years between him and his misery? Like his *Maman* said, there are always two sides to every story.

Swearing, he rose from the swing with a movement that set it to swaying jerkily, and drew deeply on the cigarette. He ought to go up there and put an end to the anger the same way he used to. Kiss her until she couldn't breathe, love her until neither one of them could remember why they were angry, and rid himself of the ache that had shrouded him for so long. Bitter laughter echoed softly through the night. Did he really think she'd let him touch her?

He flipped the cigarette butt out into the darkness, watching the red glow as it fell in a wide arc to the water-sprinkled ground. How was she feeling? Was she as shaken as he was? And in spite of the fight they'd had, did she recognize his going to her room for what it really was...a reaching out to her? And was there some small ray of hope deep down inside her she didn't want to acknowledge...just as there was in him?

Chapter Three

A night of relatively little sleep hadn't done much to improve either Ginna's state of mind or the nagging depression that had hung over her like a pall ever since Ryan had left her room the night before. She'd conjured up the sight of him standing in her doorway countless times. She'd replayed the sound of his voice over and over. *Don't ever run from me again.* Why was she plagued with the feeling that the command had nothing to do with the fact she'd turned to walk away from him? Why did she think the statement meant more? Was it only because she wanted it to?

She was feeling things for Ryan she thought were impossible, especially since she'd managed to convince herself through the years that she despised him. Which, it appeared, couldn't be further from the truth. The emotions that being with him again had stirred to life were the height of foolishness, something she couldn't afford. Shaking her head to rid herself of her fanciful thoughts, she rinsed her juice glass and set it in the dish drainer. There was nothing she could do but ask him to talk to Erin as soon as possible. The sooner the better. And then she could leave.

The rays of the sun just topping a stand of pines to the east glittered off the small pond in the infield of Catalpa's training track. Ryan squinted his eyes against the brightness. The smell of dust hung in the air, a residue left by the group of horses that had just breezed past. The promise of another scorching day was whispered on the slight early morning breeze fanning his face as he stood leaning against the rail of the training track, a cup of coffee in one hand and a stopwatch in the other.

A sound behind him snagged his attention momentarily, and he turned to see Ginna approaching him. Without so much as a word of welcome, he turned back to the horse that was thundering around the track. All the tender feelings of the night before dissipated like the dew on the grass once he actually saw her. The unwanted memory of her naked body urged forward more potent feelings, feelings he shouldn't have for a woman who'd left him and taken his child. He cursed silently, furious at her for triggering the sexual longings and at himself for feeling them.

She leaned against the railing beside him, knowing intuitively not to speak. It wasn't until the horses passed in front of them a few seconds later that he pocketed the watch, drained the cup and turned his attention fully to her. Sunlight glinted off the burnished copper of her hair, and Ryan resisted the urge to plunge his hands into it to see if it felt as warm as its fiery brightness made it look. He frowned at his own lack of control.

"Did you want something?" he asked, more sharply than the situation warranted.

"I wanted to talk to you."

"So talk," he said, turning and striding toward the barn, not shortening his stride even though he knew her shorter legs had to really work to keep up with him.

"I want to know when you're going to talk to Erin."

His head swiveled toward her. "When the time is right."

"What do you mean, when the time is right?" she snapped. "It's a hurtful subject. The time will never be right, Ryan, surely you know that."

A muscle in his jaw tightened. "Maybe not, but I think she needs a little time to get to know me again. To feel comfortable with me before I try to explain things to her. I don't want her to feel like we're ganging up on her."

He entered the barn, stepping onto the blacktopped hallway separating the rows of stalls. Out of the corner of his eye he saw Ginna blink, struggling to see in the suddenly dim light. The familiar scent of the fresh sawdust used to bed the stalls, the medicinal smell of leg paint, and the pungent odor of alcohol assailed his nostrils as he strode down the aisle.

She gave a little running skip to catch up with him as he stepped through the door of a small office situated beside a tack room. She followed him into the masculine domain. "That's exactly how I feel."

Stepping behind a massive oak desk, Ryan plopped down the empty coffee cup and turned to face her. "What do you mean that's how you feel?"

"I feel like everyone's ganging up on me," she cried. "Erin won't listen to me, you demand I leave my business at the peak time of the year, and now I can't get you to give me five minutes of your precious time! But then, I never could!"

She cringed mentally the minute the rashly spoken words left her lips. She watched Ryan pull his cigarettes from his pocket and reached for a match from the old-fashioned kitchen match-holder hanging on the wall. Resting the ankle of one foot on the opposite knee, he struck the wooden match on the sole of his boot before sinking down into the antique office chair behind the desk. He lifted a narrowed blue gaze to her fearful face.

"I'm sorry. I shouldn't have said anything."

"No," he agreed, flipping ashes into a ceramic ashtray and struggling to hold on to his anger, "you shouldn't have. But you did, so let's get all this out, hmmm? Maybe if we clear the air between us, we'll be able to help Erin more effectively. After all, that's why you're here, isn't it?"

Even though the words were spoken in a carefully neutral tone, there was no doubt he was angry. An answering anger glinted in the amber depths of Ginna's eyes. Her breasts heaved and her voice throbbed with emotion as she said, "I'm here because you insisted I come. And if you want to clear the air, that's fine with me! We can start with the reasons you left me here while you went off to race!" The festering, sixteen-year-old hurt erupted from her in a bitter accusation.

"Dammit, I left you behind because I had to prove to your parents that I could provide a stable home for you and Erin!" he yelled, rising from the chair and leaning menacingly across the desk toward her.

Whatever Ginna might have said was lost as they heard Brad's voice yelling, "Whooooo, Pigs! Soooie! Arkansas, here we come!"

A muffled curse escaped Ryan's finely chiseled lips.

Brad, wearing an Arkansas Razorback cap and followed closely by Erin, Cissy and the kids, burst into the room. He stopped short when he saw Ginna and Ryan squared off across the desk. His gaze moved from his brother to Ginna. His jubilant smile disappeared when he saw the strain on both faces. "Did I interrupt anything?" he asked belatedly, and in a significantly softer tone.

"Yes."

"No."

Ryan and Ginna spoke simultaneously. Brad looked questioningly from one to the other. Seeing the thunderous look on his older brother's face, he backed toward the door. "I just wanted to let you know that the Arkansas camping trip is all set. We were wondering if Erin could go with us. We'll be leaving in the morning."

Ryan's features wore an unyielding look Ginna remembered only too well as his brooding gaze moved from his brother to Erin and finally to Ginna.

"Can I go, Dad . . . please?" Erin begged, a beguiling look of entreaty aimed directly at her father's heart.

"Pleeease, Uncle Ryan!" chorused Brad's three little ones.

"The Logginses are going. I think Kyle would like to have someone nearer his own age come along. And it's just for three days," Brad said, flicking a glance toward Ginna. "So how about it? Can she go?"

"Certainly not," Ginna said, at the precise time Ryan said, "Sure."

Ginna glared at him and plunged her hands into the pockets of her shorts. "She's not going anywhere, Ryan. You seem to forget that I'm not here on vacation. I have things I need to get back to in Chicago, and you, Erin and I have things to discuss—the sooner the better!"

His blue eyes glittered with the hardness of sapphire. "And I told you that I'm not rushing this!"

Both had forgotten they had an audience. From the corner of her eye, Ginna saw Cissy shepherding her children out of the room and saw Erin's eyes widen in surprise at the possibility of seeing her parents argue. An uneasy look settled on Brad's face. He cleared his throat and said, "Talk it over and I'll check back with you later."

"Do that," Ryan suggested coolly. He flicked a glance at his daughter, who was clutching her hands together in a gesture that betrayed her nervousness. "Go with Uncle Brad, Erin. I'll talk to you later."

Erin looked from her father's outwardly calm face to her mother's agitated countenance. She opened her mouth to say something, then thinking better of it, whirled and left the room.

"You had no right to tell her she could go!" Ginna cried as she began pacing the room.

"She's in my care for the summer. That gives me every right," he corrected.

"Not when it keeps me from going back to my own life!" she flung over her shoulder. She stood with her back to him, staring unseeingly out the window.

He looked at the dejected slump of her shoulders. She looked tired. And if Erin had been acting as disrespectful and belligerent these past couple of weeks as she had since she'd been here, it was no wonder. The anger he'd felt at himself the night before for going to her room and his anger with her just now faded beneath an aching need to hold her close and tell her that things would work out. If he were honest with himself, he'd admit that he wanted Erin to go with her uncle because he wanted a chance to be alone with her mother. He sighed. He didn't want to fight with Ginna, but it seemed that every time they got near one another sparks began to fly. What a mess! He raked his hand through his dark hair and heaved another, deeper sigh of disgust.

Ginna turned toward the sound. The anger had fled Ryan's face and weariness had taken hold.

"Look," he said in a coaxing tone, "I know you need to get back, and I appreciate the fact that you have a thriving business, but Erin needs some time. I think we all do. If we give her a little space, what she found out won't seem nearly as bad as it did at first. I promise."

She stared unseeingly at the wall covered with pictures of winning races, her mind filled with another picture—a picture of the day Erin had found the marriage license. Some inner recording replayed the sounds of a crying, hysterical Erin. Tears filled Ginna's eyes. Was Ryan right? Would time ease the hurt she knew Erin had experienced? And would time ease the hurt Erin was inflicting in return?

"She told me I was easy," Ginna said in a voice that was nothing more than a trembling whisper. "She said I preached one code of morals to her, but that I lived by another set." A soul-deep shudder wracked her body and she turned her golden, tear-glazed eyes to him.

Something flashed briefly across Ryan's features. His lips moved and she thought she heard him swear. His hands went to his hips and he dropped his head and stared at the floor. When he finally looked at her again, there was something closely akin to tenderness on his face. He moved to stand before her.

She stared up at him, waiting...

"This isn't something that can be settled overnight," his voice rumbled softly. One finger reached out and traced the path of a tear. "You and Erin can't keep trying to hurt each other, and neither can you and I. Stay two weeks. Just two weeks. Maybe in that length of time we can find some common ground that will give us something to build a better relationship on. We need some time, Ginna. All of us."

Ginna still couldn't believe she had agreed to Ryan's suggestion to stay for two weeks, until after Erin's birthday. But there had been something in his voice, some urgency that brooked no refusal. Maybe he was right. Maybe if she and Erin were together on new, neutral territory they could find that common ground he spoke of.

The dawning of her second day at Catalpa brought to light several things she'd pondered until well past midnight. Ryan was right when he said the two of them couldn't go on hurting one another. It was time they learned to interact with one another, if only for Erin's sake.

She watched them load the station wagon with camping gear and wondered how she would fill the three days Erin would be gone. She wondered how she would fill the hours of two weeks without going totally crazy...

"Well," Brad said at last, "I guess we're all set."

"Looks like it," Ryan agreed, closing the wagon's tailgate.

Erin stood on tiptoe and kissed his cheek. The crinkles deepened at the corners of his eyes as he smiled down at her. "Be good," he warned.

"I will, Daddy." She laughed up at him. "I promise."

It was only when Ryan released Erin that Ginna was able to pinpoint her feelings at the obvious love the two shared. Pain. A soul-deep sadness and, if it weren't too ridiculous to even consider, jealousy.

At loose ends after the campers set out for Arkansas and Lake DeGray, Ginna sought the sanctuary of her room, much as she had in the early days of her marriage. Unlike the early days of her marriage, though, she was no longer content to be cooped up, feeding off her misery. And she was miserable. Miserable and jealous...of her own daughter. She envied the way Ryan treated Erin and wished he would look at her with that love and laughter in his eyes. She sighed. Wishing didn't make it happen, and sitting here thinking about it wouldn't change things. She had to do something...go somewhere.

On impulse, she went downstairs to the kitchen. "Busy?" she asked, entering her mother-in-law's undisputed domain.

Nora glanced up from the pie crust she was crimping and smiled. "Same old thing."

The way Nora said it, the word "thing" sounded like "ting"—a leftover trait of her ancestry. "Need any help?" Ginna asked.

"No, thanks." Nora pushed her glasses up with the back of one floury hand. "Bored?"

"Excruciatingly," Ginna qualified.

"Why don't you take my car and go into Bossier City and look around. Have lunch at the mall—you did know they have a mall now?" She laughed. "I think you'll be surprised how things have grown the last few years. The Bossier City and Haughton outskirts have grown so much they almost meet."

"Really?"

Nora nodded. "Go get your purse. The keys are hanging there by the door."

"Are you sure you don't mind?"

"Get outta here!" Nora laughed. "I got pies to bake!"

Moments later, her lipstick brightened and her hair freshly brushed, Ginna sailed out the back door to Nora's New Yorker. She was just getting into the car when Nora stuck her head out the door and called, "Stop by the Country Village Center. There's a neat antique and craft shop there."

With a wave of acknowledgement, Ginna got into the car, anticipation simmering inside her.

Nora was right, she thought several hours later, the area was growing. The placement of the racetrack between Bossier City and Haughton several years before probably had more to do with the growth of the small country town than anything. Highway 80, as Nora had predicted, was almost solid with new businesses from the edge of one town to the other. And the relatively new Country Village Center was only one of three recently built shopping centers. There was a new library, a pizza parlor and at least two video shops. McDonald's familiar golden arches lorded over a corner where a small ice cream shop had once stood.

The shop Nora spoke of was situated in an old, single-story house. Pushing open the door, Ginna found herself surrounded by antiques, porcelain dolls and wreaths made of everything from vines to Spanish moss. She turned slowly, absorbing the ambience of the cleverly arranged clutter. Baskets and vases of silk flowers sat atop highly polished walnut and oak antiques. The heady aroma of potpourri mingled with that of brewing coffee. A piece of exquisite stained glass in a large picture window caught the golden rays of the sun and flung them back into the room in shafts of red, purple, blue and green. Stuffed fabric chickens with wire eyeglasses perched saucily on their beaks sat on boxes of excelsior with whimsical dignity.

A smile of pure enchantment caught the corners of Ginna's lips. It was a tasteful melange of old and new, of craftsmanship and crafts, of tradition and fad. She moved into the next room. Homemade aprons and pot holders hung from hooks on the wall, a quilt in autumn tones lay draped across a rocker and the tray of an old trunk was filled with "how-to" books on every craft from doll making to stenciling—from tole to flower arranging.

"May I help you?"

Ginna turned toward the sound of the pleasant voice and saw a woman with a cut out piece of wood in one hand and a paint brush in the other.

"I was just admiring the shop," she confessed. "It's fantastic!"

"We do have a little bit of everything," the shopkeeper said. "Come on through the work room, here. There's more."

Her mind whirling with possibilities of incorporating some of these ideas into the Petal Pusher when she

got back home, Ginna followed the woman through
what was once the kitchen of the house, but now served
as a combination storage-workroom and, down a short
flight of steps, led to a small room on a lower level. She
gasped in surprise when she saw the florist's cooler.

"You're a florist, too?"

The woman nodded. "We have a florist hired, but
my boss wants to move the florist's shop next door and
make this a place for craft classes."

"It's wonderful!" Ginna exclaimed, eyeing the
quality of the workmanship of a spring bouquet. "I
have a florist's shop in Chicago, but I really like having all this under one roof."

"We are sort of unique, at least in this area, and we
really do a booming business."

Ginna spent the better part of an hour with the
woman, looking over the merchandise, comparing
prices and haggling over the price of a porcelain doll
for Nora. It was late afternoon when she left the shop
and drove back to Catalpa, pleased with her pur-
chases, pleased with the price she'd given for the doll
and pleased with herself for making something special
of what promised to be a boring day.

The following day, at Nora's insistence, the whole
family packed up to go swimming and picnicking at the
Lake Bistineau State Park. Instead of cooking out, she
packed fried chicken, sliced tomatoes and potato salad
for lunch, which left nothing to do but swim and
generally be lazy.

It was a beautiful lake, with a veritable forest of Cypress trees growing out of the green-looking water.
Ginna sauntered down to the lake to check out the
swimming area before changing into her swimming
suit. It wasn't her imagination; the water was green...

at least in the shallow backwashes. Though the water was clearer in the swimming area, Ginna couldn't work up much enthusiasm for a swim. A delicate shudder rippled through her.

"What's the matter? Cold?"

She spun around to see Ryan, clad in a pair of worn-out Pumas, faded cutoffs and an old Louisiana Downs T-shirt, standing behind her, an inevitable, but unlit, cigarette dangling from his mouth.

"No," she confessed with a smile. "Dreading the thought of putting my body in that water."

He flicked the lighter and held the flame to the tip of the cigarette, smiling slightly through the shield of smoke. "I know what you mean, but it really isn't so bad. It isn't slimy or anything." When she gave him a dubious look, he grinned. "Promise. It's just little plants—water hyacinths. The state wages battle with them every year, and they are pesty, but when they bloom, it's beautiful."

"If you say so. Do you think Nora will mind if I don't swim?"

He shook his head. "No. She just wanted us all to be together while you're here. And I think she wanted us to relax a little this week."

"Why?"

"We have a filly running in a stakes race this weekend. We're all pretty confident about her ability, but it's been a long hard row getting her to this point."

Ginna could imagine. She'd seen the pressure a good horse put on everyone before. She was a bit surprised to hear her thoughts come out in words. "It's a lot of mental strain on all of you, isn't it? I mean, she does the physical stuff, but you're the one who has all the worry about something going wrong."

"Yeah. And believe me, a lot can go wrong before you get one ready to go to the track."

"I know. I'm only beginning to understand that since I've been here following your dad around. I never really realized it before."

He looked at her strangely for a moment, then ground out his half-smoked cigarette and asked, "Do you want to go for a boat ride?"

"You don't have a boat."

"We can rent one with paddles," he explained. "You really ought to experience a ride through the Cypress trees."

She looked at him searchingly, wondering what was behind his offer. Understanding came slowly. Ryan was making a move toward the better relationship he'd said they needed for Erin's sake. Nothing more; nothing less. A part of Ginna was glad for Erin's sake. But a part of her couldn't help but be a little sad that it wasn't more. With a small sigh, she offered him a hesitant smile and a nod of acquiescence.

He was right, she thought later. This was an experience she wouldn't have wanted to miss. After renting the boat he had stripped off his shirt to give him more freedom to row. Her pulse raced at the sight of well-honed muscles rippling beneath the tanned skin of his arms and back. She couldn't help but notice how the sun glinted off the rich, dark mat of hair growing on his chest and stomach. She forcibly reminded herself that the boat ride was for Erin's sake.

It was only a matter of a few minutes of steady rowing before the trees began to swallow up the boat and the man-made beach disappeared from view. Ryan put one oar back in the boat and moved the shallow aluminum craft through the sea of water hyacinth with the aid of only one paddle, which he switched from side to side when necessary.

The deeper he rowed them into the stand of trees, the more shady and cool it became. The Cypress trees grew so closely together that she could reach out and rub the gnarled knees or grab a handful of the trailing Spanish moss if she wanted. A stillness hung suspended on the hot breath of the morning. She couldn't have explained it if she'd tried, but they seemed to have stepped backward in time. There was no sound but the soft lapping of the water against the boat and the almost imperceptible swish of the paddle through the water.

Ryan pointed silently to a white egret gliding by on quiet wings of flight. She smiled her pleasure at him, the first smile he'd seen on her face in years. His heart throbbed with the painful thought of all they'd lost.

"It's beautiful," she said softly.

"Yes," he agreed, but his gaze wasn't on the scenery. It grazed the sunlight glinting off Ginna's hair, swept to her startled golden eyes and trailed to her lips that were being moistened at that very moment by the sudden nervous flick of her tongue. His eyes found hers once more and his own tongue darted across his mouth, as if somehow by doing so it could capture the taste of her.

The raucous call of a crow shattered the building tension of the moment and drew a shaky smile from Ryan. He struggled to find a topic of conversation. "We never did do anything like this when we were married, did we?"

"No."

His smile turned pensive, almost weary. "It's too bad." He sighed. "It just seemed like there wasn't enough time..."

"Don't..." she said, shaking her head slowly from side to side.

His eyes questioned.

"Don't take all the blame on yourself. We were both at fault."

He regarded her thoughtfully for a moment. Maybe she had grown up after all. He lit another cigarette. Silence surrounded them while he smoked. Silence laced with aching regret, unasked questions and unspoken answers. Then with a flip of his fingers, the cigarette sailed out into the water. Without a word, he picked up both oars and began to turn the boat back toward the shore.

Ginna looked around at the unbroken mass of trees. "Do you know the way out of this mess?" she asked with a tentative smile.

His eyes were serious as he said, "I hope so. For both our sakes."

Something about the way he said it catapulted Ginna's mind back to the night he'd told her never to run from him again. As she had that night, she had the unmistakable feeling that while he said one thing, he meant something entirely different.

It was a feeling that was still with her the next day as she prowled Catalpa, picking the fresh vegetables Nora grew, pulling weeds from the rose garden at the back and watering off the horses in the barns at noon. The farm, which had never interested her before, was suddenly exciting as she listened to Lefty's plans for the horses they were running, and which stallion he would breed to what mare the next spring.

It was a feeling still with her Sunday night as she sat on the swing, thinking and drinking a glass of tea. She and Ryan had actually related to one another. They had talked—no matter how briefly—about their problems with no arguing. That had to be a step in the right direction . . . whatever that direction might be.

From far across the pasture she could hear the howling and yipping of the coyotes that plagued the countryside. Even farther away came the squealing and barking of Skunk Taylor's coyote dogs hot on the trail. The whippoorwill and the mockingbird teamed up for yet another duet; a cricket string quartet and a bull-frog's bass joined in as backup. Ginna sighed in complete contentment as with the wisdom that comes with age, she absorbed into her very soul the peace and the love that was the very heartbeat of Catalpa . . .

"Tomorrow is Roger and Del's last day," Ryan said the next evening, dishing himself up a generous dollop of baked beans from the table of food that had been set up on the wide back porch. Since the campers were due back in any time, Nora had agreed to a cookout so that when the stragglers got in they could throw a hamburger on the grill for them. The tantalizing scent of mesquite wafted through the early evening air.

"Tomorrow? Where they goin'?" Lefty asked.

"They're going back East with Sanderson's outfit. They said they couldn't stand the heat," Ryan explained.

Ginna sat at a glass-topped table, working steadily at lowering the level of a plate piled with more food than she could eat in two days. She looked askance at Nora and said, "I can relate to that."

Nora smiled and set her plate down next to Ginna.

"So what are you gonna do for help?" Lefty asked.

"I'm supposed to get a couple of high school boys to muck the stalls, but they won't be able to start for a couple of days. We'll make out somehow."

"I'll help." The words were out of Ginna's mouth before she could stop them. She'd explored every interesting local nook there was to see, and once she'd picked the vegetables for Nora, there wasn't much else to do to kill time. Why shouldn't she help?

Ryan sat down across from her, his eyes widening in surprise. "You?"

"Yeah," she said with a nod, "me. I'm not exactly helpless."

"I know, but it's hard, dirty work." He looked pointedly at her hands.

"It won't kill me."

He reached across the table and lifted the hand holding her fork. His eyes held something that was not quite humor and that fell just short of exasperation as he said, "Just look at these pampered hands. Your blisters will have blisters if you shovel sawdust all day."

Her breathing accelerated at his touch. His hands were big, rough and extremely capable...of all sorts of wonderful things she shouldn't be thinking of right now. She looked steadily at him and struggled to keep her voice even. "So? Besides, I keep the sidewalk at home and in front of the shop shoveled free of snow all winter."

"It isn't quite the same," he said, relinquishing her hand.

"I know. Snow doesn't smell."

Ryan glanced at Lefty, who lifted his shoulders in a purely Gallic shrug that somehow gave his approval.

Looking back at Ginna, Ryan mimicked his father. "It's your funeral," he said flatly.

The sound of a horn honking turned all heads toward the road. The Catalpa station wagon came barrelling down the driveway in a cloud of dust.

"Damn!" Lefty growled. "He must be layin' on that horn!"

In a matter of moments the new arrivals were swarming onto the porch. The three tow-heads grabbed Lefty's pants legs, demanding hugs, and then moved on to Nora for a kiss. Ryan was next, while Brad and Cissy and Erin hugged the adults. Kyle, who seemed to be along for the ride, stood politely aside and listened to the animated chatter and laughter that bubbled from the LeGrand homecoming. Even Ginna found herself hugged by Brad and Cissy, and if anyone noticed that Erin neglected to greet her mother, no one said anything.

She was swallowing the lump of disappointment in her throat when Kristi, Brad's middle child, demanded to sit in Auntie Gin's lap and have some chips. She hugged the little girl's small body close. How long had it been since she'd held Erin the same way?

Now, instead of seeking her mother, Erin wrapped her arms around her father's neck from behind, leaned over and pressed a kiss to his cheek. His hand came up behind her head and he kissed her back. When Erin straightened, her blue eyes met Ginna's with an undisguised challenge. To her chagrin and shame, Ginna felt the green-eyed monster rearing its ugly head once more.

"You and Kyle fill up a plate," she said, determined to act as if nothing was amiss. "The hamburgers will be ready in a jiffy."

"We want to wash our hands first, don't we, Kyle?" Erin said with a devastating smile in the boy's direction. Ginna watched sadly as Erin and Kyle disappeared into the house hand in hand.

"You'd better hurry it up, or I'll throw it out!" Lefty called after them.

"Were they holding hands?" Ryan asked his mother sotto voce, poking his fork in the direction the kids had gone.

"It looked like it to me," Nora said placidly.

A look common to parents the world over as they realized that their child was growing up passed silently between Ryan and Ginna whose truce was holding up remarkably well.

Brad, armed with a heaping plate and a bun readied for the upcoming hamburgers, sat down at the end of the table.

"Did she give you any trouble?" Ryan asked.

"Naw—except for having to stand guard over her every time we went swimming."

"What do you mean?" Ginna asked, frowning.

"Hell, woman, have you seen her in a bathing suit lately?" Brad said with lifted brows. "She ought to be banned."

Cissy poked her husband in the ribs with her elbow and confided to Ryan and Ginna, "I had to turn his pacemaker up to a high nine every time we went swimming. He's too old for girl-watching."

"But last summer she was just a kid!" Brad said, shaking his head in disbelief. "It's amazing what one year and a few pounds shifted around will do."

"I'd noticed," Ryan said gruffly. "But then, she'll be sixteen in a few days. I guess it's time she started looking grown-up." His gaze was drawn unerringly toward the doorway where Erin and Kyle had disappeared.

Ginna could see the hint of sorrow in his eyes. It was an emotion she'd experienced a lot lately in connection with Erin. Actually, she'd been lucky. Erin had been interested in drill team and hadn't shown more than passing interest in boys until this past year, unlike some of her friends, who had been going steady ever since junior high school. Now it looked as if all that was changing.

Erin and Kyle came back through the French doors. His head was bent toward hers as he said something that brought immediate animation to her face. She smiled up at him, her pert nose wrinkling, her sapphire-blue eyes sparkling and her teeth flashing whitely in a breathtaking smile. She slid her arm around his waist and laid her cheek briefly against his chest.

Ginna felt a tightening in her own chest. She wasn't ready for this, even though she knew it was normal and natural, a part of growing up that everyone faced... even parents. Her eyes moved from her daughter to Ryan who was looking in the other direction and hadn't seen the flirting.

"I think this is the big one," she said softly.

Ryan glanced over his shoulder at the younger couple. They were doctoring their hamburgers amid soft laughter and teasing, lingering looks.

"She's too young for that!" he growled in a low voice.

"Ryan!" his mother said, smiling at him. "C'mon! Get real. I was fourteen when I fell in love the first time."

"Yeah?" he said with a grin. "Who was it?"

"His name was Phillip Page. He was tall, skinny and very studious, but he had the prettiest smile... Besides, I remember your first big love."

Ryan looked surprised. "You do?"

"Lola White," Nora supplied unhesitatingly. "You were a sophomore and she was a senior."

Ryan's grin widened. "Aah, I remember her now. But it wasn't love, Mom. It was lust, pure and simple."

Ginna hardly heard his brash admission. Her attention was drawn inexorably toward the spot where Erin and Kyle sat shoulder to shoulder, their legs hanging off the edge of the porch while they murmured softly to one another, laughing at softly whispered secrets.

"Momma... Momma..."

The low murmured words penetrated Ginna's dream-drenched mind with the same speed they had when Erin was a baby and, like mothers all over the world, she was instantly wakened by the slightest noise made by her child.

"Erin?" she questioned, sitting up and peering through the darkened room. "What's the matter?"

The sound of a sniffling sob filtered through the blackness. "I've got a sunburn!"

Reaching out, Ginna turned on the bedside lamp, bathing the room in sudden light that caused them both to blink. Dressed in a cotton gown with an elastic gathered neckline, Erin sat on the edge of the same chair Ryan had occupied the night of her arrival, her hands clasped in her lap and tears of misery streaming silently down her fiery red face.

"Oh, sweetie!" Ginna whispered compassionately, sitting up and leaning forward to see better. "You got a doozie, didn't you?"

Erin nodded and swiped at her tears.

"Come here," Ginna urged, holding out her hand. Erin moved from the chair to the edge of the bed, turning her back to her mother. Reaching out, Ginna gingerly eased the elasticized neck opening over her daughter's shoulders.

"Ouch!" She winced in pain herself when she saw how badly sunburned Erin was. Her back and shoulders were solid red with the exception of the narrow strip where the back of her halter top had been tied in a knot. Small water blisters were already beginning to form on her usually smooth back.

Erin glanced over her shoulder at her mother. "My front is burned, too. What are we gonna do?"

Ginna made a mental checklist of everything she knew to do for sunburn. Of course any redhead knew that an ounce of prevention was worth a pound of cure, but it was really too late now to fuss at Erin for not using a sunscreen. That would only negate her tentative reaching out.

"Vinegar?" Ginna suggested.

Erin wrinkled her nose.

"I know, I know, but it's worth the smell if it will help. You stay put and I'll sneak down to the kitchen to see what I can find."

"How about some aspirin to help the pain?" Erin asked as Ginna went to the door.

"Done."

An hour and a half later, Ginna switched off the bedside lamp and stretched out beside Erin who was asleep on her stomach. Her even breathing was testimony to her deep sleep. Ginna had done everything she knew to do: extra-strength pain reliever, a vinegar bath, ice, and a coating with Erin's cooling medicated face cleanser. But even with all that she was convinced that Erin had fallen asleep from total exhaustion rather than anything she had done. Turning on her side, she reached out and touched the back of Erin's sleep-tousled hair. In spite of everything, Ginna thought, she had come to her when she really needed someone. With a smile of contentment firmly on her lips, she fell into a world of restful sleep.

By the following evening, Ginna was ready to drop. Erin had awakened that morning hurting again and, just to be on the safe side, Ryan had taken her to town to have a doctor check her out. Armed with medicine and cream, she'd returned and promptly had the entire household stepping to her commands. Nora had fixed her a special lunch, Lefty had gone to town and rented a video recorder with enough movies to last a week, and Ginna had spent almost every minute running and fetching, and keeping her entertained. She was as bad a patient as Ryan had been the few times he'd been really sick.

But what lay at the real root of Ginna's discontent were the facts that Erin's demands had dumped squarely into her lap. Facts that couldn't be denied as much as she would have liked to deny them. Things like hearing the same words coming from Erin's lips that she herself had hounded Ryan with all those years ago. Pouting expressions that she could see mirrored on her own face. And irrational demands that served no purpose but to put the person doing the demanding into the limelight.

As hurtful as it was, by the end of the day Ginna had an inkling of what Ryan had put up with from her for eight years. It had come as something of a shock to learn that she had been as much—if not more—at fault for their marriage's problems than Ryan. The thing that really surprised her was that it had lasted as long as it had. That it had survived so long was certainly not any of her doing, a fact that made her terribly sad and ashamed.

Tired from her day of catering to her daughter and worn out from her deep introspection, she was just finishing a game of Scrabble with Erin and had visions of stretching out on her bed and doing something totally undemanding, like watching sitcoms that were so boring that even laughter wouldn't be required. She rose and stretched. "Do you want anything before I go to bed?"

"Bed? It's only eight o'clock, Mom!" Erin cried.

"I know, but I'm pooped! I want a hot bath and a couple of hours of just lying around. You forget that I'm the one who made a thousand trips up and down the stairs today!"

"Just one more game of Scrabble, Mom...please."

She was thankful to hear a knock sound at the door, silencing Erin at least momentarily. "Come in!" Ginna called.

Kyle sauntered into the room, his hands thrust into his back pockets, his broad chest barely covered by an LSU half shirt that left a considerable expanse of his middle bare. Erin's face lit up immediately, and Ginna conceded with as much magnanimity as a mother could, that he was definitely good-looking.

"Saved by the knock!" she said, rising with an exaggerated weariness that wasn't too far off base. She grabbed Kyle's arm and dragged him toward the bed. "You entertain her for a while. I'm going downstairs for something to drink."

As Ginna made her way toward the door a movement caught her peripheral vision. Kyle leaned over and kissed Erin. For a moment, Ginna was shocked into stillness. Erin was her baby! She shouldn't be kissing boys. Then Ryan's words flitted through her mind. *Only a kiss. One damn kiss . . .* She shouldn't be making mountains out of molehills. There was no getting around it. Erin was growing up, and there was absolutely nothing she could do about it.

Chapter Four

It's your funeral. The words Ryan had spoken to her two days before rushed back to haunt Ginna as she hoisted a shovelful of clean sawdust into the wheelbarrow. She had begun the day already exhausted from fetching for Erin the day before. Her back ached, her eyes stung from the sweat that ran down into them despite the red bandanna tied around her head, and even with the brown cotton gloves to protect her hands, she knew his prediction had come true. She had blisters.

The barn had forty stalls to be cleaned daily. Generally, they were "picked out"—all the offal and wet places removed. Once a week, they were cleaned completely out and fresh sawdust put down. Today happened to be the day they were due to be cleaned to the bottom. It was only one-thirty, and already the confidence in her abilities she'd flaunted the day of the barbecue had been sapped by the scorching mid-June heat. They'd finished lunch less than an hour before, and she already felt as if she could use another break. Sinking her teeth into her bottom lip, she took a firmer grip on the aluminum shovel handle and scraped up another scoop of sawdust.

"Pile a little more on there." Surprised, she turned to see Ryan standing behind her, dressed in old jeans, a faded shirt and a teasing smile.

Her heart sank as she realized what a mess she must look. She frowned at him and blotted her face on the shoulder of her shirt. "Slumming?" she asked with a lift of her auburn brows.

His hand went to his heart. "Aah. A mortal blow." He reached out and took the scoop from her. "Actually, I came to help. I had things to take care of at the track this morning."

"Oh."

"Yeah. Oh," he said with a grin. "Did you know your freckles are popping out in this sun?"

Ginna's gloved hand flew to her nose, the only place on her otherwise clear complexion she was ever bothered by freckling.

Reaching out, he grasped her wrist. "They're really sorta cute."

Before she could respond, one of his helpers, a tall, thin black man wheeled his wheelbarrow out the door toward them.

"Can I believe my eyes? The boss in his old clothes with a shovel in his hand?"

Ryan's teeth flashed in a wide smile. "Yeah, Kirby, I thought I'd come help ya'll out. You know, show you how it's supposed to be done."

Kirby's dark face collapsed into laughter. "That's a good one. When's the last time you mucked a stall, anyway?"

Ryan shrugged. "I don't know. But it's like riding a bicycle. You never forget how."

"Let's see how fast you are," Kirby said. "I bet me and Trey can work twice as fast as you and Ms. Le-Grand."

"You're on!" Ryan said. "But you have to remember that my helper doesn't have the experience yours does."

"I been watchin' her," Kirby said casting a wide smile in Ginna's direction. "She'll do."

"Then let's go!" Without another word, Ryan picked Ginna up and set her atop the shavings in the wheelbarrow. Grabbing the handles, he almost ran to the barn. Ginna shrieked as he made a sharp turn into the barn. She reached for something to steady herself, came up with two handfuls of nothing and went tumbling off the sawdust onto the blacktopped surface of the hallway.

Ryan skidded to a stop, turned and raced back to her. "You all right?" he asked, squatting and helping her into a sitting position.

She clutched at his forearms and nodded. Ryan helped her to her feet. "I'd forgotten how crazy you can be," she confessed, smiling up at him with golden, wonder-filled eyes.

He smiled back. "And I'd forgotten just how loud you can holler when you're scared." His blue gaze lingering on her mouth he reached out and brushed some sawdust from her heat-flushed cheek. His head tilted to the side, lowering slowly. She felt herself swaying closer...

"Hey!" Kirby yelled from behind them. "We ain't havin' no hanky-panky on the job."

Jumping apart guiltily, they turned to see that Kirby had filled his wheelbarrow and was rushing to fill his empty stall. Ryan swore softly, his eyes filled with a regret that Ginna felt, too. They sighed simultaneously. "Let's get after it," he said in resignation. "We have some stalls to clean."

"Need a break?" he asked almost an hour later as Ginna leaned tiredly on her rake and waited for him to bring another load of sawdust to the stall. Looking up at him through the haze of perspiration glazing her eyes, she wiped her face on the shoulder of her shirt and nodded.

The hint of an I-told-you-so smile toyed with the corner of his finely chiseled lips as he went to the watercooler and got them both a cup of cold water. Their eyes met and melded as he handed her the paper cup. "Thanks," she murmured, leaning gratefully against the stall wall.

"Tired?" he asked.

"Hot."

"Yeah? Me too." Without another word, he unbuttoned the short-sleeve chambray shirt he was wearing and pulled it off, hanging it on a screw-eye on the outside of the stall. Ginna's breath hung in her throat at the purely masculine picture of beauty he portrayed. Was it possible that he was more gorgeous now than he had been eight years ago, or did he seem so because it had been so long since she'd seen him in this state of undress?

Completely unaware that he'd whipped her stifled sexuality into throbbing awareness, Ryan sauntered— there was simply no other word for that rolling, cowboy walk—to the cooler and refilled his glass. While she watched, he trickled the cup's contents over his bare shoulders and torso.

Ginna's eyes were glued to the sight of his naked chest. He was definitely driving her crazy. Even as she thought it, he trailed another runnel of water over himself. The palm of his hand rubbed in mesmerizing circular movements over the crisp black chest hair, distributing the moisture in an effort to cool himself.

Her fingers clenched into a fist at her side; she fought for control as his hand moved with unstudied sensuality to the hard flatness of his ridged abdomen. How many times had she run her palms over him, seeking the flat, masculine nipples hiding in the thatch of dark hair, and tracing the sensuous path it took down the hardness of his belly... and beyond? How many times had her lips followed the path of her hands, moving over him, teasing him, loving him until he finally put a stop to their torment by crushing her mouth beneath the brutal sweetness of his?

From across the barn, a snatch of lyrics by the Pointer Sisters infiltrated the sensual turn of her thoughts... something about being excited, losing control and liking it...which was exactly how she'd felt ever since she'd come to Catalpa...every time she came into contact with Ryan.

Drawn unerringly by her thoughts, her eyes climbed from the sleek wetness of the hair of his stomach, up over the moisture-spangled curls adorning his chest, up, up, to his mouth, with its full lower lip and the bold sweep of black mustache that only added to his unrelenting maleness—up to his eyes. Boldly blue, they assessed her flushed cheeks and the damp tendrils of strawberry-blond hair escaping the confines of her bandanna. For just a moment, his defenses were down and she saw the look in his eyes change slowly, mutating from glittering blue to smoky gray. They smoldered with a promise she'd seen there many times before, taunted her with the remembered knowledge of what they'd once shared . . . what they would still be sharing if only things hadn't gone wrong.

"How many more stalls, Ryan?" someone called loudly, snapping the delicate thread of awareness stretching between them. His gaze flew from Ginna to the man who stood nearby with a questioning look on his lined and leathered face. The tenderness residing on his face only seconds before was replaced by a businesslike facade as he answered the man.

A soft sigh of regret fluttered from her lips as she pushed from the wall and pulled on her gloves, lifting the handles of the wheelbarrow and pushing it outside for more shavings. While she accepted the stolen moment for what it was—recognizing and facing the fact that they still wanted one another—she wasn't certain if Ryan was as honest with his feelings as she was, because when their eyes met in passing, his were once more unemotional and completely unreadable.

"Rise and shine!" Ryan's voice, coming from outside her bedroom door, penetrated Ginna's confused dreams. She rolled over onto her side, gasping in sudden pain as muscles she didn't even know she possessed protested the halfhearted effort and something in her back tightened into a knot of agony.

When she didn't answer, he called again, "Ginna! You up?"

"I'm up!" she groaned, "but I'm not certain I'm alive!"

She heard as well as saw the doorknob turning beneath his hand before his dark head appeared around the corner of her door. "What's the matter?"

Raising up on one elbow she brushed a tangle of reddish hair from her sleepy eyes. "I'm so sore I can hardly move," she admitted with a groan.

"I told you it was hard work."

"I'll be fine," she told him, shifting to ease the pain in her back and wincing as another hurtful shaft shot through her.

An anxious look replaced the mockery on his face. "You've got more than sore muscles," he told her, coming into the room and approaching the bed. "Where do you hurt?"

"My back."

"You probably just strained it somehow, doing all that shoveling," he rationalized. "Let's see."

Her eyes flew to his. "What do you mean?"

"I mean, pull up your gown and let me see where you're hurting," he said, a hint of challenge in his voice.

"But..." she began, a crimson blush staining her cheeks.

Cool detachment lurked in the depths of his eyes. "I've seen you before, remember?"

"I know, but—"

"No buts. Turn over on your stomach," he commanded in a tone reminiscent of the one he'd used when he told her to be on the plane.

Catching her bottom lip with her teeth to hold back a cry of pain, she did as he told her, her forearms framing her head on the pillow, her face toward him. His Levi's-clad thigh was so close to her that his bent knee touched her side. Lingering traces of some uniquely masculine soap he showered with teased her nostrils. She drew in a shaky breath, wondering if she would she ever stop feeling this inexplicable longing for what she'd lost.

The breath she'd drawn in stopped before she had a chance to exhale when she felt the gentle upward tugging on her gown. Wide-eyed, she raised up quickly to her elbows. A sharp cry of pain was quickly followed by her grated question, "What are you doing?"

The warmth of his hand pressed against the middle of her back. "Be still," he commanded. "I told you to pull up your gown. But don't worry. I'll make certain your modesty stays intact."

Was she imagining it, or was there a trace of huskiness in his voice? She lowered her upper body against the pillow once more, steeling herself against the touch of his hands. At the first brush of his calloused fingers against her aching flesh, another pent-up breath trickled from her in a long sigh. Probing gently, his fingers moved over her back.

"Tell me where it hurts."

Eyes closed, she nodded, giving herself over to the pleasure of having him touching her again. "Ohhhh," she moaned as his fingers moved to her lower back. "There. Right there."

"Muscle spasm," he told her, diagnosing the problem while his fingers massaged the hard knot of muscle situated to the right of her spine at about waist level.

"What do we do for it?" she asked, angling her head and meeting his frowning gaze.

"We'll start with a hot bath. I think Mom has some muscle relaxers. You can take some of them. You ought to be okay in a couple of days."

"What about the stalls?"

"I'll get Kyle to help me. Don't worry about it," he said, standing up and heading toward the bathroom.

"Where are you going?"

"To run your bath."

"I can manage."

"Give in gracefully for once," he said softly, before he disappeared into the bathroom and before she could protest further. It was wonderful to have someone to take care of her for a change. She let him draw the bath, let him help her up and into her robe. She leaned on him on the long trek to the bathroom, but she drew the line at letting him help her into the tub.

"Fine," he said tightly, turning his palms outward and retreating back into the bedroom as she started closing the bathroom door. "But you stay in that tub until I come back with the medicine."

Twenty minutes later, her skin was shriveling in the cooling water when the sound of his voice on the other side of the door shattered her bath-induced lethargy. She struggled to get out of the tub, fighting the agony of the strained muscle while she dried off.

"I need another gown," she said, sticking her head out and finding him seated on the edge of her bed once more.

"Later," he said in a no-nonsense tone. "Come on. I've got some stuff to rub you down with."

"Ryan, that isn't necessary," she said, knowing she couldn't take much more of having him touch her without betraying her feelings in some way.

"It is if you want some relief. I guarantee that if you take a pill and let me rub you down with this, you'll sleep pain free for a couple of hours."

She saw the hint of a dare in his eyes. Was it possible he knew how she felt? Still, the promise of her back not hurting anymore overrode her fear of discovery. "Okay, but I want a gown first."

He sighed, rose and turned toward the maple chest of drawers standing against the far wall. "Which drawer?" he called over his shoulder.

"The middle one."

Pulling a peach-colored gown from the drawer, Ryan strode back across the room and held it out to her with the terse instruction, "Hurry up and get under those covers."

It was no time until she was back in bed, lying down and turning onto her stomach with her face away from him. Within seconds she felt the brush of his fingertips as he tugged the gown up to give him access to her back. Her stomach quivered as he pushed the damp hair off her neck and she felt the warmth of his hands as he smoothed the medicated cream onto the skin of her shoulders and back. His strong hands stroked up to her shoulders, squeezed, slid down her back and smoothed the tingling flesh down, down to her waist where the curve of her hip flared gently. His thumbs worked at the knotted muscle, creating pain, but a pain laced with pleasure. She trembled inside as his splayed fingers raked her rib cage, tantalizingly close to the undersides of her breasts.

The pungent scent of the penetrating ointment filled her nostrils. The heady touch of his hands filled her senses, mesmerizing her into a bone-deep lethargy. Ryan touching her again after all this time. Ryan touching her when she thought she would never know the excitement of his touch again. His hands, smoothing...kneading...rubbing... She sighed deeply in contentment and pleasure, totally unaware that she did so.

Damn, but it felt good to touch her again, Ryan thought as his lashes drifted shut, hiding the sudden surge of passion blazing in the depths of his eyes. He'd almost forgotten the incomparable texture of her apricot-cream flesh. Almost forgotten the smell of the light, flowery fragrance she wore. Almost forgotten the subtle woman scent that was exclusively hers. His fingers moved, brushing the little mole he remembered just below her shoulder blade. Would she still giggle if he touched it with his lips? Would it bring a moan of pleasure from her as it once had? Would...

Without conscious thought, he bent and pressed his mouth to the small, dark mole. At first her breathing completely stopped, and then he felt as well as heard the expulsion of a soft sigh. Taking it as a sign of acquiescence, his mouth continued its journey, moving slowly to the vulnerable flesh of her neck, then inching in miniscule kisses to the spot behind her ear. Slowly, so he wouldn't hurt her, he turned her to her back.

Their eyes met and, as Ryan had only seconds earlier, Ginna acted impulsively, lifting her arms and looping them around his neck. She shifted, weaving her fingers through the vibrant thickness of his dark hair. Eyes locked with his, she moistened her parted lips invitingly as she waited with suspended breath for an eternity that was actually mere seconds. Wordlessly, he allowed her to pull his head down to hers. Their breath tangled when his lips hovered momentarily before swooping to claim her mouth with a kiss that tasted slightly of chicory. Some still-rational portion of her mind told her he had already been downstairs for coffee.

Rationality flew by the wayside as his hands moved to cup her face, his strong fingers threading through the silken strands of her hair, his palms blocking out every sound but the wild beating of her heart. His tongue invaded her willing mouth. He kissed her hungrily, demandingly, asking for everything she was willing to give and, as she'd always been with him, she was willing to give everything...

A sound desecrated the quiet of the room—a whimpering, lost sound that came from her throat and stilled the rapacious hunger of his kiss. He lifted his head slowly; she was powerless to stop the clenching of her fingers in his hair, a gesture that was designed to hold him, but failed. He reached up and disengaged her hands from the back of his neck. Holding her wrists in a loose clasp, he put enough distance between them so that he could look down into her eyes.

"So...so easy," he said softly, a funny sort of smile curving his lips. Her body went suddenly still. "Nothing's changed, Ginna. You're still so damned easy to..."

Ginna's cry of rage and shame shattered the sexuality throbbing throughout the room and between them. She tried to jerk her wrists free of his hold. "Let go of me!"

Ryan's eyes widened in disbelief.

"Get out of here! Now!"

He rose automatically from the side of the bed, his confusion written clearly on his face. "What happened?" he asked, his heavy brows drawn into a single line of query.

Ginna, her pain forgotten, scooted into a sitting position, her breasts, barely covered by the lacy-topped gown, heaving with anger. "Easy!" she spat.

The perplexity on his face faded beneath a rapidly dawning comprehension. She thought he was saying she was easy, when that wasn't what he was about to say at all. He should explain . . . tell her what he really meant.

No. He wouldn't tell her. He scrubbed a palm over his face. She was doing it all over again. She was behaving just as she had eight years ago, jumping to conclusions and condemning without even trying to communicate and get to the real problem. Almost as angry as she, he moved to leave the room. At the door he half turned, a sudden ache squeezing his heart. He smiled, a wry smile that somehow looked sad, defeated. "Like I said, Ginna, some things never change."

Ginna spent the day in bed, being generally lazy, her mind roiling with unanswered questions about what had happened between her and Ryan that morning. She felt she had his feelings pegged pretty well. Desire. Pure and simple. Or lust pure and simple, she thought with a bittersweet smile, recalling his words the evening he and Nora had been discussing first romances. Whatever you called it, it translated to one thing. If his kiss was anything to judge by, he still wanted her. And the feeling was mutual.

Easy. He'd said she was easy. And why wouldn't he think that after the way she'd behaved? Oh, sure, he had instigated the entire kiss by kissing her on the back. But the moment he'd turned her to face him, there was no doubt about who had been the aggressor. Her face burned with shame as she remembered how wantonly she'd thrown her arms around him and pulled him down to her for that kiss. After the way she'd acted, it was no wonder he'd said what he did. With a moan of dismay, she eased to her side and curled into a ball of misery. It promised to be a long day.

Lefty peeked in on her at midmorning and, at her confession of boredom, brought her a small portable television. Brad and Cissy stopped in, and even the coolly lovely Darlene brought Ginna up a glass of iced tea. Nora checked in on her throughout the day and promised to fix her favorite dinner: fried potatoes, chicken-fried steak, sliced tomatoes and field peas.

In spite of his resolution, Ryan found himself standing outside her room just after lunch. His hand rested indecisively on the doorknob. Everyone said she was doing fine, but he just wanted to see for himself. He didn't know why he should want to after the way she'd blown up at him earlier, but he did. Drawing in a deep breath, he lifted his hand to knock. No, he thought, lowering it almost at once, he couldn't do it. The newest wounds she had inflicted were still too raw, or that damnable LeGrand pride was too strong—one or the other. He leaned his head against the door for just a moment, sighed, then turned and went down the hall to his room.

Erin, who was going to check on her mother at Nora's insistence, stopped dead in her tracks when she saw her father standing outside the bedroom door. A frown puckered her forehead. She was still wearing the puzzled look when she entered Ginna's room and found her propped up in bed doing her nails. "How are you feeling?" she asked her mother, taking refuge in the stock question.

Ginna was still buoyed up about Erin coming to her in the night. "Better, thanks. How's the sunburn?"

"It's still sore and feels tight," Erin said with a shrug, "but it's better." Her eyes brightened suddenly. "Dad says if I feel like it and wear a long-sleeve shirt I can drive the tractor and pull the manure spreader this afternoon. Did you know you can get your driver's license at fifteen in Louisiana? I could have been driving for a year!"

"No, I didn't," Ginna said. "But the tractor driving should be some good experience."

"Yeah." A dreamy sort of secret smile curved her beautifully shaped mouth. "Kyle says that at least I can't hit anything out in the pasture."

Aah, Kyle, Ginna thought. She'd been right the other day. Her daughter was definitely in the throes of her first major romance.

The sharp rapping of knuckles on the door sent two pairs of eyes winging toward it. Ryan stepped inside. His ruggedly handsome face looked solemn, even defensive as he said, "I'm looking for my help."

"I'm coming," Erin said, scooting past him into the hallway. "Give me a minute to change." The last request was made as she ran down the hall away from Ginna's room.

Ryan's eyes met Ginna's. "How's the back?"

"Better," she replied, allowing her gaze to drop to the sheet where her fingers were busily pleating the flowered fabric. For some obscure reason she was glad she'd taken time to put on some makeup earlier and pleased that her hair was brushed into its usual gleaming pageboy. She force her tone to a deliberate lightness as she said, "Those pills really are great. I'm going to try to come downstairs for dinner tonight."

"Good," he said, sounding as stilted as she felt. "I'll see you then."

But she didn't make it to dinner. Though she was still pretty uncomfortable, she could have gone down if it hadn't meant facing Ryan. It was too soon. Her emotions were still too lacerated by his words—however true they might be—for her to risk facing him over a dinner table.

The dinner hour came and went, and Ginna ate the meal especially prepared for her in the loneliness of her room. She watched television alone and played several desultory hands of solitaire. Later, when the house quieted and the sound of the last doorway closing faded into the night, she lay in bed, tears pooling in her eyes, listening to the soft hum of the air conditioning and the even softer beat of her heart. Ryan was in the room across the hall. Was he staring up at the ceiling and thinking about the kiss? Was he sorry he'd refused to take what she offered? Did he wonder how they let their marriage slip from their careless grasps? And did he wish with all his heart that they could pick up the pieces and put them back together again?

Across the hall, Ryan lay on his back, his left arm pillowing his dark head, while his right hand carried a cigarette to his lips. He dragged the nicotine deep and blew the smoke upward, his mind, as it had been every night since her arrival, on Ginna.

He still couldn't believe he'd actually talked her into staying for two weeks. Two weeks that were already half gone. But he had, and just knowing she was so close had given him an immense amount of satisfaction—until tonight. Tonight his feelings were light years away from satisfaction, and all because he'd kissed her and she'd kissed him back. He shoved the memory aside. What followed the kiss was too painful.

Instead, he forced himself to think of the way he could look up at any given time throughout the day and see her in the garden, with the horses, or in the kitchen with his mother, doing things he could never remember seeing her do before. Surprisingly, she seemed to be enjoying life on the farm, seemed willing to take a part and make herself useful. Like helping him in the barn. Her offer had surprised him, but then, so had her uninhibited response that morning. They'd been getting along just fine until then. Damn! Was there no escaping that kiss? Was there no escaping the fact that he still wanted her as he had no other woman before or since he'd walked into the florist's shop almost seventeen years ago?

She wanted him, too. That much was clear, if her kiss was anything to go by. He leaned on one elbow and ground out the cigarette. What a helluva mess! He hadn't expected to feel all these things when he'd asked her to come with Erin. He hadn't done it just to have the opportunity to be near her again, to hold her and touch her . . . to feel her warm response in his arms. He hadn't ask her to come hoping something would spark between them once again . . . had he?

It took two to make love. It took two to make a baby. It took two to destroy a marriage. But, in some lonely and hopeful corner of his heart, was he hoping that it only took one to put it back together again?

Ginna went down to the kitchen late the next morning, hoping Ryan had already gone. She pushed the door open hesitantly, but found only Nora, busily loading the dishwasher. At the sound of the door opening, the older woman turned. "Good morning," she said with a smile.

"Good morning," Ginna replied as her mother-in-law wiped her hands on her apron and reached into the cabinet for a coffee cup.

"Did you rest well?" the older woman asked, setting the steaming brew on the table's polished surface.

"Pretty well. My back is a lot better," Ginna hedged. She couldn't tell Ryan's mother that she'd spent a good part of the night fighting erotic dreams of her son and wishing she could turn back the clock and change the outcome of their union. Instead, she added two heaping spoonfuls of sugar and poured a generous amount of cream into the viscous, blacker-than-black chicory-laced coffee the LeGrands thrived on. She took a cautious sip. A visible shudder trembled through her.

Nora's laughter brought Ginna's woebegone eyes to hers. "Can't stand the stuff, can you?"

"I've tried for a week, Nora, I truly have."

"I'll pick up some Folgers this afternoon. No sense a body not having their quota of caffeine in the mornings."

"Thanks."

"What do you want for breakfast? I have some pancake batter left."

"Just some toast. I've been eating so much since I've been here, I'll have to diet when I get back home."

Nora's smile faded at the casual comment. Wordlessly, she turned to get the bread for the toast.

"I can do that," Ginna said, rising and crossing the tile floor and taking the bread from Nora. "You don't have to wait on me," she said with a smile. "I'm not company; I'm family."

As soon as she said the words, she wished she hadn't. She wasn't family. And she wasn't company. Truthfully, she really didn't belong here. She turned abruptly and untwisted the wire tie from the bread sack, popping two slices into the almond-hued toaster.

Silence filled the room. "You've been here over a week. Has Ryan talked to Erin yet?" Nora asked at last, deliberately changing the topic of conversation.

"No," Ginna replied. "He says he wants to give her some time to settle in and get used to him again before we try to explain things."

"She'll get over it," Nora prophesied. "Something hurtful always gains perspective with time and age."

"That's what he says, but I'm not certain I can survive until she's old enough to understand," Ginna confessed, staring at a wall hung with an odd assortment of baskets.

"She's been better since she's been here, hasn't she? I haven't noticed her being openly defiant."

A wry smile twisted Ginna's peach-glossed lips and she cut her eyes to Nora's. "No, she wouldn't dare do anything overt in front of Ryan. But I still get the smug smiles and the looks that could kill."

"But she came to you with the sunburn. That's encouraging."

A sigh soughed from Ginna. "Yes. I keep holding on to that one small thing. It's all I've had for a good while. I just wish it was all settled. I really need to get back to the shop. I shouldn't have stayed this long."

"Do you have to go?"

Ginna gazed with a sinking heart into her former mother-in-law's earnest face. "Yes."

"Why?"

Ginna shook her head slowly from side to side. "Because nothing has changed, Nora. Ryan told me that yesterday."

"But it has," Nora insisted. "I know Ryan has changed. He isn't so driven to prove himself these days. And I've watched you. You've been happy here, haven't you?"

Ginna nodded. "Yes." She laughed softly. "I wonder why I never noticed before how interesting Catalpa is?"

"You were too tied up in misery before," Nora said sagely. "You're different now."

"Am I?"

It was Nora's turn to nod. "You've grown up. Matured. You've learned to be comfortable with who and what you are. More importantly, you *know* who and what you are. You were nothing but a frightened, selfish child before—even though you were twenty-six when you and Ryan split up. When he left to go race, you were scared he wouldn't come back, and you held on so tightly when he did come home he was glad when the time came to go again."

"I know." Ginna's voice held the sorrow she'd been living with the past few days. "I realized while I was taking care of Erin that she was behaving exactly as I had back then."

"Ryan wasn't without fault either," Nora was quick to clarify. "He should have talked to you more... explained things."

"Maybe," Ginna agreed, feeling suddenly melancholy at the turn of the conversation.

Ginna was thankful that the toast popped up, necessitating at least a temporary lull as she went to the refrigerator for the butter. She had the butter dish in hand when movement outside the kitchen window caught her eye. Two people were coming around the corner of the barn. A man who had his arm around a woman's shoulders. Ryan and Darlene...

"Ginna, do you—" Nora began, but stopped when she heard the butter dish clatter to the countertop. She started to ask what was the matter, but when the path of her gaze followed Ginna's, she knew. When she spoke, her voice sounded unnaturally loud in the stillness of the kitchen.

"Do you still care for him?"

Ginna's eyes, carefully devoid of emotion, found Nora's. "He's Erin's father. Of course I care for him."

"That isn't what I mean, child. Do you love him?" Nora probed.

Ginna fought the helplessness of her sinking heart and tentative hopes. Could she deny the hurt she'd experienced just now? If she didn't care, why would it hurt so badly to see him with someone else? She stared into Nora's dark eyes, seeing genuine compassion and love. Could she deny truth to this woman who accepted her so wholeheartedly in spite of her many faults?

Her eyes glittered with unshed tears and her voice shook as she admitted softly, "When he walks into a room I can hardly breathe, my heart is beating so fast. When he touches me I remember everything we had and how poorly I handled it. And knowing what I lost makes me unbearably sad. If that's loving him, then I guess I do."

Nora's eyes shimmered with tears of sympathy. "Good."

Ginna's bitter laughter trilled through the room. "Good? Why? Ryan isn't interested in me. Look!" She gestured toward the couple standing so close to each other. There was no denying the intimacy they shared.

Nora saw the jealousy in Ginna's eyes and hesitated a moment—struggling between easing the younger woman's mind and protecting the privacy of someone she loved. Finally, she said softly, "You should know by now that sometimes things aren't what they seem, Ginna."

Ginna's fair brows drew together uncomprehendingly before she turned back to the window. A small smile of satisfaction curved Nora's lips. It just might be that a little jealousy would do Ginna LeGrand a lot of good.

Chapter Five

Ginna fidgeted with the belt of her gray linen slacks, turning and casting a glance over her shoulder at her mirror image. A thousand butterflies battered about in her stomach at the realization that she was going to spend the afternoon at the track with Ryan's family. Le Grand Lady was running, and the whole family was confident she would win, even to the point that they had planned a victory celebration for later in the evening. She couldn't help but be caught up in the excitement even though she didn't feel she was a real part of the family festivities. Her immediate concern was the fact that she would once more be thrust into an unfamiliar world and be introduced as Ryan's ex-wife. She wondered how the LeGrand friends would respond to that.

Ginna hadn't seen much of Ryan since the morning before when he'd been with Darlene outside the barn.

She worried about her confession to Nora that she might still love him. Did she? Or was it just that old, forbidden feeling of desire holding her captive? What was Ryan feeling? It was impossible to tell. Whenever they were in the same room he was pleasant, polite, even friendly, but never once had she surprised a look of anything in his eyes that could be compared to what she'd seen there the day in her room.

She sighed, pulled on a matching linen jacket and gave her bouncy pageboy a final spritz of hairspray as she pushed thoughts of him from her mind. She would share her afternoon with Nora, Darlene and Cissy and have a good time. She would go to the races and bet some of her carefully saved money. And she wouldn't think about losing... anything.

As usual, Louisiana Downs on a weekend was a montage of different types of people and a cacophony of voices, all bound together by an invisible skein of excitement. There were long lines at the windows and money was exchanged for tickets with amazing speed. At the table the LeGrands shared in the dining area, the tantalizing aroma of gourmet cooking mingled with the scent of dozens of expensive perfumes and the acrid smell of cigarette smoke. The low babble of voices provided a lulling backdrop for the female LeGrand's luncheon conversation.

"I'm having the gumbo," Ginna said after a thorough study of the menu's offerings. "That's one thing you definitely can't find in Chicago."

"It isn't as good as mine," Nora said with a smug smile, "but it's pretty good."

"Such modesty," Cissy taunted goodnaturedly, softening the cutting remark with a wink and a smile at her mother-in-law.

"Lefty always says 'if you've got it, flaunt it,'" Nora bragged with an answering smile. "What about you, Darlene?"

All eyes were focused on the elegant blonde, whose thick hair was twisted on top of her head in a becoming, timeless Gibson-girl style. "I'm just having the chef's salad," she said decisively, handing her menu to Nora. "I have to watch my figure."

As if she needed to, Ginna thought acidly, eyeing her companion's sleek, model-thin body, whose svelte lines were enhanced by the soft molding of a raw silk dress of jade-green. She wished she had a couple of her sister-in-law's spare inches to add to her own height.

Echoing Ginna's thoughts, Cissy rolled her eyes and said, "As if you need to. I don't know why you have to watch your figure; every guy in here seems to be doing it for you."

Darlene lifted one perfectly arched eyebrow. "Aah, but there's only one guy I want eyeing my figure."

A picture of Ryan walking around the corner of the barn, his arm holding Darlene close to his side, paraded through Ginna's mind.

"You betting the Double, Ginna?" Cissy asked, bringing Ginna's thoughts abruptly back to the present.

"N-no," she faltered, "I don't think so. I'm not familiar enough with the horses to make an intelligent wager."

"So who makes intelligent wagers?" Cissy asked. "Everyone has their own system. I close my eyes and bet whatever two numbers pop into my head first."

"That's about as good as my system," Nora said with a laugh. "I bet eight and three and three and eight—mine and Lefty's birthdays. I've been doing it for years, and I win a few and lose a few."

Ginna glanced over at Darlene, determined not to let the scene with Ryan upset the tranquility of the day. "What about you?"

"I don't bet the Daily Double. I like the Exactas."

Ginna raised her brows in question. "What's an Exacta?"

Darlene flashed a grin at Nora and Cissy. "My, my, she is a greenhorn, isn't she? I suppose if the horse you pick comes in first, you'll tell everyone it won the race."

"Well," Ginna said, looking from Nora to Cissy and back to Darlene, "sure. After all, it did."

"Wrong, Chicago. The horse *win* the race."

"But that's incorrect grammar."

Nora reached over and patted Ginna's hand. "No, honey. That's racetrack talk."

Ginna sighed. Unbelievable! All those years ago when she'd heard Ryan and the others say their horse win a race, she'd supposed it was just because they'd done poorly in English class. She even admitted that the language had grated on her nerves. Now she was beginning to realize there was more to this racetrack thing than met the eye.

She lifted her frowning gaze to Darlene. "Just what is an Exacta?"

She wasn't surprised at the sudden laughter shared by the women at the table. She was more surprised when she joined in, laughing at her own expense.

The gumbo was delicious, Ginna thought later, and she was surprised to find she was enjoying the outing more than she'd expected. Several people she'd met while she and Ryan were married stopped by the table just to say hello, and she was introduced to several others she'd never met. If any of them were surprised to find his ex-wife visiting Catalpa they were too polite to say so.

They were just finishing lunch when Brad stopped by the table. "Excuse me," he said, holding his cowboy hat against his stomach. "Have you seen the LeGrand ladies? They were supposed to be sitting here, but instead of a bunch of small-town hicks I find a table of Hollywood starlets."

Cissy batted her eyelashes at him amidst a burst of laughter, grabbed his hand and asked, "Do you have anything to do with pictures? I'll do *anything* to get a part."

Brad leered down at her and whispered something into her ear that brought a quick blush to her piquant features. "Even that?" he taunted before he straightened and said, "Actually, if you all want to be in pictures all you have to do is wait for our race and head to the winner's circle. You look great."

"How is the filly?" Nora asked.

"Cool as a cucumber," he said with a smile. "Which is more than I can say for Dad."

And he was right. Lefty joined them later, sat still through a race and left, saying he needed to see someone. Nora only rolled her eyes and shook her head with the comment that he should have learned to take the pressure by now.

After the dishes were cleared away, Cissy gave Ginna a quick lesson in how to read a racing form. An hour and a half later, she had won twenty-two dollars from picking a place and show horse and had a horrendous headache from studying the form so diligently. Tossing it aside, she decided to go to Cissy's method of picking horses since she was playing with the track's money now.

Much to Ginna's surprise Lucas stopped by the table briefly. He kissed his mother on the cheek, spoke to Cissy and Ginna, and pinned Darlene with a penetrating look. "Having a good time?" he asked politely.

"Yes," Darlene said, suddenly subdued.

"That's good."

Ginna watched the exchange covertly. It was amazing how much Luke and Ryan looked alike and more amazing how much they acted alike, she thought, seeing many of Ryan's actions recreated by his brother.

Lucas smiled tightly at them, said he had to go and with a final probing look at his wife, left the women to their betting. Like Cissy, Darlene blushed, but the enthusiasm seemed to drain from her like air from a pinpricked balloon. Only the arrival of Ryan, just before the ninth race and the proposed LeGrand victory, brought a semblance of the former sparkle to Darlene's perfect features.

"Have you ladies won a lot of money?" he asked, his eyes resting momentarily on each woman at the table.

"Ginna won sixty dollars," Cissy said.

His heavy brows rose in surprise. "Ginna LeGrand betting? Tsk, Tsk," he said with a lopsided grin aimed at her. "What would your mother say?"

"I quit worrying about what Momma would say a long time ago."

"That right?" he drawled, before turning to his mother. "Dad wanted me to ask if you all wanted to go down and watch me saddle Lady."

Nora looked at her three daughters-in-law. "Sounds good to me. What about you girls?"

"Sure!" Cissy said, reaching for her purse.

Darlene offered a dainty shrug of her shoulders and Ginna nodded, too undone by Ryan's presence to do anything but acquiesce.

The paddock area, fifteen three-sided enclosures that backed up to the racing secretary's office, was familiar to Ginna. Gaily colored pennants atop the building waved weakly in a desultory breeze and a bed of summertime flowers drooped tiredly beneath the sun. Not much had changed. What wasn't familiar was the surge of excitement gushing through her veins as she saw Kyle leading a leggy chestnut filly into the number seven hole where Ryan stood leaning negligently against the wall.

Her heart lurched crazily as a lazy smile of welcome curved Ryan's lips when Kyle led the filly in and turned her so she faced the crowd that leaned against the chain-link fence to get a better look at the horses.

"She's a gorgeous thing, isn't she?" Nora asked.

Ginna nodded. Le Grand Lady was a beautiful horse. Delicately and daintily built, her bright, copper-colored coat gleamed in the glaring June sunlight like a newly minted penny as she stood calmly and let the identifier check the tattoo inside her upper lip. How could she not win, Ginna thought with atypical pride.

She watched as the valet put a saddle towel with the number seven on it high on the horse's back, watched Ryan's hands adjust it just so and smooth all the wrinkles out...in much the same caring way he'd massaged the ache from her back, she thought with a sudden pang of longing. The rest of the saddling was lost to Ginna, whose intent amber gaze focused instead on the man.

Once the jockeys were all mounted and the horses were headed for the track, Ginna and the others trooped inside to wait until race time. It was only when they'd reached the coolness of the grandstand that she realized Darlene was nowhere to be seen and reasoned that she, like Nora and Cissy were about to do, had gone to bet the upcoming race. Once they had placed their bets and were settled at the top of a section of bleachers outside the grandstand, it seemed only a matter of minutes until the track announcer clipped, "They're at the starting gates."

From across the width of the track's infield, Ginna could see the loading of the horses into the starting gates. She wondered where Ryan was. She wondered if, as the person who was responsible for the training that had enabled the filly to come this far in her three-year-old career, he was as nervous about the outcome as she was. After all, this was his life. A life she was only beginning to understand. Only seconds after the last horse walked into the metal enclosure, the announcer said, "The horses are in the starting gate…and they're off!"

Tension seemed to radiate from the spectators as the field of twelve fillies erupted from the gates and thousands of voices were raised in a loud roar as each person yelled for his particular favorite. Ginna found herself clutching the racing form tightly, losing sight of the Catalpa Farm silks as they moved down the backstretch.

The announcer's voice came crisply over the speakers. "Breaking from the gate with a slight edge is Steph's Silver, closely followed by Smoothly Crimson and Semi Pretty.'' He listed the order of the other horses and finished up with, ''and Le Grand Lady and My Kinda Girl trailing.''

Ginna groaned in disappointment, then felt Cissy grasp her arm. Her dark eyes sparkled with nervous excitement as she tried to explain what was happening to Ginna. ''We were in the seven hole and it looks like Keith is letting her settle in. Ryan says she likes to be off the pace a bit and come running at them down the stretch.''

''Down the backstretch,'' the disembodied voice droned, ''Steph's Silver holding the lead, Smoothly Crimson second by a length and Semi Pretty.'' This time when the rest of the field was called Le Grand Lady was ahead of three horses. She still had seven to beat, and the distance between her and the gray filly in first place looked depressingly far to Ginna who said as much to Cissy.

''I know, I know. All we can do is trust Keith to know what he's doing. She really likes making up ground.'' She gnawed on a fingernail. ''I just hope she isn't too far out of it.''

''Coming into the turn,'' the announcer called, ''is Steph's Silver, followed by Semi Pretty who takes second by a head, Smoothly Crimson third...''

Catching sight of the farm colors, even Ginna could see that Le Grand Lady was moving up closer to the pack. She found herself clutching her form even more tightly while she chanted softly, ''Come on, Lady... come on!''

''At the head of the lane, Le Grand Lady coming around the outside...''

The din of the spectators' voices rose even higher. Cissy and Nora were yelling, and without realizing it

Ginna found her own voice raised in excited urging as the filly stretched out, her smooth, even stride shortening the distance between her and the lead horses with seemingly no effort, her muscular rear end propelling her forward with raw power, the shiny copper of her coat rippling with each movement of sinew and bone beneath.

"And Le Grand Lady passes Smoothly Crimson and Semi Pretty," the announcer yelled. If possible, the din of voices grew louder. Cissy grabbed Ginna's arm in a death grip when the jockey atop Steph's Silver began to whip the horse to even greater speed in an effort to hold her position. Ginna saw Keith pop Le Grand Lady once with the whip and the filly surged forward, overtaking Steph's Silver in three easy strides, pulling away and crossing beneath the wire in first place just seconds later.

"She did it! She did it!" Cissy squealed, jumping up and down. Ginna felt tears stinging beneath her eyelids at the pure beauty of seeing a perfect animal performing at its peak. Now she understood more fully the LeGrand obsession with horse racing. She glanced at the tote board and saw that the horses had run the mile and sixteenth in a minute, forty-five and two-tenths seconds—a fast time.

Nora grasped Ginna and Cissy's elbows, a radiant smile wreathing her lined face. "Let's go have our picture made!"

Laughing jubilantly, the three made their way through the crowd to the winner's circle. Ginna saw the jockey standing up in the stirrups to slow the prancing filly to a halt as the trio approached Ryan and the other LeGrand men whose faces reflected their pride and happiness. She neared the beautifully landscaped area, her own pleasure triggering the smile that curved her lips.

Ryan was there, exchanging handshakes with his brothers. Ginna saw Darlene approach Ryan, who was standing at the filly's rump. Her smile faded abruptly as her gorgeous blond sister-in-law slid her arms around Ryan's lean middle. She watched helplessly as Darlene lifted herself up on tiptoe and pressed the ripeness of her mouth to his.

Newspaper cameras flashed and television cameras rolled, saving the moment for posterity, while Ginna's heart, the same heart which had been so buoyed up with happiness only moments before, crashed to the bottom of her soul.

Ryan pulled suddenly away, breaking the contact of his lips and Darlene's. His gaze zeroed unerringly in on Ginna who stood near the gate. Her amber eyes were wide with shock. She clutched her racing form to her breast.

She stood stock still while a picture of Ryan's kiss with Carol swept through her with the force of an Arctic wind, freezing her emotions to a blessed numbness…a numbness that thawed beneath the heat of the flashing cameras and left her lacerated heart open to the stinging salt of the tears she fought desperately to hold inside. Just as he kept telling her…some things never change.

Three hours later, Ginna still warred with the feeling of incipient tears. The victory celebration Lefty and Nora had planned so confidently was going off as expected, and Catalpa swarmed with dozens of people who had come to savor the victory in the form of freely flowing food and drink.

Several times throughout the evening, she had suffered the uncomfortable feeling that comes from someone staring. When she turned to see who it was she invariably caught Ryan's intense gaze stalking her. But she hadn't seen him or Darlene the past hour or so.

She sighed in defeat. She'd mingled as best she could, knowing as few people as she did, and longed for nothing more than a place of quiet escape where she could be alone with her thoughts and heartache. She soon found there were none. The kitchen, the study and the porches all held varying numbers of people. Finally, in a gesture born of self-preservation, she made her way around back. Surely if she went far enough away from the house she could find someplace to be alone.

It was almost dark when she started down the driveway, her heels crunching on the gravel as she walked. The evening was still, and the first stars winked saucily in the nearly navy sky. The moon, a giant sphere of yellow approaching its fullness, illuminated the buildings beyond the house. An owl hooted from the stand of trees edging the mare pasture, and the scent of newly mown grass filled her nostrils. Peace. It flowed from the night through Ginna like a healing tonic, alleviating to a degree the pain she'd been suffering since seeing Darlene kiss Ryan earlier that afternoon. Déjà vu. Instant replay. Her life ending the second time.

It was funny really. Somehow during the time she'd spent at Catalpa she had subconsciously begun to think that maybe, as Nora seemed to hope, she and Ryan could get back together. Yet all she really had to base that hope on was the way she felt about him and a single kiss. A kiss that she'd initiated and Ryan had stopped, she reminded herself with brutal honesty. She heaved a deep sigh.

Kisses. She didn't want to think of kisses because that brought back the scene that afternoon with Darlene and Ryan...and before that, Ryan and Carol. She hurt as badly now as she had all those years ago. The feeling of betrayal was just as great. Her heart was a lump of cold hurt inside her that expanded with each mental picture of Darlene's mouth against Ryan's.

She was kissing me. The sound of his voice flitted through her consciousness, implying that he hadn't done the kissing. She pictured again the way Darlene had put her arms around him, recalled how his head jerked back and relived the look in his eyes as they had met hers across the throng of people. What emotion had they held? *A kiss. One damn kiss...*

Her footsteps slowed to a stop. She looked around, surprised to find that she was inside the door to the barn. She would go to the office. Maybe there she could find some solitude and thrash out the conflicting emotions battling inside her. She made her way slowly down the hallway, taking comfort in the sounds of the horses shuffling around in the semi-darkness. Her spirits took another nosedive when she saw that the door to the office was partially open and a light was on.

She was turning to go when the sound of Darlene's soft, sexy laughter stopped her. Darlene...and... who? Even as she wondered, she heard the answering sound of masculine laughter. Darlene and Ryan had been missing for how long now? In spite of telling herself not to, she found herself moving through the darkness to the door. Her heart pounded out a jerky offbeat cadence inside her chest as she approached the crack in the door. The sight that greeted her stole the breath from her body. Darlene, in a state of dishabille and . . .

A brawny arm circled Ginna's waist from behind at the same time as strong fingers covered her mouth to silence the scream building in her throat. Her head fell back against a broad chest and she struggled to see her abductor. Ryan! The tension holding her captive drained as quickly as it had come, leaving her limp in his embrace. His mouth formed a low, "Shh." She nodded, and he released her slowly. With his arm still around her, he led her to a spot beneath the outflung arms of one of the huge live oak trees, well away from the lovers inside the barn.

"What were you doing in the barn?" he asked.

"I was trying to get away from the people. I . . . needed to think."

"About what?" His cigarette lighter flared in the darkness. "Never mind. Let me tell you. You were thinking about Darlene kissing me in the winner's circle this afternoon, weren't you?" Without waiting for her reply, he continued, "And you were comparing it to the kiss you saw before. I saw the look on your face, and I'd bet my part of Catalpa that your narrow little mind has come up with the same answer. Ryan LeGrand is guilty. Guilty of messing around with his brother's wife just as he was guilty of cheating on his own wife eight years ago. How'm I doin'?" he asked sarcastically.

His answer was so close to the truth that she was shocked at his perception. But she hadn't actually condemned him this time. She was learning that things weren't always black and white. There were often shades of gray. Like the look she'd seen on his face, and finding Darlene and Lucas in the office. What did it all mean?

Instead of answering his question, she asked one of her own. "What's going on with Luke and Darlene?"

The tip of Ryan's cigarette glowed more brightly as he took a long drag from it. She heard, rather than saw, him exhale the draft of smoke. He leaned against the tree. "Like a lot of couples, Darlene and Luke have their share of marital problems. But I'm not the cause of them," he tacked on for her benefit.

"What is their problem?" she asked, nearing the place where he stood and peering up at him in the moon's light.

"A child. Or rather, the lack of one."

She frowned. "I don't understand."

"Luke has wanted a baby ever since they got married. Darlene wanted to have her career as a model and the 'gorgeous young married couple' image and kept putting him off. Things have been really bad between them this past year. I've been expecting them to call it quits for months, but somehow neither one can take that step. The truth of the matter is that they love each other too much."

"But she hangs on to every word you say!"

"Sure. I'm her sounding board. She has to talk to someone. Darlene talks to me to have some way to gauge how he's feeling. She's realized Luke means more to her than her career and her figure. She really wants to work things out, but unfortunately, Luke is cursed with an extra dose of LeGrand pride."

"Then what about that kiss today?"

His rich, warm chuckle tickled her taut nerves. "Darlene is a gutsy lady. She isn't opposed to stirring up some jealousy, and from the little scenario in the office, I'd say it worked, wouldn't you?''

An invisible load seemed lifted from Ginna's shoulders. Nora's statement the previous morning about things not always being what they seemed suddenly made sense. Her answer was a soft, ''Yes.''

Silence stretched between them while Ginna assimilated what he'd told her, and Ryan struggled to find something safe to discuss. ''So tell me. How did you like the race today?'' he asked suddenly.

''It was exciting,'' she admitted, taking his lead and changing the topic of conversation. ''I'm beginning to see how people get hooked on racing.''

''Yeah,'' he agreed, tossing the cigarette to the ground and grinding it out with the toe of his boot. ''It's like a lot of things...it can get in your blood.''

Their eyes clung. *Like you.*

He exhaled a gust of air. ''Look,'' he said softly, ''I'm sorry. All right?''

''Sorry?'' she echoed. ''For what?''

''For kissing you that day. It was a mistake. You were just lying there, and I was still remembering the night I saw you just out of the shower, and...aw, damn!''

She stiffened, hardly able to think for the anger raging suddenly through her. He was making excuses for kissing her!

He lunged away from the tree and stood facing her. ''I'm sorry,'' he repeated. ''Let's just say that I'm as susceptible as the next man to a naked woman.''

She laughed bitterly. ''Oh, it was my fault. As long as we're distributing blame, here, I'll take my share. I put my arms around you. I kissed you. There's no need to apologize." *A kiss. One damn kiss.* Would the words—whatever the context—haunt her forever?

Ryan hooked his thumbs in his belt loops, an action that was achingly familiar. "Right. You did. But only after I started things by kissing your back."

"Yes," she whispered. "Why did you?"

His face, gilded with moonlight, wore a to-hell-with-it look as he confessed, "I don't know. I think it had something to do with getting my feelings for you into focus. I wanted to see if there was still anything there after all these years . . . to see if I could still get a reaction from you."

Ginna's temper rose along with a scorching sense of shame at how easily and quickly she'd responded. She reacted accordingly, her hand lashing out with all the strength of her one hundred ten pounds. Ryan's arm came up to ward off the blow, catching her by the wrist with hard fingers and securing her other hand just as deftly.

Struggling to free herself, she spat, "So I was an experiment! Something to boost your male ego! And you found out, didn't you, Ryan? You can still arouse me. I'm just what Erin said I was. You said it yourself after the kiss. I'm easy!"

"Shut up!" he snarled, shaking her slightly.

"I won't shut up! Yes, you still turn me on! But then if you and Erin are to be believed, any man with a modicum of talent in the sex department could. Isn't that right?" Her breasts heaved with the force of her anger. "Tell me, Ryan, what does that do to your macho image?"

"Damn you, Ginna! Will you ever stop jumping to conclusions? I don't know that I consciously set out to prove anything. Maybe the thought was there, but that isn't really why I came on to you." He released her abruptly and raked his hand through his hair, struggling to control his temper. "You're still beautiful, and I'm not immune to that beauty. I made a pass and you responded. It just happened. It's over."

"You came; you saw; you conquered," Ginna retorted scathingly, fighting her own sense of shame.

He scraped his hand through his hair and managed a low humorless laugh. "I didn't quite conquer."

"Thanks to your magnificent control!"

He let that pass and offered her a half smile whose charm she fought to resist. "If you would have given me a chance to explain the other day you'd have realized I wasn't saying you were easy."

"You did! I heard you! That's exactly what you—"

The rest of her tirade was silenced when, with a growl of anger, he jerked her into his arms. The growl mutated to a sound that was closely related to a groan before he crushed her accusing lips beneath the roughness of his. He made no concession to the fact that they had been apart for so long. He took no consideration for the possibility that she might not respond to him. Eliciting a response had never been one of their problems.

Ginna forgot her anger of seconds before, forgot the reason she was here with Ryan, forgot the aching heaviness of her heart. There was nothing...no one but the two of them and the pulsing throb of her blood as it raced through her veins, escalating her heartbeats to a choppy staccato. A whimper of pain and need struggled up through the arch of her throat. Her hands groped their way blindly to the back of his head and her fingers plowed through the rich blackness of his hair.

She felt his hands moving over her back, sighed as they slid down to cup the rounded contour of her bottom and felt tears stinging beneath her eyelids as he shifted and half lifted her into the vee of his legs, fitting his hard masculine body to the waiting, wanting heart of her femininity. Denim and cotton were meager barriers to the heat flowing from her to him and back again. Heat generated at each spot their bodies touched. Heat that fused them mouth to mouth, hard length to soft, aching heart to aching heart.

His mouth ravished hers with a bruising hunger, his tongue urging her lips to part, thrusting deeply, roughly, while his lower body moved against hers, rhythmically matching every silken stroke of his tongue. It seemed as if he sought to erase everything that had gone before them by the very force of his will, striving for the impossible, attempting in a few brief seconds to make up for eight long years of abstinence and hoping he could stamp her with his mark of possession once more.

What the kiss lacked in finesse, it more than made up in emotion. Ginna had relived Ryan kissing her many times...so many times. But dreams, she realized, were a poor substitute for the reality. Dreams made the image of the remembered pleasure blurred and smudged at the edges, a faded copy of the actual taste, smell and touch of this man.

Slowly, slowly, his hands moved to her shoulders and she felt his mouth leaving hers, felt the shudder that wracked his body as he struggled to put distance between them both physically and emotionally. He lifted his head and looked down at her. Her lashes dropped to block out the blazing passion in his eyes. It had always been this way between them. Probably always would. The realization stole quietly into her mind, a peaceful thought contrasted against the harsh sounds of their labored breathing.

More than sixteen years ago, as an emotionally handicapped girl, her reaching out for touching and kissing had been motivated by her longing and need for physical proof of love. As a woman grown and matured, she couldn't lean on that excuse. There was no excuse that would justify her response just now. No rationalization that would make it anything other than what it was: desire for the man who still held her in a loose embrace. A tentative, fragile thread of wanting that even now was unfurling throughout her lower body in bright, sensual ribbons of longing.

She couldn't deny it. She didn't want to. But beyond acceptance of that irrefutable fact, she couldn't think. Gambling mentally on where it might lead was a risk she was afraid to take. The stakes were too high. She couldn't even afford to think of what he might say or do next.

His hand lifted and his thumb traced the moonlight tracking across the sweep of her eyebrow. His voice was low, husky as he said, "Like I keep telling you, some things never change."

"I don't know what you mean," she whispered, both fascinated and frightened by the intensity in his eyes.

His hand slid around beneath her hair to the back of her neck. "Yes, you do. I still ache with wanting you, and if you're honest, you'll admit you still want me."

Her lips parted to deny his statement, but before she could say anything, his fingers tightened warningly on her neck. "Don't say it, Ginna. I kissed you. Twice. You responded both times. We need to face it, no matter how angry it makes us. Why we keep trying to destroy one another is beyond me."

She tore her eyes from his, letting her gaze fall to the crisp hair peeking from the vee of his shirt. She swallowed the lump that suddenly appeared in her throat.

His voice was a sweet caress against her cheek as he leaned down and whispered into her ear, "No more fighting over the past. What's done is done. No more recriminations. Agreed?"

She nodded and raised troubled amber eyes to his face. "And no more kisses?" she asked in a trembling voice. "Promise?"

Ryan's head moved slowly from side to side. "I'm not sure I can manage a promise."

Her heart sprinted forward at the heat in his eyes. She watched his face blur in its movement toward her and barely had time to breathe a soft "no" of protest before his parted mouth found hers again. There was no anger in his kiss this time. Anger she could have withstood. He attacked her crumbling fortresses with a tender bombardment of her senses. Tears squeezed out from beneath her tightly closed eyelids. A small, involuntary moan escaped her lips as they moved in an unwilling response to his. She wanted to tell him to stop, but instead she held him close while his mouth moved hotly over her jaw line in a series of nibbling kisses.

A shout of laughter from somewhere off in the darkness shattered the sexually charged tension of the moment.

His smile was crooked and a trifle sad, and the sigh that lifted his chest was deep and heartfelt. "I can't make any promises, babe. And not because I think you're easy. But I'm beginning to think that maybe I am."

The girl and boy walking toward the barn stopped when they saw the couple standing beneath the tree.

"What's the matter?" Kyle asked softly.

"It's my mom and dad," Erin said, unable to pinpoint the feeling that seeing them standing so close together generated inside her.

Kyle smiled in the moonlight. "That's great! Maybe they'll get back together."

Erin's gaze was troubled and more than a little sad. "Yeah. Maybe."

Chapter Six

Ginna stretched and rolled to her back. Her eyes were closed not so much to block out the brightness of the early morning sun as to keep the dreams of Ryan closer. Dreams that increasingly invaded her waking as well as her sleeping hours. Dreams that wrapped her in a fog of pleasure reminiscent of those enveloping her after their first encounter seventeen years before. A picture of Ryan was etched into her heart. The touch of his mouth was branded onto hers. The magic he worked with his hands a crystal-clear mind memory.

If he was forever on her mind, he was also forever in her sight. If she was pulling weeds in the rose garden, he soon showed up with something cool for her to drink. If she helped Nora in the kitchen, he was in there sampling their cooking. The change in their relationship the past two days, though tentative and as fragile as a tender shoot of grass in the spring, was obvious even to the most casual onlooker. It was no wonder Erin noticed.

Erin. Ginna's eyes fluttered open. A frown drew her auburn brows together and tugged the corners of her mouth downward. She knew Erin noticed the attention Ryan was paying her. There was no mistaking the jealousy in her daughter's eyes, nor was there any mistaking the revival of the negative attitude that had abated somewhat after the sunburn incident.

Ryan had been solely Erin's the past eight years, and she obviously didn't want to share him with anyone . . . not even her mother. Especially her mother. A part of Ginna understood, but part of her still wanted to throttle her capricious, aggravating daughter. Of course she couldn't say anything about it, not with the problems they were already having. So there was nothing to do but wait and see what would happen after Ryan had his talk with her, Ginna thought, throwing back the sheet and heading for the bathroom. Maybe then they'd see a change. And as far as she was concerned, it couldn't happen soon enough.

Thirty minutes later, she stood leaning against the kitchen cabinets, looking out the window at the early morning activity. Today there was no sign of either Ryan or Darlene as there had been a few mornings ago. There was only Kyle and Erin out near the yearling paddock, and Trey and Kirby rolling the wheelbarrows back and forth between the sawdust pile and the barn. Where was everyone? It was only eight-thirty, but the kitchen was spotlessly clean and no one was about, not even Nora. Ginna wasn't certain how long she'd been standing there looking out the window before she was aware of someone in the room.

Whirling around, she found Ryan standing just inside the door. He could have posed in a cigarette ad, she thought randomly, taking in the totally masculine picture he made standing there with his booted feet slightly apart, his thumbs hooked into the belt loops of his Levi's and a burning cigarette between the fingers of his right hand.

Heat swept through her at his perusal that moved with maddening slowness from her sandaled feet up over her lightly tanned legs in the loose-fitting shorts, up over her striped T-shirt and on up to the short ponytail that was already slithering down at the nape of her neck. "Hi," he said softly.

"Hi," she replied, her breathless response giving away much more of her feelings than she liked. Her gaze slid from his to roam the empty room. "Where is everyone?"

"Already gone. Mom wanted me to tell you she had an appointment for a permanent this morning. She said for you to go ahead and fix whatever you wanted for breakfast, but to leave the dishes. She said she'd clean things up when she got back."

Ginna smiled. "That sounds like your mother." She went to the coffee pot and poured herself a cup, then turned back to face him. "She's a very giving person. I think all the LeGrands are."

"What's this?" he asked with a half smile. "A testimonial?"

"No. It's just that I'm learning a lot about you and your family this time, Ryan . . . things I never realized before because I was too wrapped up in myself and how I felt."

He moved to within a foot of her, tossed the cigarette into the garbage disposal and washed it down. His brows were a straight slash across the bold sweep of his forehead. "What are you trying to say, Ginna?" he asked in a husky voice threaded with a silken whisper.

Without realizing that she intended to do it, her hand lifted to his cheek. The scent of his musky after-shave sent her heart into a wild calypso. Her index finger traced the deep groove that time and life had carved into the lean hardness of his cheek. Her own voice was the barest wisp of sound as she murmured, "I'm trying to say I'm sorry."

His hands closed over her narrow hip bones. "Sorry? For what?"

"I'm sorry I set myself up as judge and jury. It was wrong."

Before he could respond to her confession, the phone hanging on the wall across the room began to ring. They jumped apart guiltily. Swearing mildly, Ryan strode across the room and picked up the receiver.

"Yeah?" he growled into the receiver, his attention torn between the voice at the other end of the line and the woman standing across the room. "Oh, Mom. What? Sure thing. Yeah. You bet. Bye."

He cradled the receiver and faced Ginna, a deep sigh issuing from his chest. "That was Mom. She forgot to tell Dad that there's a big load of alfalfa coming in from Paul's Valley this morning. I have to go tell him so he can have some help around to unload it."

Ginna was silent.

He moved to stand in front of her. One hand reached out and cupped her cheek. "We need to have a talk."

She swallowed and stared up into his eyes, waiting. Her tongue darted out to wet her lips. She was completely mesmerized by the gleam in his eyes and captivated by the hope in her heart as his head lowered and his mouth found hers in a kiss of gentle promise. Then he lifted his head, brushing the shiny fullness of her lower lip in a feather-light caress with the pad of his thumb. Giving her a slow smile, he said, "I'll see you later, babe."

Nine fifty-two.

Somehow Ginna had made it through the interminable day and an evening spent watching television with Nora, Lefty and Ryan. Kyle and Erin had driven into Haughton for some frozen yogurt, Cissy and Brad had taken the kids to see a movie, and Darlene and Luke had gone out to dinner.

Ginna's gaze shifted from the grandfather clock to Ryan who sat sprawled on the sofa across the room from her. It was hard to concentrate on the TV movie when all she could think about was his comment earlier about their need to talk. Her nerves were stretched to the snapping point with wondering just when the talk would come about.

Suddenly he stretched and returned the chair to its upright position. "I'm going to go water off," he said offhandedly. He flicked her with a questioning look. "Want to come with me?"

"Sure." Ginna hoped her answer sounded breezy and nonchalant, but feared it betrayed the breathlessness brought on by her palpitating heart. She pushed herself up from the chair.

"There's a spoonin' moon out tonight," Lefty said, winking at his son.

"Lefty LeGrand!" Nora admonished with a shake of her head and an apologetic look at Ryan and Ginna. "Don't pay any attention to him. He's getting senile."

"Senile!" Lefty jumped up from his chair and scooped a shrieking Nora up from the sofa. "I'll show you who's senile!" he taunted, a leer spreading across his face.

Ryan's blue eyes rolled ceilingward. He cast the kissing couple an indulgent look and turned to Ginna. "Let's get out of here before we see something we're too young to see," he said teasingly. Ginna returned his smile, and with a hasty good-night to his parents, followed him from the room.

The obvious love Lefty and Nora still shared left her wrapped with a warm feeling of happiness. If there were any sadness to blight the moment, it was the fact that she would be leaving in four more days and wouldn't be a part of this caring, loving family anymore...and the fact that she'd destroyed her own chance for such happiness. She wished for the thousandth time that things could have been different and wondered if Ryan felt the same.

Once outside, they found that though Lefty's spoonin' moon had begun to wane, the night was still bright. Nightbirds calling in the dark and the sound of an occasional car speeding down the distant highway were the only sounds intruding on their self-imposed quiet.

When they reached the barn, Ryan stepped in front of her to turn on the lights. Bathed in the moon's warm glow, Ginna stood before him, a trusting, waiting expression on her face. Instead of connecting with the lightswitch, Ryan's hand fell onto her hair, his fingers winnowing through the thick richness that looked as if it had been spun from moonbeams into a rich mane of coppery gold.

The unique male scent of him coupled with his cologne wafted to her sensitive nostrils, causing her to shake her head in negation of what she knew was coming. "Ryan," she whispered halfheartedly, protesting with words something that at this moment she wanted more than life itself.

"Yes," he insisted, overcoming her objections with a single word. His hands moved to the sides of her face, holding her captive and blocking out every sound but the frantic beating of her heart as his mouth moved inexorably toward hers. Their lips met softly, sweetly, and Ryan tilted his head to a position to better accommodate his tentative tasting of her.

A groan of exquisite agony rasped from her throat as his mouth began to move in a series of soft, grinding kisses over hers. He had always been a consummate kisser, always able to mold her to his every will with the touch of his lips that could tease, provoke, incite and even punish... just as he was doing now with the tip of his tongue that sought entrance to the warm and waiting cavern of her mouth.

One part of her cried out that she would be a fool to be taken in by his wiles the second time. But his mouth wooed her slowly, convincing her that history repeated itself and that there was such a thing as a second chance. With a moan of surrender, her lips parted. She insinuated two fingers between the buttons of his shirt in an effort to really touch him. Her reward was the increased speed of his heartbeats.

"Touch me, Ginna," he whispered against her mouth. "Touch me..." His hands slid down to her shoulders, moving gently, exploringly over her, dragging the straps of her sunshine-yellow sundress with them. Their calloused roughness was as exciting as his words, words that shattered her slumbering sexuality with the force of a piece of delicate crystal being hurtled carelessly into a fireplace.

Half-remembered feelings of his clever hands and fingers touching and exploring every millimeter of her body exploded in her mind. Feelings she wanted to recapture fully. Feelings she wanted to experience again and again. Thinking only of that end, her fingers moved with unforgotten swiftness at the buttons of his shirt, pulling it from the waistband of his low-riding Levi's and drawing a murmur of acquiescence from lips that moved hotly, wetly over hers.

When her hands, shaking with nervous anticipation, touched his bare chest and found the flat brown nubs of his nipples, Ryan tore his mouth from hers.

"I want you."

The words were spoken with the harshness of an undisguised and unrelenting need. They didn't seek permission. They held no unspoken promises. They were confession. Statement. Demand. They were exactly what Ginna wanted to hear. She smothered the niggling voice of her conscience that reminded her that she wasn't married to Ryan any more and that this was wrong... wrong... Yet how could it be wrong, when she felt so right for the first time in eight years? "Where...?" she whispered in a voice husky with her own need.

Without another word, he took her hand and led her around to the back side of the barn, away from the view of the house to the shadows of the oak tree where he'd kissed her before. He dropped to his knees and reached out in silent invitation. She placed her hand in his; warm fingers closed gently around hers. When he tugged slightly on her hand she sank down before him, her dress billowing out around her.

Their eyes met in the glow of moonlight. Slowly, silently, he reached behind her, his fingers sliding the metal zipper down past her waist. He eased the cotton downward, helping her to free her arms. The fabric pooled at her hips, leaving her covered with a scanty wisp of wire and lace that left precious little to the imagination.

"Ginna?" he asked in a trembling voice.

She knew what he was asking. Her palms brushed his hair-roughened chest and her answer was swift, sure. "Yes."

Wordlessly, he pulled her against him, arching her back and crushing the softness of her breasts against him. Her arms went around him and her head fell back, exposing her neck to a series of rough, impatient kisses while his fingers worked with the hooks of her bra. His mouth left hers and a sound of frustration preceded the scream of tearing cloth. Though their bodies still touched, the tightness beneath her breasts gave. The scratching slide of crisp lace abraded the sensitive tips of her breasts when he pulled the bra away, freeing their fullness to nest in the curling mat of his chest hair.

"Ryan..." she said on a sigh. Her arms tightened around him, and her mouth moved in nibbling kisses over his whisker-stubbled chin. He was warm. Unbelievably, wonderfully warm. It had been so long since she'd held him, so long since he'd held her. Too long. And it was so very good to feel him this close. Ginna reveled in the feel and taste of him.

He shifted slightly and wrung a sigh of dissatisfaction from her... a sigh that changed to one of delight as his hand slipped between them, palming the softness of one creamy mound of flesh. Capturing the sound with his hungry mouth, he asked for—and got—every drop of sweetness hers contained. His other hand slipped beneath her dress and slid the length of her thigh before coming into contact with the thin, silken barrier of her panties. Cupping her bottom, he pulled her closer to him, an action that forced her to a full realization of the extent of his arousal.

"Ryan?" This time the name was both question and supplication.

In answer, he eased her slowly onto the dew-wet grass. The dampness was cool to the heated flesh of her bare back. Due to some calculated move of Ryan's, he knelt between her legs. Her skirt was bunched up around her hips, exposing her slender thighs to the molten, silver moonlight filtering through the branches of the oak and dappling her bare legs and breasts. An instinct as old as time brought one of Ginna's knees up.

He shrugged out of his shirt and, reaching out a trembling hand, traced meaningless hieroglyphics on the skin of her midriff. Their eyes mated. There was no mistaking the message in his. Her tongue darted across her lips and a shiver of longing rippled through her, tautening her blooming nipples into tight, rosy buds of desire. Ryan lowered his body into the cradle of hers.

"Am I too heavy?" His voice was a deep rumble in her ear.

"No..." she whispered, loving the way the denim of his Levi's chaffed her inner thighs. Her fingers traced the sweep of his mustache. "Never."

Smiling, he captured the aching heaviness of one breast and lowered his head. Her fingers raked through

the cool thickness of his hair while his mouth moved
with maddening slowness over her middle.

She should stop him. A pang of hurt pierced her as
she realized she was opening herself up to a new, different heartache. One based on a mature woman's
emotions—not those of a woman-child. Any minute
now he might push away from her as he had that
morning in her bedroom. She didn't think she could
take that sort of rejection again. With that hurtful
memory fresh in her mind, Ginna vowed to push him
away. Just as soon as he stopped nuzzling the undersides of her breasts, she would put a stop to this mad-
ness . . . in just another moment. Her hands tightened
in his hair.

Her newly found resolve scattered to the four winds
as his mouth moved to the peak of her breast and
closed with excruciating care over the turgid tip.
Squeezing her eyes tightly shut, her lower body arched
against him while he laved her with feather-soft strokes
of his tongue. Coherent thought was an impossibility.
All she could do was feel . . . the softness of his hair
beneath her fingertips, the delicious weight of his body
against hers, the tugging of his mouth against her
breast, drawing out the pain of the past, drawing the
very heart from her. Need, so long suppressed, escalated to a devastating crescendo, hammering for freedom. Freedom that could only be purchased with total
possession. She pressed him closer.

His hand left her breast and whispered along her
thigh to her satin-clad hips. He cupped her femininity
in the warmth of his hand, and slowly, so very slowly,
his questing fingers inched to the elasticized leg opening, moving it aside. He touched her. His cheek rested
against hers. "You feel so good, babe," he whispered,

the rhythm of his skillful stroking quickening imperceptibly. He had always known just how to touch... just when... and where...

"Ryan?" she questioned in sudden panic, her eyes opening wide and her nails digging into the flesh of his shoulders. "Ryan!"

"Ssshh..." he crooned into her ear. "Let go..."

At his whispered command, her body arched against his touch and her teeth sank into her bottom lip, biting back a cry of unparalleled pleasure while ripple after ripple of release coursed through her, leaving her breathless in his embrace.

His lips nuzzled her ear. She felt him smile against her cheek as he whispered, "No fair."

She traced the line of his ear with her index finger and whispered, "I know. Now it's your turn."

He leaned back to look at her, a lecherous grin on his face. "Yeah?"

Her hands cradled his cheeks and she turned his face to hers. She smiled. "Yeah."

He groaned when she pulled his head down to hers and her teeth closed gently onto the fullness of his bottom lip. Her hands glided to his bare shoulders and farther, sliding between them over his chest and the flat, hair-whorled planes of his stomach. It was amazing how quickly her nimble fingers unbuckled his belt. Astounding how simple it was to unfasten the catch of his jeans. Astonishing how easily the zipper slipped downward.

"You haven't forgotten much," he told her in low approval.

"It's all that on-the-job training you gave me." she said softly. Her hands pushed the denim fabric aside, cupping his heavy maleness with hands that moved in soft seduction. His readiness was clearly evident and the heat of him radiated through the cotton of his jockey shorts.

Ryan thrust against her caressing hand. His voice was a low, throaty growl as he said, "Lady, you're playing with fire."

Ginna's hands moved to the elastic waistband, her palms turned inward against the crispness of the hair covering his belly. With one quick, deft motion, she freed him to the eagerness of her waiting hands, her fingers closing around the hot, pulsating length of him. Her voice, as sensuous as the slide of lips against a rose petal, taunted softly, "So burn me."

The implication of her words sent Ryan's clambering libido over the edge. His jeans and their underwear were barely tossed aside before he lowered himself over her and slid into her velvet softness. He heard her quickly indrawn breath. Buried deeply inside her, he was still, savoring the reality of the moment. His chest heaved as he fought the rush of emotion clogging his throat and the impending threat of tears.

Ginna absorbed the aftershocks of the slight pain piercing her so sweetly. But it was a pain worth bearing, laced as it was with a promise of pleasure. Her eyes flooded with tears. She touched her lips to his cheek. When he lifted his head to look at her she was dazzled by the tenderness written on his face.

"Yes," she whispered, gazing up at him with moondrenched eyes.

He began to move against her then, slowly, so that each could reacquaint themselves with the pace of the other's need. He was surprised to find her hunger matched his own. He had forgotten that it always had. His hands continued to move over her breasts and he watched the emotions chasing one another across her face. Searing her throat with a kiss, his mouth moved to take hers. He wanted her, needed her...for so many reasons he was unable to separate them into a single, coherent thought.

Ginna tore her mouth from his. "Now," she panted, struggling to speak around her ragged breathing.

"Easy..." he soothed. "We've got forever."

Her head moved in negation. "Now!" Rising up on one elbow, she fastened her mouth roughly to his, invading the warm, moist cavern with rapierlike flicks of her tongue while her hips urged his to a faster rhythm.

"All right, babe...all right..." Ryan filled his hands with the roundness of her bottom and moved against her in a quick succession of deep, grinding thrusts that carried them to the edge of a mind-shattering fulfillment.

"Aahhh, dammit, Ginna!" he rasped as his love spilled into her on wave after wave of sweet sensation. She held him tightly to her, his name a melodic chanting that grew softer and softer as the crashing curls of desire settled to rippling eddies that washed onto the shore of her soul.

Night sounds gradually overcame the sounds of harsh breathing and pounding hearts. The call of the whippoorwill drowned out the sound of his name. With their bodies still fused, he rolled onto his back, taking Ginna with him. Reaching up, he traced the curve of her love-swollen lips with his fingertips. "It's never been this way with anyone else," he said in an awe-filled voice.

A moonbeam sliced the blackness of the night, illuminating his strongly masculine features. She pressed a kiss to the hollow of his throat. "I know." Ever so gently, she lowered her head to his chest. His hands moved caressingly over her back. His heartbeat filled her senses just as he filled her.

"Why did you leave me here?" Without considering how she knew, Ginna realized that now was the time to ask.

His hands stilled at the softly spoken question. Whispered low against his chest, it was impossible to tell, but it seemed to Ryan that besides the hurt behind the question, there was a hint of accusation in her voice. The possibility brought him up short. Why would there be accusation in her voice, unless... Was it possible she thought he'd left her behind to escape the confines of an unplanned marriage? Of course it was possible. Even probable.

He knew he had to choose his words very carefully, because his entire future hung not only on the reasons for his actions in the past, but his ability to make her believe them. His arms tightened around her and he drew in a deep breath.

"I left you here because of your father."

A sudden tension tightened her features. She lifted her head and looked down at him. "My father? What did he have to do with it?"

He smiled wryly. "He was always very vocal about my life-style. He even told me that I couldn't provide you with a stable home life. I was trying to prove him wrong by leaving you here while I traveled the race circuit."

She was quiet a moment, then suddenly she relaxed against him, her face once more resting on his sweat-slick chest.

When he spoke she could feel his lips moving in her hair. "I was really glad when you decided you wanted to come with me after Erin was born."

"Then why did you leave me day after day?"

His hand held her cheek against him. His voice held an earnestness that couldn't be denied. "Because I was trying to make a living the best way I knew how. You have to stay on top of things in this business. I felt I had to go out there every day to do that."

"I can see that now," Ginna confessed, lifting her gaze to his once more. "And...Carol?" she asked, needing to hear his denial once more.

"The backside is full of women who are looking for someone to latch onto. And some of them don't care if the guy is married or not." His voice rumbled from deep inside him. "Carol was one of those. Like I told you—she was doing the kissing. If you would have stayed around, you'd know I fired her that day. Things weren't terrific between us at the time, but they weren't so bad I'd start looking for another woman."

The tears Ginna had fought to hold back for so long trickled down her cheeks in silvery moonlit tracks. "I've been such a fool!"

"I think maybe we should have had this talk a long time ago."

"Yes."

The mockingbird sang a series of sweet songs, the sound at once joyous and sad. The brief moment with Ryan was drawing to an end. And who knew what daylight would bring to them? Ginna moved away from him and sat back on her knees, struggling to cover the lushness of her breasts with the bodice of her dress. "We need to get back."

"I know." Ryan lifted himself to one elbow and threaded his fingers through his hair. He was a perfect sculpture of masculine grace and power as he reclined in naked splendor against the grass. "And what happens now, Ginna? We can't ignore what just happened—or what it means."

She shook her head. "I don't know," she told him honestly, turning her back to him so that he could fix the zipper. She didn't add that she wasn't sure what their lovemaking meant to him.

Ryan zipped her up, then reached for his jeans and stood, thrusting his long legs inside without bothering with his underwear. She made a forlorn picture sitting on her heels in the shadows of the night. Stepping over to her, he cradled her head against his hard thighs, hoping somehow to ease whatever ache might be bothering her. Her arms closed slowly around the back of his knees.

"I'm flying down to Lafayette early in the morning," he told her, tilting her face up to him. "I'll be home about four or five tomorrow afternoon. That will give us some time to get things into perspective. And then we can talk."

You haven't said you love me!

She wanted to shout the words, wanted to ask him if he did, or if what they shared was nothing more than an insatiable sexual craving for one another. Instead, she nodded her agreement and allowed him to pull her to her feet. Gathering up the evidence of their stolen hour, they went back to the house.

At the bottom of the stairs, Ryan pulled her close and pressed a chaste kiss to her forehead. It wasn't until much later, when she lay staring up at the ceiling that she realized that maybe he was waiting for her to make the first move. After all, she hadn't told him she loved him either.

The moon hung low in the sky, silhouetting the shape of a dilapidated barn and glinting off the shiny surface of the car parked behind it. Inside, a radio played softly, the sound of Journey's one-time hit, "Faithfully," a background for low murmurs, soft giggles and masculine laughter. Suddenly, muscular arms pulled the girl close. The laughter stopped, and lips wise beyond their years coaxed hers into a melting pliancy.

She whispered his name, the sound a mixture of wonder and excitement. It was the only sound heard in the car for a long time, while formerly undiscovered feminine feelings quivered in anticipation of release from the bonds forged in years of training. It was only when fingers—accidentally, or otherwise—brushed her breast that Erin pushed Kyle away, her fear and uncertainty overcoming the newer, more fragile emotions...this time.

Chapter Seven

Ryan. The word stole through Ginna's consciousness slowly, with all the brightness and warmth of the early morning sunshine beaming through the frilly priscillas hanging at her bedroom windows. Had the night of loving been only a dream? She tried to recapture the feel of his body against hers but, while she could make mental pictures and hear the words he'd spoken, it wasn't the same. Only the reality of seeing him again, of having him hold her, could compare in any way.

Eyes still closed, she arched her back and stretched, a smile of pure contentment crescenting her lips. The protesting ache in her body and the slight soreness between her thighs were adequate testimony that the night hadn't been a dream. The smile faded. Somehow, instead of bringing her satisfaction, the reality nudged forward a barrage of doubts and apprehensions she wasn't certain she wanted to face.

She sprang from the bed, headed for the bathroom and stepped into the shower, determined to put off thinking about possible repercussions and problems . . . at least for the moment. All that mattered was that Ryan had belonged to her once more. For one night, anyway.

She reached for the shampoo and began to work her hair into a rich suds. *For one night.* Her hands paused. The words haunted her, in spite of her vow not to let anything mar her perfect morning. Had it been for only one night? What did Ryan mean by saying they would have the day to get things into perspective? Was it possible that he was entertaining the idea of a reconciliation? And if he was, what were his reasons? Love for her . . . or Erin?

She shook her bubble-capped head to free herself of her fanciful thoughts and lathered a washcloth with clean-scented soap. Closing her eyes, she rubbed the softness slowly and caressingly over the fullness of her breasts. Her tender nipples puckered at the light stroking, much as they had beneath Ryan's ministrations, but without that same hot rush of sexually charged pleasure. The mound of creamy flesh surrounding them bore pink abrasions from the day's growth of beard he had sported.

All right, babe . . . all right . . .

The words came out of some secret place inside her . . . out of the hissing spray of steamy water cascading over her . . . out of nowhere. Her breath caught in her throat as she recalled the feel of Ryan sliding into her. She could see the look of hunger in his eyes and almost hear the soft expulsion of his breath. *Aahhh, dammit, Ginna!*

Ginna's own breathing quickened at the memory. *He never mentioned love.* The thought ran through her mind as it had the night before, wiping away the sound of his voice, wiping away her tentative hope. Tears rushed to her eyes and she began to scrub at her body with renewed vigor. Just because she still loved him, she shouldn't get her hopes up.

And just because Ryan made love to me, doesn't mean that he returns that love. Her scrubbing movements stopped. All it meant was that the sexual attraction they had always felt for one another still burned as brightly as it always had. The thought both excited and frightened her. She was almost afraid to think of her next meeting with him. Still, it couldn't happen soon enough.

She ducked beneath the warm spray. Streams of iridescent bubbles sluiced over her body and disappeared down the drain. She slicked the hair back from her face and turned the water off. If only she could rid herself of thoughts of Ryan as easily.

The sounds of bedlam assailed her ears half an hour later when she went down to breakfast and stood in the doorway taking in the familiar scene. Lefty, Ryan and Brad's brood all sat at the long ash table devouring fat links of hickory-smoked sausages and stacks of golden pancakes that dripped butter and maple syrup. A laughing Darlene and teasing Luke were just coming in the back door. Like Brad, they lived close enough that dropping in for meals was common.

Erin was pouring more coffee, Cissy wiped sticky chins and Nora tended a griddle where even more pancakes browned. Ginna watched Luke drop a kiss to his mother's cheek. Nora hugged both her son and his wife.

"Hey, boy, you been lookin' mighty tired these past few days," Lefty bellowed teasingly to Luke while he cast a sidelong look at Darlene, who blushed to the roots of her blond hair.

Luke pulled his wife close, placed a slow, hot kiss on her beautifully shaped lips and favored his family with a Cheshirelike smile. "Yeah, well, I hope I get to lookin' worse before I get better." He led the still-blushing Darlene to two empty spaces at the table while the rest of the family roared at the implication of his words.

Closeness. Friendship. Love. All were words that applied as Ginna stood taking in the family gathering. There was something here in his house, something so special about this family that it defied categorizing...or analyzing. She only knew that she wished with all her heart that she'd had it in her life while she was growing up and was thankful that Erin had at least had a sampling of it in hers these past few years. A lump formed in her throat when she contemplated the possibility of becoming a part of it all once again.

Her sorrowful gaze moved back to Ryan. He looked wonderful. The breadth of his shoulders filled out the striped knit shirt he wore. His teeth flashed whitely beneath the sweep of his dark mustache and his eyes danced with laughter. Then, as if he felt her scrutiny, he lifted those laughing sapphire eyes to where she stood.

The merriment fled his face when he saw the regret on hers. His heart—lighter than it had been in years—skipped a beat before regaining its normal rhythm. The look on her face could only mean one thing. She was sorry about what had happened between them. She

wasn't going to give them another chance. She was...
Why, Ginna, Why?

She smiled at him. Slowly. Tentatively. As if to ask
permission to join them and whatever it was they were
celebrating. As if to say she was sorry. As if to ask if
the night had really happened...and if so...where did
they go from here? The giant fist squeezing the hope
from Ryan's heart eased its grip. Maybe the doubts
hadn't taken too strong a hold yet. The questions in her
eyes were ones he wanted so badly to answer, but only
with her tucked securely in the haven of his arms.

He smiled back; Ginna's smile widened.

Suddenly Lefty's voice boomed out over the ordered chaos of the kitchen. "Ginna! Good mornin'.
Come sit down and have some pancakes. Erin, get your
maman a cup of coffee."

Smiling a welcome that was echoed on the faces of
the whole LeGrand clan—minus Erin—Cissy scooted
one of her toddlers down the bench and made a place
for Ginna between the child and Ryan. The roar of
conversation with its different topics hummed
throughout the room again, and it seemed to Ginna
that she and Ryan were alone in the room full of
laughing, talking people. Their eyes clung in mute tenderness. "Hi," she said, stepping self-consciously over
the bench and sitting down. Her thigh brushed his;
their bare arms brushed. Electricity sparked.

"Hi," he said quietly.

"Wanna kiss Auntie Gin!" The demand was made
by the child at Ginna's side and drew her attention
momentarily from Ryan. She couldn't be sure, but she
thought she heard Ryan utter a low, "Me, too!" as she
turned to a smiling, dimpled countenance generously
smeared with portions of breakfast. Chubby, sticky

hands touched her cheeks and a gooey kiss was planted at the corner of her mouth. It was one of the sweetest kisses she had ever received . . . in more ways than one. "I wuv you, Auntie Gin," three-year-old Kristi Le-Grand cooed with a wide smile.

Ginna's smile matched Kristi's. "I love you too, *petite,*" she said, the French endearment slipping out with a naturalness that surprised her. Satisfied, the child went back to demolishing her pancakes and Ginna turned back to Ryan, a wide grin on her face. "She's adorable."

"So are you," he said solemnly, "and you have about as much syrup on your face as she does." He dipped the corner of his napkin into his water glass and grasped Ginna's chin gently between his thumb and forefinger. Tilting her face, he dabbed at the smears of syrup on her cheeks and chin. Ginna was entranced by the concentration on his face as he worked at cleaning hers. When the cloth and his attention moved to the corner of her mouth, the tip of her tongue peeked out from between her peach-glossed lips and made a swipe at the sweetness lingering there.

Blue fire flashed in Ryan's eyes. His finger brushed the corner of her lips. While she watched, he lifted it to his mouth. His tongue curled around the tip in much the same way it had curled around her nipples. She watched him suck the stickiness of the syrup away. Her breasts swelled and their peaks tightened. She could feel the gentle suckling to the innermost heart of her femininity. The simple act resurrected memories that had no place at the breakfast table.

"Here's your coffee."

Both Ginna and Ryan jumped at the sound of Er-in's voice and his hand dropped quickly from Ginna's chin. Erin's face was impassive except for the antagonism glittering in her eyes.

"Thank you, Erin," Ginna said, gathering her senses and taking the cup. She gave her daughter a slight smile and silently berated herself for letting the girl intimidate her.

"May I have some more, please?" Lefty asked in an effort to ease the potentially awkward moment.

Erin complied, and Nora brought Ginna's pancakes. The mood was broken, and though she was aware of every move Ryan made, she made it a point not to make any direct eye contact with him during the remainder of the meal. It would never do to antagonize Erin any more than she already had.

The children had gone out to play, and everyone was finishing their last cup of coffee before anyone mentioned Ryan's trip to South Louisiana.

"What time are you leaving?" Brad asked.

Ryan lit a cigarette and blew a draft of smoke upward, flicking Ginna with a glance. "In just a minute."

"You're coming back this evening, aren't you?" Nora asked, setting her coffee on the table and lowering herself to Lefty's knees. Lefty gave her behind an affectionate pat and took another swallow of his coffee.

He nodded. "I ought to be home by nine or so."

"I won't wait supper if you're going to be that late," Nora said.

"No need. I'll catch something in town." He flipped his ashes into an ashtray and turned to look at Ginna. "Want to come along?"

"Me?"

"Yeah."

Fly! In that little bitty plane of his? No way! Not even to be with Ryan would she do something as fool-hardy as that. She cleared her throat of the annoying squeak. "No thanks. I think I'll just stay here."

"Chicken!" Ryan scoffed, but his eyes held under-standing. "How about you, honey?" he asked of Erin who was loading the dishwasher.

Erin looked at her mother and then back to Ryan. "No. I think I'll stay here. Kyle and I are supposed to go to the lake this afternoon."

Ryan heaved an exaggerated sigh. "Well, then, I guess I'll go by myself," he said, grinding out the cig-arette and standing up. He looked at Ginna. "I'll go on up and get my clothes. Walk up with me. I want to talk to you about something."

She nodded and followed him from the room as he called good-byes over his shoulder. As soon as they were out in the hall he grabbed her wrist, backed her against the wall and pinned her there with his body. His chest flattened her breasts and one Levi's-clad leg in-sinuated itself between hers before his mouth swooped and took hers with a searing kiss. He tasted of chicory and tobacco and Ginna thought that the feel of his mouth on hers and the erotic dancing of their tongues might possibly be the most wonderful sensation in the world.

He drew away slowly and trailed a string of kisses along her jaw line while his fingers worked some but-tons free of their moorings and pushed her shirt off her shoulder. She angled her neck to give him freer access. "What was that for?"

Pulling back to meet her eyes, he said, "When you walked into that room I could see the regret on your face."

She shook her head. "Regret? But I didn't . . ." she began, then remembered. "Yes, I was. I was regretting that I hadn't known a family like yours while I was growing up. And I was sorry that I hadn't taken more a part while we were married."

Relief spread across his taut features. "I was afraid you were sorry about last night."

Her cheeks washed with the pale pink of embarrassment. Her finger whispered along his bottom lip. "No. I'm not sorry."

"Good," he told her around a sigh. He shackled her wrist in his tanned fingers and carried her palm to his mouth. His tongue tickled the sensitive area. "The kiss was originally meant to remind you how good things were . . . to make you sorry that you were feeling regret. But if you weren't having second thoughts, I guess it will have to be a kiss to hold you until tonight when I get back," he told her solemnly.

She smiled up at him, the love in her heart shining from her amber eyes. "Oh. If that's what it was, then maybe I'd better have another . . . just to be sure."

"You and Ryan are going to get back together, aren't you?" The question was spoken by his mother while she cut up chicken for dinner.

Ginna was sitting at the table peeling potatoes. Her startled gaze flew to Nora's. "What makes you say that?"

"It sure took you a long time to water off the horses last night," Nora said, a sly smile spreading across her face.

The blush, which Ginna was beginning to think was perpetual, stained her cheeks once more. "I still love him, Nora. I know that now."

"He loves you, too."

"Do you really think so?" Ginna asked earnestly.

"I think I know him well enough to safely say that I truly believe so."

"But I'm not certain where we go from here."

"That's up to you and Ryan, isn't it?"

Ginna rose and walked to the sink, laying the knife on the countertop and putting the colander full of peeled potatoes beneath the running water. She turned to Nora, a troubled golden gaze meeting one of steady brown. "I don't know. Is it?"

"What do you mean?"

"What about Erin?" Ginna's voice was laden with doubt and concern.

"I think she'd be glad to see her parents back together again and happy," Nora said.

"Then you don't know Erin very well," Ginna said with a wry smile. "You should have seen the look she gave me this morning when Ryan was trying to wipe Kristi's syrup off my face."

Nora laughed. "Oh, I don't think that's anything to worry about. From what I hear, it's natural for a young girl to be in competition with her mother for her father's attention."

"I know that's what they say, but with Erin it's more. She blames me for her conception, Nora. She's put all the blame off on me and pardoned Ryan completely," Ginna said, cutting the potatoes into a copper-bottomed pot. She shrugged. "God only knows I've never been able to say no to him—" her eyes met Nora's squarely "—either then or now, so maybe I am to blame."

Nora's face held a trace of sadness. "I don't deal in blame, Ginna. That's for someone mightier than I am.

And I try not to deal in guilt too much either. Guilt is too easily acquired and too hard to get rid of. I think you and Ryan need to decide what's best for the two of you, because in the long run that will be the best thing for Erin."

Ginna searched her mother-in-law's face for confirmation of her words. "Do you think so?"

Nora nodded. "I know so."

"What if Ryan wants to get married again?"

"I think that's a distinct possibility."

"But nothing has really changed, Nora. We would still have the same problems. Ryan is still in the same business."

"Yes, he is. But all the boys share the workload more evenly now since there are families involved. Ryan doesn't go off and stay for long periods of time any more. None of them do. Besides, even if he did, it would work this time. You're different. I told you that the other day."

"You're right. I am different. Ryan is used to having a hot lunch ready at noon, and a big meal at night. I have my own business, and I like working. My work is what ultimately made me grow up, I think, and I don't want to give that part of myself up. How would Ryan feel about a working wife?"

"I can't answer that. But if he loves you, and I believe he does, then you'll be able to work everything out."

Tears glittered in Ginna's eyes. "I don't know how you can be so nice to me after all the heartache I've caused everyone."

Placing the chicken in the sink, Nora wiped her hands on a towel and turned to her daughter-in-law. Reaching up, she framed Ginna's cheeks with her work-worn hands. "I think there's blame on both sides, child. Ryan's as well as yours. You, Cissy and Darlene are the daughters I never had. You're the women my boys chose to share their lives, and I couldn't have chosen better myself."

With a small cry of joy, Ginna let herself be wrapped into the healing warmth of Nora LeGrand's embrace. For that one moment it was so easy to believe her, so tempting to think that everything would be all right.

Unlike breakfast, dinner that evening was a quiet meal. Luke had taken Darlene into Shreveport for dinner at Firenze's and to the Strand theater for an evening of ballet, which, he bemoaned, his brothers and Lefty would never let him live down. Brad and Cissy had gone to friends' for another cookout.

Conversation was more personal since there were only the four of them, and Ginna was pleased to see the rapport between Erin and her grandparents, even though she had little to say to her mother.

When everyone was stuffed with Nora's spicy Cajun fried chicken, Nora and Ginna agreed to clean up the kitchen while Erin moved the furniture in her room. Ginna was wiping off the last countertop when the phone rang.

"I've got it!" Lefty called from the den.

"Probably Brad to tell me if he'll be over for breakfast in the morning," Nora said.

"Doesn't it bother you to have them all living so close and dropping in so much?"

"Bother me!" Nora said with a laugh. "I love it! You have to understand how we Cajuns were raised— always a passel of folks around. You get used to it." Her petite shoulders lifted in a shrug. "It's a way of life."

"Ginna!" Lefty called out. "Ryan wants to talk to you."

Ginna's eyes flew to her mother-in-law's face. "Ryan? Why is he calling? He's supposed to be home in an hour."

"Maybe he wants you to meet him in Shreveport or something." Nora winked at Ginna. "I'll just go watch TV a while."

With her heart beating ninety to nothing Ginna picked up the kitchen extension. "Ryan?"

"Hi, babe."

"Ryan, aren't you supposed to be on your way home?"

He laughed. "I just called to let you know I won't be there until some time tomorrow. My landing gear tried to hang up on me. I want to have it checked out and the mechanic can't get to it until tomorrow. No big deal."

Ginna's heart did a nose dive. "What happened?"

"Nothing. Absolutely nothing. Just calm down," he said soothingly.

She swallowed the lump of fear clogging her throat.

"Ginna? Are you okay?"

"Yes," she wheezed. "Yes."

"Miss me?"

If the possibility of something happening to Ryan had partially robbed her of her breath, those words finished her off. She could only nod, an action she be-latedly realized he couldn't see. "Yes."

"I miss you, too. I'm supposed to be selling shares in a stallion, and all I can think about is you. You're beautiful. You know that?"

"I'm not."

"And sexy."

"No . . ." she moaned.

"And when you kiss me, I go absolutely crazy with wanting you."

"Ry-yan..." she muttered in protest. "*You're* driving *me* crazy."

"Yeah?" She could hear the smile in his voice.

"Yeah."

"Good." He paused. "Have you been thinking about things?"

"Yes."

"And?"

"And now isn't the time or place," she said. "This is serious. It deserves more than a quick telephone conversation."

She could almost see him running his hand through his hair. "Don't I know it! Tomorrow, then. As soon as I get back. We'll go to the lake or something."

"Okay."

A deep sigh came across the lines. "I hate to hang up."

"I know."

"There's so much to say...so much to tell you..."

Ginna knew how he felt. The need to clear up the past and get on with the future was burning inside her. But, as she'd said, now wasn't the time. Tears stung beneath her eyelids as her heart swelled with love and the promise of a second chance. "Tomorrow," she whispered.

"Tomorrow," he agreed softly.

"I'll see you then," she said, wanting to hang up before she made a fool of herself and broke into tears.

"I'll see you then."

They each sat staring at the phone, hundreds of miles separating them, and neither could hang up. Finally,

Ginna made the move. As if he could see her, he said suddenly, "Ginna!"

"Yes?"

"Dream about me."

She nodded once more. "I will."

"Promise?"

"Promise."

"Good night, then."

She heard him hang up. She sat there with her eyes closed and the phone pressed to her ear for several seconds. Then, so softly she could barely hear it, she heard another click. Lefty had probably forgotten to hang up the den phone. She shrugged and cradled her own receiver, anxious now to finish the dishes and go up to bed so that she could keep her promise to Ryan. She was longing to dream about him and what the following day would bring.

Upstairs, Erin sat staring at the phone, a disbelieving look on her face before she fell onto the bedspread and let the tears fall.

"They're going to get back together!" Erin spat out the following morning.

Kyle stood leaning against the fence, his elbows resting on the top board. "How do you know?"

"After dinner last night I heard Poppa tell Mom that Dad wanted to talk to her on the phone, so I listened in from my room."

"You did what!" Kyle exclaimed, lunging from the fence and grabbing her by the shoulders. "You had no right to do that, Erin."

Erin wrenched herself free. "He's my father!" she shouted.

"And Ginna is your mother," Kyle reminded her. When he saw the anger on her face, he sighed. Combatting Erin's anger with his own was useless. He'd already learned that reason worked much better. "Okay, so what makes you think they're getting back together?"

Erin plunged her hands into the back pockets of her jeans. "The things they were saying. How much they missed each other. Had she been thinking about things. How sexy she was..." Erin kicked at the ground. "I don't know! Lots of junk." She rolled her eyes heavenward. "He told her to dream about him. Can you imagine?"

Kyle planted his hands on his hips and nodded. "Yeah. I can. I think it's great. He's right. Your mom is beautiful, sexy and a really nice person. Your dad has been a different person since she came. He's been more content...happier. It sounds to me like you're just jealous of the attention he's giving her."

"I am not jealous!" Erin yelled. "And he's probably so content because she's letting him have a little."

Kyle looked as if Erin had just slapped him. His voice held shock and anger as he said, "I can't believe you'd say such a thing. Not about your mother."

Erin's eyes filled with tears. She dropped her head to hide them and mumbled, "Yeah? Well, nice person or not, she's no saint."

"None of us are," Kyle said, beginning to see that there was more to this than just jealousy. He reached out and lifted her chin. "Do you want to explain that last statement?"

"I don't know," she told him, tears and truth sparkling in her eyes. "It might make you feel differently about me."

Kyle smiled. "I doubt it. I scoped out all your bad faults a long time ago, Erin, and in spite of them I think you're okay."

"What faults?"

Kyle took both her hands in his. "You're stubborn as a mule, have a terrible temper..." She tried to pull her hands free and his grip tightened. "...and have a smart mouth. Want me to go on?" he asked, a wide grin splitting his handsome features.

Her head tilted to a regal angle, and she fought back the tears once more. His criticisms hurt, even though deep down she knew he was right. "So why do you keep hanging around?"

Kyle pulled her resisting body into his arms and rested his chin on top of her shining head. "Because you're pretty and funny, and you make a mean oatmeal cookie."

"Get serious!" Erin grumbled against his chest.

"I am. Besides, you're too much like both of them to turn out too bad."

"I'm not like my mom!" she said, pushing away from him.

"Sure you are. You look so much like her it's a joke. And you have that same determination she does, even though you channel it differently."

"I'm more like my dad."

"Nope. He's too easygoing. You're uptight like Ginna. And he's forgiving. You're not. At least not yet."

Erin burrowed closer, anchoring herself to him and seeking solace from his stability. She didn't want to hear this, but somehow, hearing it from Kyle made it easier to take. Suddenly she knew she could trust him with her secret. "They had to get married," she mumbled into his chest.

His only response was to hold her more tightly. "When did you find out?"

"A few weeks ago."

She felt him shrug. "It's common enough. Happens all the time. So what?"

Erin pulled from his embrace. "So what? Kyle, they're my parents!"

Kyle's face wore a strangely tolerant impatience. "They're people, Erin."

"I know that!" She turned and crossed her forearms on the fencetop. "Mom has always told me not to go all the way. But she did."

"Is that what all this is about?"

Erin didn't answer.

Taking her by the shoulders, Kyle turned her toward him. She had lost the battle with her tears and the crystalline droplets scored twin trails down her cheeks. He brushed them away with his fingertips. "It's time you faced a few facts of life, Erin. Sometimes things like that just happen in spite of what we've been told. Even in spite of how we feel about it. You don't seriously think they planned to sleep together, do you?"

"How should I know!" she cried, thankful he was taking it so well.

"Well, think about it."

She had. Every time she pictured her mother and dad in bed together she couldn't help feeling betrayed. But Kyle's comments made a lot of sense. Sometimes he made her feel so young. She squinted up at him in the bright sunlight. The tears sparkled against the darkness of her lashes like drops of dew. "How old did you say you were?'' she asked, already feeling the weight of her burden ease by just sharing it with someone.

He ran his finger down the nose so much like her mother's. ''An ancient nineteen to your tender fifteen.''

''Sixteen in two days,'' she corrected, her heart's wings spreading in sudden contentment and pleasure.

''Ah, yes,'' he lamented. ''Sweet sixteen—never been kissed.''

Erin lifted her smiling face to his and looped her arms around his neck. ''Wanna bet?'' she whispered, rising on tiptoe to meet his descending mouth.

Chapter Eight

The scent of damp earth assailed Ginna's nostrils as she bent to place several yellow squash into her wicker basket. Lefty's natural fertilizer and his slow, nightly watering were definitely paying off, she thought, eyeing the stately rows of corn and okra and the healthy tomato plants that already bore clusters of green tomatoes. She smiled, remembering his prediction of tomato and mayonnaise sandwiches by the end of the month. Her mouth watered just thinking about it.

The unwelcome realization that she might not be around by then intruded with rude abruptness, drying up the pleasant turn of her thoughts and her watering mouth simultaneously. What would happen between her and Ryan was a question—one of many whose answer would continue to evade her until she could see him face to face—that had plagued her until the pink of dawn had stained the eastern sky. She wanted to believe that the night they'd made love meant as much to him as it had to her. Still the doubts crept in. There were so many things to settle. Maybe too many things. She and Ryan had to bury the skeletons of the past before they could build a future. A marriage couldn't be built on physical attraction alone. If nothing else, their first attempt had taught her that.

Ginna wiped the perspiration beading her face onto the shoulder of her cotton shirt. It was much too hot to be picking vegetables, but she'd needed something to keep her busy. The long hours would have passed even more slowly if she'd just sat around waiting for the sound of Ryan's truck. She glanced at the plain gold watch circling her wrist for the fourth time in as many minutes. It was just after two o'clock—long past the time she had set in her mind for his arrival. She wondered what was keeping him. With a sigh, she bent over and began searching through a dense patch of green leaves for the ever-hiding cucumbers.

"I see your underwear."

Ryan's low observation several moments later sent her whirling around, cucumbers scattering in all directions. He stood leaning against the garden gate, his straw western hat shadowing his face, wearing a half smile and his overwhelming masculinity with a carelessness that never ceased to amaze her. The inevitable cigarette resided between his fingers and, as usual, his thumbs were hooked in the belt loops of his snug-fitting Levi's.

Ginna was well aware that the cutoffs and old T-shirt of Erin's she wore didn't present the most attractive picture in the world. She was also aware that the shirt was damp with perspiration, her ponytail was straggling into her eyes, and her face, already tingling from too much sun, was undoubtedly the color of Lefty's beets. She wished she could crawl into the crawdad hole she'd seen over by the zucchini. Yet incredibly, the doubts that had plagued her all day dissipated like night mists before an early morning sun the instant she had turned to see him standing there.

"You're back," she said inanely, while her hands tugged to no avail at the frayed bottoms of the shorts she wore. A warm feeling of happiness that he'd made it back safely infused her.

"Yep." He tossed the cigarette to the dark, rich soil and ground it beneath the heel of his boot. One long finger flicked toward her basket of vegetables. "Finished?"

"Not really."

"Oh, yes you are." He walked over and picked up the heavily laden basket. "It's too hot for this. We can pick the rest late this evening."

Lifting her hand to shield her eyes from the sun she looked up at him. "We?"

"Yes, we." He flipped her a jaunty Boy Scout salute. "Promise."

"Okay. But I'm holding you to it," she told him as they started across the yard. She gave a little running skip to catch up with his ground-eating stride. "Where are you going?" she asked, noticing that he was headed for his truck instead of the house.

"You look hot and sticky. I'm taking you someplace to cool off."

She stopped in midstride, suddenly uncertain about what she would do and say alone with Ryan in an intimate setting, and not at all sure she was ready for the talk they both knew could only be put off so long.

Though he sensed her hesitation and knew why she was so reluctant to be alone with him, he never stopped walking. He knew where she was coming from. If they were alone, they would be compelled to talk things through, and he didn't think he was ready for that yet, either. But he still wanted to be with her.

"Come on," he urged, tossing her a grin over his shoulder. "I know where there's a great pond. I'll stop and get us something to drink and a bag of chips. We'll just swim a little and rest. Okay?"

She wanted to go. To be with him. And he seemed to be saying that they would do nothing more than enjoy some time together. A sudden smile broke across her face. "Let me run in and tell your mom."

He hoisted the basket into the bed of the truck, a semi-naughty smile deepening the creases in his cheeks. As he opened the door he confessed, "I already told her."

Ginna hurried to the passenger side, wrenched open her door and got inside. Her eyes narrowed as she faced him in the close quarters. "Pretty sure of yourself, aren't you?"

He settled in beside her and turned the key in the ignition. "Not really. Just hopeful."

Fifteen minutes later, armed with a Coke and a package of crackers with peanut butter for Ginna and a beer and bag of pretzels for himself, Ryan sent the truck barrelling down the highway toward the secret destination.

"Did you get the landing gear fixed?" Ginna asked suddenly.

Taking his eyes off the road long enough to flick her with a brilliant blue glance he said, "I had it checked out, but the mechanic couldn't find anything. I'll have Luke look at it."

"He and Darlene went to Dallas for a few days," she told him. Then, suddenly realizing what he'd said, she asked, "Luke can fix airplanes?"

"One of his many talents," Ryan quipped, turning off the main highway onto a pocked and rutted road bordered on both sides by a dense growth of hardwood trees. "Actually, he's very good at it."

"I guess having an airplane mechanic in the family saves you a bundle," she said, bracing herself against the dashboard as they hit a particularly deep pothole. Without waiting for his answer she asked, "Are you sure you know where you're going?"

"Uh huh," he replied, keeping his full attention on the road before him and trying unsuccessfully to avoid the craterlike holes. He offered her a quick smile. "This is an old logging road. No one uses it but hunters anymore." He hit another pothole and grinned. "Dad always says it takes a good driver to hit them all."

Ginna rolled her eyes. "You're undoubtedly the best, then."

He cast her a wounded look as the front wheel fell off into a deeply scored rut and threw Ginna against the door. She yelped when her head hit the window.

"You okay?" he asked. She rubbed her throbbing temple and gave him a short nod. "Almost there," he assured her with an encouraging smile.

Sure enough, they soon approached a gate. Ryan got out, unlocked it and drove through. Innumerable acres of slightly hilly pastureland, knee-deep in lush green Bermuda grass, rolled out before them. Ginna cranked down her window to get a better view. A large pond with a rickety looking boat pulled ashore at one end, and shaded by trees at the other, beckoned with the promise of a cooling dip. Cattle egrets dotted the field of green that sustained a motley herd of cattle. One brave bird actually sat on the back of a Brahma heifer with a wilting hump.

"How did you ever find this place?" she asked, turning to him with wonder in her eyes.

"We lease it for deer hunting," he explained, driving the truck over a worn path through the grass. "I usually make that trek on my four wheeler."

"I can understand why. I think I'll walk out."

"No you won't," he predicted. "You'll be too tired."

When she looked at him with a question in her eyes he only gave her another of those bad-boy smiles that set her heart to racing.

Driving as close as possible to the shaded end of the pond, he stopped the truck and got out. Ginna followed, throwing back her head and looking up at the canopy of leaves. The huge tree's branches spread protectively out over the spot, shielding it from the heat of the afternoon sun in the same way a mother hen spreads her wings to shield her newly hatched chicks from harm. Her gaze shifted to Ryan who was watching her with an intensity in his eyes that made her want to seek that same protection.

"What kind of tree is this?" she asked with a forced smile.

He noticed the way her eyes refused to meet his. He lit a cigarette before he spoke. "It's a black gum. You should see them in the fall. They turn a bright red. The sweet gum turns almost purple." He flashed her a smile filled with an apology. "Sorry. I never meant this to be a nature lesson."

The tension eased somewhat. Returning his smile, Ginna tucked her fingertips with her palms outward into the back pocket of her cutoffs and headed toward the water. It didn't have the green stuff growing on top of it like the lake did, but it didn't look very appealing, either. She wasn't certain she wanted to get in it.

"I don't think I want to swim in there."

He flicked his cigarette out into the water and leaned against a tree, bending over to pull off one boot. "Aw, c'mon, spoilsport. A little muddy water won't hurt you."

She cast the murky depths another woebegone look and put the toe of her right tennis shoe against the heel of the other to pull it off. The shoes were sitting neatly beside a tree trunk when a sudden thought assailed her. How could she have been so naive? Was it because she and Ryan had been intimate for so many years that she'd forgotten?

"Ryan," she said over her shoulder. "We don't have any swimming suits."

One heavy black brow lifted questioningly. "So?"

"So I'm not going skinny-dipping with you," she told him, knowing for some reason that she couldn't let him touch her again...not until they had settled things between them and she had some idea where this new relationship was going.

He saw the resolve in her eyes. Instinctively, he knew how she felt. The same thoughts had been bombarding him for two days. "We can wear our underwear," he proposed logically. "It'll probably cover us up better than a swimming suit would anyway."

Shrugging, she peeled out of her clothes and moved quickly for the water's edge.

Ryan tried to keep his mind on his own stripping and off the fact that Ginna's underwear didn't cover more than a swimming suit. To the contrary, the sheerness of her lavender bikini panties allowed him a tantalizing glimpse of the shadowy delineation of her sweet-curving derriere. Thankfully, he was afforded only a back view. Maybe, he thought, drawing a shaky hand over his face, this wasn't such a good idea after all.

Ginna squealed, drawing his attention from her anatomy to her surprised face. "It's muddy!" she cried, staring in disbelief at the black mud oozing between her toes.

"Of course it's muddy. It's a pond." He piled his jeans next to his boots and shirt and started toward her, a half smile on his face, determination in his eyes.

"I'm not getting in that nasty stuff," she said, turning and starting back for her clothes, attempting at the same time to keep her eyes averted from Ryan who wore nothing but his pale blue briefs. When they were face to face he stepped in front of her and stooped to hoist her over his shoulder before she knew what was happening. He hadn't even broken stride.

"Ryan LeGrand, you put me down!" she yelled, pounding on his back with her fists and pummeling his hard abdomen with her feet.

"Ouch! Dammit, Ginna, stop that! Kick a little lower and I'll be ruined for life!" he grumbled, giving her bottom a hard smack.

Her squirming and kicking stopped immediately. The humor of the whole thing hit her, bringing a wide smile to her lips. "I'm going to tell your mother you threw me in the pond," she threatened, her breath warm against his back.

His hand brushed caressingly down the back of her thigh. He turned his head and pressed a moist kiss to her bare side. "Oh yeah?" he taunted softly. "Before or *after* you tell her you were swimming with me in your underwear?"

Her laughter gusting against his lower back caused frissons of sensation to scamper down his spine. "Point taken. Put me down, Ryan."

"Okay." His hands clamped at her waist and he lifted her up from his shoulder, pushing with all his might as he thrust his arms out straight, propelling her away from him with a hard shove.

She felt herself going out and up and then, without warning, his hands left her and she was falling down, down into the pond's water. She barely had time to scream before she hit the surface and went under. Flailing and kicking, she fought her way to the surface, only to hear the rich, warm sound of his laughter.

"You rotten . . . no-good . . . !" she sputtered, trying to tread water and push her hair from her eyes at the same time.

"Tsk, tsk," Ryan interrupted from his place further down the pond. "Such language."

"I'll 'such language' you!" she threatened, swimming toward him. She launched herself at him in an all-out effort of her one hundred and ten pounds to push him under, a task that only made him laugh harder.

"Laugh, you sorry—"

Her tirade was cut short as his arms went around her and he jerked her body up close to his. Dancing blue eyes met those of glittering gold. "It's that funny, huh?" she asked tartly.

"Yeah," he said, trying his best to control his mirth. "It's sorta hard to push someone under who's standing on bottom."

"Why, you..." she began. "I thought you were treading water."

"That's what you get for thinking," he told her with a cocky grin.

She pushed back from him a bit and said, "Just look at me!"

His eyes moved leisurely from her red-gold hair that was plastered to her head, down over her pouting mouth that begged to be kissed on down to her breasts. The flimsy covering of lace had lost all pretense of modesty with its recent dunking and clung wetly to her rounded fullness. Pink nipples, tight from the coolness of the water, pressed impudently against the sheer barrier of lace and brought a surge of heat to his loins.

She felt the growing hardness of him against her belly. "Ryan..." she began.

"Shh," he whispered, lowering his head and pulling her close once again. "Kiss me."

She was helpless against the soft command. It was, after all, what she wanted. Her lips parted, her eyes closed and her head fell back. His open mouth met hers sweetly, persuasively. With a moan of surrender, she let her tongue join his in an erotic dance of love. It was so right...so very right. How could anything go wrong?

But when his hand moved between them and she felt him unhook the front catch of her bra, she tore her mouth from his. "No," she told him in a shaking voice.

He looked deeply into her eyes. Desire still shimmered in their golden depths. Desire and something else. Fear. Uncertainty. She was right, he thought with a sigh. They couldn't afford to let these newly found feelings lead them any deeper into a relationship until they knew exactly what that relationship was.

He smiled at her then. A smile of understanding. A smile that told her without words that he wouldn't push and that he, too, knew they needed to talk, to come to an understanding. But not now. Not this moment. The talking could wait. Right now they needed to just be with one another. Wordlessly, Ryan rehooked the catch of her brassiere and pressed a quick dispassionate kiss to her mouth.

"Race you to the other side," he challenged.

She reached up and rested her palm against his cheek in a gesture of thanks. Then a mischievous smile arced her lips. She pushed away from him and started out across the water. "You're on!"

"Cheat!" Ryan called, watching for a second before starting out after her. In spite of the fun of the moment, there was an unaccountable ache in his heart, and for the life of him, he couldn't figure out why. It was only later that he realized what it was. Like Ginna, he was afraid. And he wasn't certain if he'd survive losing her a second time.

The drive back to Catalpa was made in almost total silence. The time at the pond seemed almost unreal—the legendary moment snatched out of time. They had played in the water, finished their drinks and talked. Ginna couldn't even say what they'd talked about. She only knew they didn't talk about the night they'd made love, or where they would go from here, and that they stayed longer than they should have. It was almost as if they each realized that the afternoon spent innocently together was a planned effort to put off the inevitable. Now they both realized that things had been put off about as long as they could. The tension between them grew the closer they drove to Catalpa, stretched more tightly with each passing minute.

Ryan turned off the ignition. By mutual consent they were silent on the trek from the truck to the house. He set the basket of vegetables inside the kitchen door and ushered Ginna in ahead of him. He gave the kitchen a quick once over. "I wonder where Mom is?"

"Watching PBS. Where else?"

Ryan's smile looked strained. "Yeah. I forgot." His gaze raked the still-damp tangle of her hair. He reached up and plucked a twig from it. "Why don't you go up and shower? You smell like Louisiana mud."

Ginna's color deepened at his customary bluntness. She laughed uneasily and attempted to lighten the moment. "I know I look terrible, but it's awfully ungentlemanly of you to say so."

Ryan's own discomfiture eased somewhat in the face of her gallant effort to maintain the camaraderie they'd shared at the pond. A wry smile twisted his lips. His fingers curled around the back of her neck and pulled her closer. "I never claimed to be a gentleman, babe. Just a man." He squeezed the nape of her neck briefly. "Besides, you're such a prickly pear. I didn't mean you looked terrible. You're as cute as a bug and sexy as hell in those shorts."

He leaned down and pressed a kiss to the tip of her sunburned nose. "You also got a burn, and your freckles are poppin' out like popcorn. We'll both feel better after a shower."

"You're right," she said with a sigh. "I won't be but a minute, okay?"

The corners of his eyes crinkled. "No hurry. I'm not going anywhere."

Thirty minutes later, showered and sweet-smelling, her hair in it's usual sleek pageboy and dressed in a peppermint-striped sundress, Ginna gave every appearance of being calm and cool. Inside, her heart was doing a tap dance on the stage of her quivering stomach. The doubts had returned with a vengeance. *Get hold of yourself, Ginna LeGrand. There is no reason why the thought of one man should make you so nervous. You're a grown woman who runs a business singlehandedly.* Her business. She didn't want to think about that now. She took a deep, fortifying breath and paused to check her makeup in the mottled mirror of an antique hall-tree before opening the door.

Ryan, his hair still wet from his recent shower, was sprawled in one corner of the sofa, his booted feet resting irreverently on the battered trunk that once served as Nora's hope chest and now doubled as a coffee table. Nora was seated on the other side, engrossed in the TV. Both heads turned when she walked into the room, but it was Ryan's silent appraisal that started the singing in Ginna's heart and turned her blood to the consistency of warm honey.

His look started at the pink-lacquered tips of her toes peeking from the hot-pink crisscrossing of straps up over smoothly shaven legs to the dress of pink and white stripes that left her lightly tanned shoulders bare, nipped in at the waist and flared gently at her hips. His eyes lingered on her breasts before moving to her lightly made up face.

Entranced by her cool prettiness, but worried by the way her eyes refused to meet his, he pushed to his feet and walked toward her. "You look like a peppermint stick," he observed with a slow smile.

Ginna couldn't have stopped her answering smile if she'd wanted to. "That unshapely, huh?"

Nora's laughter joined her son's. Ginna felt Ryan's lips brushing her forehead as he mumbled, "The clothes, the clothes. There's nothing wrong with your shape." Tucking her into the curve of his embrace he announced, "We're going to go outside awhile. If anyone wants me, I'm not back yet."

"Done," Nora said, watching them go through to the kitchen with a smile of hope gleaming in her eyes.

Five minutes later, Ginna and Ryan faced each other across the width of his desk in the barn office. The window unit breathed cool air into the small room, easing the unrelenting heat of late afternoon.

She watched him light a cigarette and thought the scene could serve as an instant replay of the day after her arrival when she'd argued with him about Erin. She only hoped that this discussion wouldn't end in the same way.

"Well," he said at last, blowing a cloud of smoke toward the ceiling, "did you have a chance to think things through?"

She nodded and straightened in her chair, thinking how like him it was to jump into things with both feet. Now that the time was here, he had no intention of beating around the bush. The happiness and fun they'd shared only an hour ago seemed light-years away, maybe even imagined.

"And?"

"And," she began in a voice that sounded stilted even to her own ears, "I think you should tell me just what it is you think we should do."

He looked at her silently for a moment, then flipped his ashes into the ashtray and ran his fingers through his hair. His gaze met hers, bounced to the doorway and returned. He dragged air into his lungs and blurted, "There isn't any doubt in my mind that the attraction I feel for you is as strong as it ever was. Or that you feel the same way about me. Otherwise, the other night would never have happened."

"Yes," Ginna agreed.

"You're gonna make me spell this out, aren't you?" he asked, his mouth curving wryly.

"I just don't want to make assumptions about your feelings."

He nodded and took a long drag off the cigarette, speaking quickly before he exhaled the smoke. "I think we should get married again."

The small bit of starch keeping Ginna's back straight wilted. She slumped in her chair. Why did she feel like crying when his words were exactly what she wanted to hear? If only there weren't those nagging doubts... *Tell me you love me and everything else will work out.* "You think we should get married again because we feel a sexual attraction for one another?" She forced herself to say the words that needed saying. "That isn't a very strong foundation for marriage, Ryan. We found that out once."

His eyes met hers steadily. "That isn't the only reason. There's Erin. I think she needs both of us right now."

Erin. So much for love, Ginna thought. Her laughter held the bitterness of self-preservation. "Erin doesn't need me in the least. In case you haven't noticed, she hardly speaks to me, and if her looks could kill, you'd have buried me yesterday morning after breakfast. To tell you the truth, Ryan, I think she senses something between us, and it's only made a bad situation worse.''

"Maybe. But I think knowing we are trying to work things out will make a big difference in her attitude, once she gets over the initial shock.''

"Why?''

"Because she'll realize there was something strong between us back then, and that we found it again. She'll know we felt more for one another than she seems to believe right now.''

"You don't seem to understand that it isn't you she blames. It's me,'' Ginna said, placing her hand against her breast. "And no matter what you say, I don't think her attitude will change overnight.''

"No, I guess not.'' He ground out the burned cigarette. "Is that any reason we shouldn't give ourselves another chance?''

"No, not for that reason alone.'' She sighed. "Has anything really changed, Ryan? Or are we the same people?''

"We've changed,'' he said positively. "I know I have. I was blind to too many things before. I'd never make the same mistakes again. Besides, there's a big difference in you, too.''

"Yes,'' she said, nodding. "There is. And I'm not certain the new Ginna is what you really want.''

"What's that supposed to mean?''

She smiled a bittersweet smile. "It means that when I was eighteen I thought you hung the moon and the stars. You were the sun in my life, and my whole life revolved around you and your world. Your family. Your business. Your wants and needs.'' Her eyes, full of candor, met his. "Well, I don't feel that way anymore, Ryan."

Pain flashed across his features so quickly she wasn't certain that she hadn't imagined it. "I'm trying to be honest. Yes, I'd like us to try again—for a lot of reasons—but I'm my own person now, Ryan, and while I'll always be proud of your accomplishments and your hopes and dreams, you'll have to realize that I have hopes and dreams and accomplishments of my own after eight years of taking care of myself."

"Your business."

"Yes." A spark of something he couldn't put his finger on lit the earnestness of her eyes. "You're used to having someone at your beck and call. Lunch at eleven-thirty, and a huge evening meal. I'm not used to doing all the little things your mother does for you. I'm good at what I do, Ryan, and I don't want to give it up."

"You're asking me if you can still work if we marry again?"

"No. I'm telling you that I will work. I would want to invest in my own business down here." Defiance and a need for understanding conflicted in her eyes. "I won't ever again be in the position of having nothing to fall back on."

Ryan regarded the solemnity of her features. He heard the words and tried to put himself in her place. While it would be nice to have her at home whenever he dropped in—and he was enough of a chauvinist not to want his wife to work—he thought he could adjust to her new qualifications with little problem. There was validity in what she said, but the fact that she felt she needed to say it cut at his heart. What hurt was the fact that she was making provisions for herself in case their marriage failed a second time. In short, Ginna just wasn't as sure about a reconciliation as he was. She was afraid she would be swallowed up by his life again, just as she had been before.

He was afraid, too. Sometimes the remembrance of past failures threatened to overwhelm him, but he knew without a doubt that if Ginna loved him half as much as he still loved her, they could work things out.

He wanted to tell her he loved her, but somehow he couldn't. Call it masculine pride. Call it wounded ego. Call it whatever. The fact was that he wanted her to say the words first. She'd destroyed some portion of his heart by refusing to listen to his pleas of innocence and love when she'd walked out on him. Maybe, he reasoned, by wanting her to say the words first he was putting her through some sort of childish test to prove her love. But as silly as his intellect told him it was, he knew it would take her saying the words first to heal the bruise she'd left on his heart. He sighed. Maybe what they both needed was more time . . .

Ginna's heart beat raggedly as she watched the emotions within Ryan fighting for supremacy of his features. The ultimatum had to be a blow to his masculine pride, but surely he realized she was fighting for her own life this time. She waited for his answer, longed for reassurances from him, needed him to tell her he loved her . . . wanted him to say that love, rather than sex, or because it was the best thing to do for Erin, was the reason he wanted to marry her again. Yet she was afraid to say the words herself. After she'd thrown his love in his face eight years ago, he might not want that binding emotion from her anymore.

"I understand where you're coming from," he said at last, the sound of his voice jerking her from her worry and insecurity. He pushed from the desk and rose, rounding the desk and half-sitting on the corner.

"You do?" She breathed a soft sigh of relief, allowing the hope to take hold once more.

"Yes," he said. "And maybe you're right. It would be unfair of me to expect you to just give up something that's been a major part of your life for so long." He paused and scraped his hand through his hair, obviously choosing his words with care. "I can understand you wanting to work and have your own business even though I'd like for you to be at home." His smile looked almost apologetic as he continued, "But I get the feeling that wanting to work is more than just that."

"What do you mean?" Unease stirred to life inside her.

"It seems to me that when you say you don't ever want to be in the position of not having something to fall back on you're automatically assuming we won't make it. And I'm not certain that's a good way to start out a marriage." *Why can't you trust me to make this work, Ginna?*

Her unease escalated to full-fledged panic. The death of her dreams was imminent. "What are you saying, Ryan? That you won't let me work?"

"No. I'd never try to tell you what to do about something as important to you as this is."

Her face paled. "Then what?"

Leaning forward, he took the hands clenched tightly in her lap. He pulled her to her feet and into the vee of his legs, facing her forehead to forehead, nose to nose. His breath was a sweet vapor against her lips as he spoke. "I want this a lot, Ginna, but I don't think you're as sure as I am about it. You're supposed to go home in a couple of days—" he paused, drawing in a breath of air before he continued "—and I think that might be a good idea."

Her head jerked back and her shock-filled eyes met his. "You want me to go?" The words were hardly more than a whisper.

"This all happened so fast, so unexpectedly, that it's no wonder we both have doubts," he said, answering her indirectly.

"You have doubts, too?"

His hand came up to rub at the frown wrinkling her brow. "Of course I do. The only difference is that I sincerely believe we can work our problems out this time. I just think you need a little space to sort things out in your mind before you come to any decision." He smiled a sad sort of smile. "What you don't need is to see me every day and feel I'm pressuring you for an answer."

"So you want me to go back to Chicago and think about it?" she repeated in an attempt to clarify things in her own mind.

"No, dammit! I don't *want* you to go," he said in a savage whisper, "but I think you *need* to go." He pulled her close and felt her arms slide around his waist. She pressed her face into his chest. His cheek rested against hers and his mustache tickled her ear as he said, "When you come to a decision, whatever it is, you call me. I'll be here waiting."

When Ginna and Ryan returned to the house, Brad, Cissy and the kids had come over for dinner, and any direct conversation with Nora was postponed. Several times, though, she caught her mother-in-law's gaze focused intently on her. It made it hard to look Nora in the eye. Ryan was unusually quiet. Thankfully, Brad's brood talked and and made enough noise that it covered the strain between Ginna and Ryan.

In spite of the undercurrents, the meal went off well, with most of the conversation centering on Erin's birthday party the next night. Besides the family who would participate in a shrimp boil, she was inviting several kids she'd kept a running friendship with from year to year to stay for a party afterward. To her delight, Lefty was hiring a live rock band from Shreveport to provide the music, and Brad and Cissy—the least stuffy of the adults—had volunteered to chaperone.

"What about you, Ginna?" Brad asked. "Are you going to hide out in the bushes and check to make sure no one sneaks off for a little kissy-kissy or tries to spike the punch?"

Ginna glanced at Erin, who was holding her breath in anticipation of her mother's response. She gave her daughter a smile edged in sadness. "No," she said softly, looking directly into Erin's eyes. "I can't chaperone. I have to get up early. My plane leaves at nine Friday morning."

Chapter Nine

It would be months before Ginna forgot the looks on the faces around the dinner table. The disappointment in Lefty's eyes. The shock on Brad and Cissy's faces. Nora's anger. The way Erin's eyes shifted from hers, and the bleakness carved into Ryan's granitelike features. Even now, a full twenty-four hours later, guilt, sorrow and an anger that had no real direction stampeded her heart, leaving her vulnerable to an ever increasing sense of loss. She was thankful that with Erin's birthday party in full swing, no one noticed how distracted she was.

Even though they had been threatened by low-hanging clouds to the west, the cookout had gone off without a hitch. Soon after eating, all the adults made themselves scarce, leaving the teenagers to their dancing and any other mischief they could put over on Brad and Cissy.

Ginna, sitting in the back porch swing, saw a couple glide by in the shadow left in the wake of the rapidly waning moon that was dressed for the occasion in wisps of gossamer clouds. It was hardly half full now, and the daily lessening of the moon's light seemed somehow a fitting way to signify the end of her stay at Catalpa. Maybe it was even significant in representing her relationship with Ryan. Things between them seemed to have been waning like the moon ever since the night they had made love bathed in its shimmering silver light.

Sighing, restless, she rose from the swing and moved with lethargic slowness down the steps. The darkness beckoned with memories of another magical evening, and she yearned to recapture a bit of that magic to take back with her. Her footsteps carried her across the backyard, past the tire-swing that hung from a branch of a Catalpa tree, and past Nora's heart-shaped bed of tea roses. Their light, spicy scent hung on the humid heat of the night, surrounding her suddenly with an onslaught of memories.

How many dozen roses does she need, for heaven's sake?

How many times had she heard her sister, Kay, voice the question when a big wedding was coming up? How many dozens of roses had she prepared for others' enjoyment throughout the years, using a paring knife to remove the wicked thorns that hid among the dark green leaves? How much wire had she used, piercing the fat hips of the roses then twining the thin length around the long, slender stems for support? How many miles of ribbon had she looped into bows? How many hours? How long since she'd looked at a rose in appreciation of its beauty instead of its freshness? How long since she'd regarded it as the symbol of love it was, instead of in terms of a profit?

Ginna stopped and retraced her steps to the rose bed. Impulsively, she reached out to pluck a single fragrant blossom, carefully pulling and twisting the woody stem. The rose gave unexpectedly and, when it did, her hand closed just as unexpectedly around a thorn, bringing blood. With a small cry of pain, she carried her hand to her mouth.

Roses. Love. Dealing with either exacted a price. Bleeding fingers or bleeding hearts, you paid. She brought the rose to her nose. The dewy softness of the petals caressed her skin, and the sweet tea smell assaulted her nostrils. The pinprick of the thorn was forgotten in her enjoyment of the flower, just as the pain of failure was forgotten in the joy and healing power of love.

She knew then that she was wrong in not accepting what Ryan offered. She knew that if she went back to Chicago and her stable, uneventful life, she would spend the next eight years just as she had the past eight—creating beauty and happiness for others instead of herself. And she knew without a doubt that the shop wouldn't be a panacea for her heartache this time. This time it would only be a place filled with roses and regrets because she hadn't tried harder to create that happiness and beauty in her own life.

She and Ryan had loved once, perhaps unwisely. They had made mistakes, and they would make more. But love—a mature love—could help make everything all right. She wouldn't need a business for a cushion in case their marriage didn't work out this time. Even if Ryan never said "I love you" to her and she never said it to him, she would still feel it. She could *show* him.

That had to make a difference. The heaviness inside her lifted.

There was only one problem, and that was finding the right way to tell him of her change of heart. An even harder task would be making him believe it. She looked around her at the encroaching night. She didn't even know where he was. Then she saw the light in the barn office. Maybe...

The first thing Ginna saw when the door to the office swung open on well-oiled hinges, was Ryan lying on the battered sofa with one arm flung up over his eyes as if to keep out the offending light. He must have heard her approach the door; perhaps he only sensed her presence. His arm came down and their eyes met across the width of the room. A frown scored his forehead. His voice was a husky bass rumble as he asked, "What is it, Ginna?"

There was no coquetry in Ginna, no hesitation. Instead, she took a page from his book and plunged. "I don't want to go back tomorrow."

He stared at her with eyes flooded with surprise and disbelief, then he swung his legs to the floor and sat up. "What?"

The petals of the blood-red rose dropped like confetti to the floor, victims of nervous fingers that unwittingly shredded the flower's perfect beauty as she moved closer to him. She couldn't say the words, but she could still make a commitment. "I don't want to go back, Ryan. I want to stay here with you, no matter what happens."

She stopped in front of him and looked fearfully into his upturned face. He didn't speak. Instead, his hands came out and fastened on her hips, drawing her into the wedge of space between his legs. The tattered rose fell forgotten to the floor and her fingers sifted through the clean softness of his dark hair. Circling her hips in a strong embrace, he nestled his face against the flatness of her abdomen. She could feel the warmth of his breath through the thin cotton of her shorts as he asked, "Are you sure?"

"Yes." She cradled his face with her palms and forced his head back until their eyes met again. "Yes," she repeated solemnly, even though her eyes smiled at him.

Drowning in the promise of her gaze, he pulled her down onto his knee. His brow knit in query. "We'll tell everyone tomorrow." It was as much a question as a statement.

Ginna nodded.

"They'll all be ecstatic," he predicted with a slow grin, unable to keep a note of exultation from his own voice.

"Erin..."

"Erin will be fine, babe," he assured her, his hand running up and down her bare arm in a light caress. He frowned suddenly. "I guess I'll have to let you go back to Chicago and clear things up."

"Yes."

"I'll start looking for a place for you to put in a florist shop here."

Ginna's eyebrows flew together; her eyes widened. "That isn't a condition of my deciding to stay, Ryan."

"I know that. But I also know it's important to you."

Gentle fingertips traced the outline of his upper lip that hid beneath his mustache. She knew just how much this concession must have cost him in terms of LeGrand pride. She loved him all the more for his willingness to make it. The smile she offered him was laced with tenderness. "When I started thinking about things, I realized the shop wasn't what I really wanted."

"What do you really want?"

I want to love you forever. I want you to love me for the rest of my life.

But she couldn't say that, not knowing if he wanted to hear it or not. Instead, she said, "I want what I've wanted since the day you walked into that shop seventeen years ago. You. And," she continued, almost as if her tongue had a mind of its own, "I want you to make love to me. Now. Tonight. And for all the tonights there are left for us."

She watched his face and waited with suspended breath for his reply. Her honesty was too revealing. Perhaps the statement was too forward as well as too revealing. She'd been too presumptuous. Too possessive. Too... She added one last word, a word unbelievably compelling in the very intensity behind its soft utterance. "Please..."

Ryan's eyes deepened to near black before his mouth met hers in a tender contact that held both the promise for tomorrow and the passion simmering just beneath the facade of insouciance he wore so well. She slid from his lap. "Don't go 'way," she whispered, going to the door and bolting it shut. It was amazing how bold she'd grown suddenly. She started to flip the light off, but he stopped her.

"I want to see you."

She blushed with delicate color, but complied, walking across the room toward him. Even as she moved nearer, he was busy unbuttoning his shirt.

"Let me," she commanded lowly, covering his hands with hers. There was an excitement shimmering in the depths of his eyes. Something she'd never seen there before. Something brought about by the fact that for the first time ever, she was taking the lead and acting the aggressor in their lovemaking. His hands fell obediently to his sides.

Ryan began to think that Ginna was going to make a career out of undoing his shirt, so slowly did she free each button from its mooring. He sucked his breath in sharply when, pushing the opened edges aside, she ran the palms of her hands over him. Leaning forward, she pressed a series of kisses over the bronze breadth of his chest, bringing the brown nubs of his masculine nipples to pebble hardness beneath the ministrations of her tongue. Her mouth worked its particular magic while her hands skimmed the hard planes of his middle. Inch by tantalizing inch, she worked the bottom of his shirt from his jeans and, easing it off his wide shoulders, tossed it onto the desktop. Then with a gentle pressure of her fingertips, she pushed him down onto the sofa and knelt on the floor before him, working off first one boot and then the other before peeling off his socks and leaving them on the floor.

With a smile that straddled daring and hesitant trembling on her lips, she reached to the hem of her tank top and started to take it off.

"No. Let me," Ryan said, his repetition of the words she'd spoken only moments before vanquishing the burgeoning aggression inside her. Her tongue darted across her lips.

He groaned at the unstudied provocation of the simple act. She hadn't changed, he thought, aching to taste the gleaming wetness of her mouth. She was still as unaware of the little sexy things she did as she had ever been.

He pulled her up onto the sofa and stood himself. Facing her, he unfastened the snap of his jeans. Her fingers clenched as the sound of the zipper's downward grind gritted through the silence of the room. Her eyes, already languid with a growing desire, turned to hot, molten gold. Pushing the denim slowly down his thighs, he stepped out of the jeans and straightening, moved toward her.

Her gaze climbed from the proof of his arousal straining against the pale blue of his briefs up over the taut musculature of his abdomen and up over his chest to his face. Without a word, she rose to her feet. His hands found her waist and slipped beneath the knit top she wore, moving quickly to the front hook of her bra. She felt it give, felt the sudden freedom of her breasts and the quickening of her nipples as his thumbs brushed them with exquisite tenderness. The all-too-familiar need his touch evoked was gathering within the heart of her womanhood, urging her closer...closer...

When she pressed her lower body against him Ryan responded by plunging his hands inside her elasticized shorts, panties and all, and peeling them downward. Their eyes meshed. Wriggling her hips to help him, she stepped free of the shorts, relegating them to an aqua puddle against a dark floor. His hands gathered the bottom of her top and pulled it upward until the folds rode the upper swells of her creamy breasts. He pulled her closer so that their rosy tips barely brushed the dark hair covering his chest.

"Ryan—" she choked out.

"What, Ginna?"

She looked up at him with desire and embarrassment sparring in her eyes. Desire was victorious. "I want you."

"You have to learn to take what you want, babe." Splaying his fingers, he molded the roundness of her hips with his calloused hands, pulling her closer to the heat and hardness of him.

The message was unmistakable. Now that he knew for certain how the scenario was to be played out, Ryan was returning the role of aggressor to her. It was a role she had longed to portray so many times in the past, but a role that, perhaps because of her strict upbringing, she'd never found the courage to play before.

Now, with maturity sitting securely on her shoulders and her long-suppressed sexuality screaming for more of his lovemaking, she found she wasn't afraid anymore. The imp of provocativeness that had prompted her to tell him she wanted him and had whispered to her to lock the door returned. Ginna moistened her lips with the tip of her tongue and, standing on tiptoe, fastened her mouth to his with a ravishing hunger that to Ryan still seemed filled with a breathtaking innocence.

A shudder rippled through him. His hips pressed into hers. And when her hands scaled his chest and cupped his lean cheeks to pull his dark head down and whisper excitingly naughty things into his ear, he groaned his impatience and stripped her shirt and bra from her with loving roughness.

Impatience was a demon who rode Ginna as well. She pulled from his embrace and dropped to the sofa, arching her back in a perfectly feline imitation, while she lured him with a seductive smile and an uplifted, beckoning hand.

Stripping off his briefs, stripping away any doubts she had about the strength of his passion, Ryan bared his eager, aching masculinity to the hunger of her gaze. The sharp intake of her breath was amazingly gratifying and he knew he couldn't wait much longer to seek the stronger gratification he knew awaited him when he buried himself in the willing warmth of her body.

Nudging her legs apart, he knelt between her thighs. His hands curled around her knees, skimming up her legs with a touch so light that if it weren't for the increased tempo of her heartbeats she might have believed it was her imagination. When his hands moved to her hipbones, she reached down and covered them with hers. Ryan looked at her questioningly and smiled when she carried his hands to her breasts. "What do you thing you're doing?" he asked.

Ginna raised herself on one hand and reached out to capture him with the other. "I'm doing what you said—taking what I want," she told him huskily, before crushing her mouth to his.

Warm and mobile, her lips twisted beneath his, transposing every move he made into something more as she gave it back. Each darting foray of his tongue was met with a dancing riposte by hers. His stroked; hers danced. Meeting, twining, mating. Something—a cross between a growl and a groan—escaped Ryan's mouth and, unable to wait any longer, he lowered himself against her.

She felt the first tentative probing, and with one quick, sharp movement, thrust upward. It was hard to say who was more shocked. Ryan, surprised but thrilled that she'd once again taken the initiative, or Ginna, who felt tears squeezing from beneath her eyelids at the perfectly complete way he filled her . . . body and soul . . .

I love you Ryan . . .

"Babe . . . babe . . ." he breathed, pressing his lips to her tightly closed eyelids. *I love you so much . . . so damn much.*

Ginna's hand lifted to his cheek. Her eyes, the color of warm honey, opened. She was drowning in the blue sea of his. Her thumb brushed the sensual fullness of his lower lip, still wet from their kisses. Lowering his head, his mouth found the pouting peak of one breast.

Sighing, her heart full, Ginna held him to her. "Love me, Ryan," she begged. "Please, love me now."

And he did.

Much later, they lay front to front, Ginna wedged between the hard length of his body and the sofa's scratchy back, one smooth leg nestled intimately between his. Ryan cradled her to him, rubbing slow, concentric circles on her upper arm and smoking another of his inevitable cigarettes.

"We need to go in," she said on a sigh.

"Uh huh."

"It's still good, isn't it?" She lifted her head to look at him, gauging his reaction to her question.

One of his eyebrows raised indolently, his eyes gleaming in merriment. "It was okay," he observed laconically.

"Ry-yan!" she cried, tugging sharply at a handful of his chest hair.

Low bass laughter filtered throughout the room. "You haven't changed. I can still get a rise out of you."

"Oh yeah?" she said huffily. "Well, unless my memory fails me, I can still get a rise out of you, too."

Ryan, who was in the process of blowing a smoke ring almost choked. "Why, Ms. LeGrand," he told her with a definite leer smeared on his handsome features, "I do believe that was a crude remark."

"And you liked it," she taunted.

"I liked it when you did it," he agreed. "Do it again."

Smiling, Ginna shook her head. "You can't make me."

Ryan leaned to stub out his cigarette in the ashtray on the floor. He threw her a decided smirk and shifted her until she lay atop him. "You're wrong, babe. I just did. And I think I will again."

Replete with loving, Ryan and Ginna started arm in arm back toward the house. She was drunk on the taste and feel of him. Satiated with something much deeper and more complex than just experiencing fantastic sex, she felt whole again for the first time in eight long years.

Whispering, laughing softly, they stumbled across the backyard, stopping to indulge in another satisfying series of kisses near Nora's roses, whose fragrance wafted to them on the freshening wind of the impending storm. Then stealthily, they moved on toward the house.

Ginna never remembered what happened next. She wasn't certain if it was the stiffening of Ryan at her side that alerted her to the couple near the Catalpa tree, or if she saw them first and transmitted her surprise to him.

A feminine body was pressed into the trunk of the tree by the muscular weight of the man whose hips pressed against hers in an obvious message, even though they were fully clothed. Pale arms twined around his neck while his hands moved with an urgent feverishness over straining feminine breasts. They were so engrossed in a deeply passionate kiss that Ginna doubted if anything would penetrate their total absorption with one another.

But she was wrong. When the wind chased the clouds from the face of the moon, briefly illuminating the unmistakable gleam of red-gold hair and wringing a gasp from Ginna's throat, the couple sprang apart.

Erin! Reeling from the force of her pain and shock, Ginna clutched at Ryan's biceps to steady herself. Some part of her mind was aware of the guilt and embarrassment on Kyle's features, of the shame and sorrow on Erin's, but any compassion she might have felt for them was lost in the jumble of emotions tumbling through her. History repeating itself. Erin was too young...Kyle was too old for her, too experienced...just as Ryan had been. How far would things have gone if they hadn't been interrupted? And, dear God, what if this wasn't the first time? She fought back the hysterical sob rising in her throat.

Racing to Erin and vaguely aware that Ryan reached out to stop her, Ginna grabbed her daughter by the shoulders. "How...could...you...do...this?" she cried, punctuating each gritted word with a sharp shake that set Erin's head bobbing on the slim column of her neck. Dimly, Ginna realized she'd lost her battle with the tears. Liquid misery sped in silvery runnels down her cheeks. "I tried to tell you not to make the same mistakes!"

"Ginna, stop it!" Ryan's voice cracked like a rifle shot through the electric silence surrounding them. She stopped shaking Erin so abruptly that Ryan knew their daughter would have fallen without the steadying touch of Ginna's hands on her shoulders. His own heart broke as he saw Erin's eyes go wide and bright and her mouth begin to quiver as she stared up into her mother's face. She didn't fight Ginna's wrath; she welcomed it.

Ginna's trembling hands crept up to Erin's face, the face she'd watched change from baby plumpness to the beautiful countenance of a woman. "How could you?" she whimpered again.

Erin stared at her mother, aware that she had single-handedly brought her to this point. The victory was hers. But the sweet taste of that victory was suddenly bitter in her mouth. Unable to bear those condemning eyes any longer, she jerked her head aside, freeing herself of Ginna's touch.

"I'm sorry, Mrs. LeGrand. It was my fault."

Furious, Ginna whirled at the sound of Kyle's quaking voice, thankful to have someone else to vent her fury on.

"You're too old for her!" she said. "I knew it! I—"

"Ginna." Ryan's voice held a warning she ignored.

"Nothing happened, Mrs. LeGrand," Kyle protested, swallowing the lump of fear in his throat as he caught sight of Ryan's approach out of the corner of his eye. "I swear to you, nothing happened!"

"Nothing happened tonight," Ginna spat, grabbing Kyle's arm. "But what about all the other nights? How many other nights have you tried to seduce her?"

"For God's sake, Ginna," Ryan said, moving between her and Kyle. "Take it easy. Let me handle this."

His piercing gaze raked her in the moonlight. Where had the carefree woman who had kissed him so passionately only a few moments ago gone? This Ginna was a stranger to him. A stranger who flung accusations and reeked of bitterness. A stranger who had not one ounce of compassion for a troubled girl-woman struggling with a problem in her own life plus the demands her body was making on her with her first rapidly growing physical attraction. As shocked and hurt as he was over finding Erin in a compromising situation, Ryan knew the proper handling of it required much more tact than Ginna was currently wielding. He reached out and gave her shoulder a light squeeze. "He said nothing happened."

"And you believe him?" Incredulity edged Ginna's voice.

Without answering her, Ryan reached out with his other hand and turned Erin's head toward him. Her face was carefully wiped free of emotion and her eyes were dry, but they screamed out a message he had no difficulty reading. *Help me. Somebody please help me.*

The need to get to the bottom of things was almost overshadowed by the need to "kiss it and make it well" as he'd done when she was a child. But she wasn't a child. Physically, if not emotionally, she was a woman, as the scene he and Ginna had interrupted proved only too well. He hardened his heart against the pull she exerted on his heartstrings.

"If you've ever told me the truth, Erin, you'd better do it, now." She acknowledged his command with a nod of her head. Ryan's tongue slid across his lips. "Have you and Kyle ever gone all the way?"

The pain in his voice was unmistakable. Erin glanced quickly at Kyle and then her mother. Her father's pain matched the hurt in her mother's eyes. She shook her head. "We never did, Daddy. I promise."

His pent-up breath hissed through his tightly compressed lips. Ginna slumped against the tree in a relief so great she wasn't certain her legs would support her. Kyle passed a shaking hand down his face, and Erin's tenuous control over her tears snapped. With a small cry, she launched herself into her father's embrace and sobbed out the misery of her aching heart.

He held her, his hand smoothing her hair with consummate gentleness. His blue gaze flicked to Kyle. His voice held a sharp note of command that the younger man couldn't contradict. "You go wait in the barn office. I'll be there in a little while. If I'm not, you wait until I get there."

Obediently, Kyle slunk off into the shadows. Ginna stood leaning against the tree, watching Ryan give Erin the balm of his love that she needed so badly herself. Their eyes met over the top of Erin's head.

I need you.

Ryan's hand stopped stroking Erin and moved to disengage her hold. She only burrowed closer and clung tighter.

"Go on up to your room," he suggested pleadingly to Ginna. "I'll be there shortly." His eyes begged for understanding.

She blinked and swallowed a choking disappointment. Fledgling dreams crashed at her feet. Oh, she understood all right. She understood that whether or not she'd done it intentionally, Erin had pulled off the coup de grace. When it came down to a choice, Ryan picked Erin. It was that simple. She stared at him in stunned disbelief.

Watching her closely and reading the emotions chasing one another across her face with no trouble, Ryan knew the precise instant she reached her mistaken supposition. He gripped Erin's shoulders to push her away, instinctively knowing Ginna was about to run away from him again. Even as he stood helplessly by, she uttered a strangled cry and pushed from the tree, racing through the darkness toward the house.

"You're wrong!" he yelled to her back, feeling his newly created world shift and hurtle him into a deep pit of depression that was as black and unending as the night around him.

The raw agony in his voice penetrated Erin's own misery. She tilted her face up and saw the heart-wrenching sense of loss sketched on her father's handsome face. Her tearful gaze followed the direction of his to the figure of her mother running toward the house. With an intuition that was as old as time, she knew. He wished he were with her mother instead of her. "Daddy?" she questioned in misery and confusion.

Ryan tore his eyes from Ginna's rapidly retreating back and struggled to focus on the sound of Erin's voice. How could Ginna possibly think he would choose Erin over her...especially after what they'd just shared?

"Daddy?" Erin queried again, accompanying her entreaty with a shake.

Gathering every bit of strength within him, Ryan forced his attention back to Erin. He would talk to Ginna later. He'd make her listen to him. But right now he had to take care of their daughter. He was suddenly sorry he'd put off the talk with her. Maybe if he'd explained before, she wouldn't have sought comfort in

Kyle's arms. Maybe if he'd— He swore silently. "Maybes" wouldn't change things. He'd done what he thought was right. Unfortunately, God didn't send a "how-to" book along with a child's birth. Parents just had to struggle along as best they could and hope the many mistakes they made along the way weren't the kind that left lasting scars.

He willed his mouth into a semblance of a smile and cradled Erin's cheek with one hand while his heart beat out a slow, aching cadence in his chest. He fought back the sting of bitter tears for all the mistakes he'd made— both with Ginna and Erin.

Poor baby, he thought, stroking the rounded curve of her chin that was so much like her mother's. She hadn't asked to be brought into this world. That act could be laid squarely at his and Ginna's feet. And now, just at an age that was unbearably difficult even at the best of times, she had learned the hard way that the parents she'd always looked up to were only too human. They'd fallen from their pedestal, and now it was up to him to see if he could pick up enough pieces of Erin's shattered image of them to create something she could recognize as good. It was up to him to make her see that he was as much to blame as Ginna for her conception. Ryan threw back his head and looked up at the cloud-riddled sky, blinking the moisture from his eyes. Somehow he had to find the right words to set all their worlds straight again.

Breath gusted from him in a soul-deep sigh. Sliding an arm around her shoulders, he pulled Erin close to his side and pressed a kiss to the shining top of her head. With the fraudulent smile still bravely in place, he tipped her face up and said, "Let's go sit on the back porch. It's way past time we had a talk."

* * *

Ginna raced across the yard as if demons chased her. Harsh sobs tore at her throat and pain clawed at her heart, leaving it in shredded, bleeding tatters. If she lived to be a thousand, she would never forget this night. It was a toss-up to whether finding Erin so perilously close to a sexual encounter with Kyle was the source of that pain, or whether it was the fact that when her soul had cried out to Ryan for comfort, he'd chosen Erin instead.

Pressing a trembling hand to her lips in an effort to muffle the sobs threatening to escape, she sneaked through the back door. She flitted through the darkened kitchen and down the hallway to the stairs, careful to make no sound, fearful of diverting Nora and Lefty's attention from the television and necessitating a explanation of her appearance.

Like a thief, she crept up the stairs and hurried down the hall to her room. The doorknob clicked beneath her touch and she slipped into the black anonymity of the room. She leaned against the door and covered her mouth with both hands to hold back the wail of hurt battering for release. Tears slid unchecked down her face as she stared unseeingly into the blackness of the room.

She groped her way to the bed, sinking onto its welcoming softness and staring up at a ceiling she couldn't see. Warm, womblike, the darkness surrounded her, offering her the solace of sightlessness. Here in the black of the night, she couldn't see the pictures of Kyle with his hands on Erin's breasts. Or the way his body moved so suggestively against hers.

Until she closed her eyes.

Images she had no control over flashed in fast-forward onto the screen of her mind. The look of surprise on Erin's face when she'd pushed Kyle away. Surprise followed by what? Shame? Sorrow? Regret? Another picture of Erin's head bouncing like a cork on the water as she was shaken unmercifully. Erin staring up at her with wide, tear-glossed eyes...

Ginna's head moved back and forth on the pillow. Her mind must be playing tricks on her. The defiant, willful child Erin had become lately wouldn't have just stood there taking it without saying something. Yet no matter how hard she tried, Ginna couldn't visualize the scene any other way. Erin had meekly submitted to—even seemed to accept—her punishment. Had it, like so many other things she'd done since they'd been at Catalpa, been solely to impress Ryan? Knowing Erin, it was likely.

And Ryan seemed to take it all so well. While she had felt as if all the years she'd spent trying to teach Erin right from wrong were going up in proverbial smoke, he had been calm, rational. How could anyone be rational coming upon the scene they had? Didn't the fact that Kyle had *touched* their only child, their *baby*, mean anything to Ryan?

Kyle's hands were touching Erin. Without warning, Ginna's mind zeroed in on a close-up of herself and Ryan on the sofa in the office. She saw his hands caressing her breasts. Felt the tug of his mouth on her nipples.

Kyle's hands were on Erin.

With a moan of protest, Ginna's hands came up to cover her own breasts and press against them as if to negate the memory.

His hips were pressing, grinding...

Her lashes flew open to erase the sight from behind her closed eyes. It didn't help. Even with her eyes wide open she could picture her own legs twined about Ryan's hips, keeping time to an ancient rhythm that shuddered to a halt as they reached the edge of ecstasy and he spent himself inside her.

"No..." Ginna moaned as the truth of the situation hit her squarely in the center of her misplaced morality. A truth that hurt more than anything else that had transpired the whole night.

Erin was right about her. She did have double standards. She had punished Erin for participating in something she believed was wrong, the same something she'd been participating in herself only moments before. Ginna drew in a shaky breath; fresh tears flooded her eyes. There was no getting around it. She was as guilty as Erin.

For the first time, she had an inkling of how her daughter must have felt when she found the marriage certificate. Something she believed in was smashed. For Erin, it was the belief and trust she'd given to her mother. For Ginna, it was her image of herself.

Chapter Ten

Thunder rolling in the distance could barely be heard for the sound of the rock music coming from the front of the house where the band and a small, temporary dance floor had been set up inside the grassy area created by the circular drive.

Ryan sat down beside Erin in the porch swing. Lighting a cigarette, he drew in a much-needed draft of nicotine and tried to think of a way to begin. How did you tell your beautiful teenage daughter that it was okay to flirt, to tease, to kiss, to touch... but not okay to kiss and touch too much? How did you tell her that necking was normal, but not to go too far... don't go all the way?

Erin just sat there, her long, slender legs crossed Indian-style in the seat, staring at the hands laced tightly in her lap. Dear God! She looked so much like Ginna! Or so much the way Ginna had looked seventeen years ago—short, petite, slender, but with a long-legged look nonetheless. And her face...Ryan couldn't help the sad smile that lifted one corner of his mustache. The profile was Ginna to a T, even down to the long, golden length of her lashes.

Nostalgia, a feeling of déjà vu, or just plain old memories, taunted him. His initial attraction to Ginna came rushing back with all the force he remembered. Shy, quiet, dependable Ginna. Ginna learning to laugh and enjoy life. Ginna in his arms in the back seat of his car, wanting so badly to please him. He recalled how he'd been only too anxious to show her how.

In a voice husky with emotion, he said, "It wasn't all her fault, you know."

Erin's head snapped toward the sound of his voice. Her blue eyes—sometimes the only thing he felt she got from him—stared out from her tear-ravaged face.

"Remember that old saying Grandma has? It takes two to tango? Well, it's true. I'm as much to blame as your mother. Maybe more so, because I was old enough and experienced enough to know better."

"I know it takes two to make a baby," Erin said, "but she always told me it's the girl's place to say no. She should have told you to stop."

"Like you did Kyle."

Erin blushed to the roots of her red-gold hair. Ryan was afraid she might start crying again. "I would have."

He nodded. "This time. Maybe."

"I could have made him stop whenever I wanted to!"

"Yeah?" Ryan exhaled a blue cloud of smoke that was carried away on the night wind. "Foolin' around, even with the intention of stopping somewhere along the way, is a dangerous game."

Contrition scored her features. "I know."

Silence fell on them while the swing groaned slowly back and forth.

Suddenly, Erin looked back at him. "Why didn't you and Mom stop?"

Ryan became extremely preoccupied with grinding his cigarette butt out beneath his heel, aware of the vital importance of his choice of words. "That's the other pitfall, Erin. Sometimes things seem so good, so right, that the girl forgets to say no." He offered her a wan smile. "Of course, she's convinced that she loves him and he loves her, so that's supposed to make it all right."

"Is that what happened between you and Mom?" Erin questioned.

"Yes." Ryan's smile was edged in sorrow. He watched her digest this new information. She looked even more like Ginna with that look of total concentration on her face. Reaching out, he grasped a lock of her hair. "You know, you're the spittin' image of her when she was about your age."

"I am?"

"Uh-huh." Ryan leaned back in the swing and stretched his arms along the swing's back, crossing his leg ankle to knee and pushing the swing desultorily with one foot. He stared out into the night and began to talk, almost as much to himself as to her. "The first time I saw her she was working in a florist shop. I was racing in Chicago and had stopped by to order a dozen red roses for a girl I'd met. But I walked in and saw your mom writing up an order for someone else. It was late afternoon, and the sun was shining through the window onto her hair. I thought it was the prettiest hair I'd ever seen. Then she looked up." He glanced over at his daughter. "I'd never seen eyes the color of hers before. Sort of like that gold stone you see in cuff links and rings—what is it?"

"Tiger eye?" Erin offered.

Ryan smiled and snapped his fingers. "That's it. Tiger eye. Anyway, she smiled at me and asked me what I needed. I was a goner from that moment on. I ordered the roses, but instead of taking them to the other girl, I gave them to your mom and asked her out."

"And she went?"

"Yeah," he said with a smile.

"What was so special about Mom?"

His hand dropped to Erin's shoulder in a gentle caress. "Funny you should ask, because I've asked myself that a million times the last seventeen years. All I can tell you is what Grandpa told me. He said, 'Son, when you meet the right one, you'll know it.' And I did."

Erin unwound her legs and drew them up under her chin. She clasped them loosely with her arms and rested her chin on her knees. "So you started to date."

"Sort of."

"What do you mean, 'sort of'?"

"Grandma and Grandpa Cassidy didn't like me too much. They told her she couldn't date me."

Erin's eyes widened in shock. "Why?"

"I was too old for her, and I was a horse trainer. They thought racetrackers weren't much better than the carnival people who blew into town every year. So...we began to sneak out."

"You and Mom?" she squealed.

"Yeah. Me and Mom. It was wrong, Erin. We shouldn't have."

Intensity burned in his eyes. Making her understand was so vital to not only her future happiness, but his. He drew in a deep breath and released it. "And then things happened just like I told you they could. And I don't have any excuses. Somehow, I felt like your mom was looking for love. Like kissing and touching and showing someone how much you cared was missing in her life. I told myself that I was only trying to fill that void, but that didn't make it right, babe. And neither did the fact that I loved her."

"You loved her?"

Ryan's face mirrored the surprise he heard in her voice. "Of course I loved her. And she loved me. I thought you'd have enough sense to know that. Your mother was a virgin, Erin. She didn't mess around. Surely you know she isn't the type to fool around with anyone?"

Erin had the grace to look embarrassed.

With an edge of anger sharpening his voice, he said, "Well, if you didn't know, you do now."

"I'm sorry." She looked decidedly contrite, but still confused.

"Anyway, it happened, and I've never regretted it for one minute. Not even the fact that we had to get married because of you. Especially not for that."

"You were *glad* she was pregnant?"

"Very glad. We both were. If she hadn't gotten pregnant, your grandfather would never have consented to our marriage."

Erin's forehead was furrowed with a frown. "What happened, Daddy? If you loved each other so much, what happened?"

Ryan's arm dropped around around her shoulders, and he pulled her against his side. "Sometimes love just isn't enough, babe. Things that happened in the past and things that are happening in the present have a way of interfering. I guess we just weren't able to figure out how to keep life from coming between us. Maybe we should have tried harder."

Erin pulled back to look into his eyes. "You still love her." It was a statement, spoken in bewildered realization as she recalled the look on his face when her mother was running toward the house.

"You bet I do," he said softly, trying to swallow back a growing lump of emotion. "That special feeling I told you about before, well, I haven't felt that way about a woman before or since your mother. A day hasn't passed that I haven't thought about how much I miss her."

He cleared his throat in an attempt to dislodge the persistent obstruction and pressed a kiss to her temple. "But the most important thing for you to know right now is that I love you, too. It's a different kind of love, but one that's as strong and lasting as what I feel for her. You do know that, don't you?"

Erin nodded.

Ryan stopped swinging. He looked at her intently. "She loves you, Erin. You've hurt her terribly the last few months by the way you've acted. And that was wrong. You shouldn't have put all the blame on her. Hell, if I'd been any kind of man, I'd have seen to it she was protected."

"Then you wouldn't have had me."

He shook his head. A tender smile shaped his lips. "Nope. No Erin. Probably no Ginna. And in spite of all the heartaches, I wouldn't have liked that at all.

That's what real love is all about, honey—accepting the hurt as well as the good things. Don't cheat yourself by settling for anything less."

Erin looked into his eyes and for the first time felt she understood. She struggled to match him smile for smile, but instead her eyes filled with tears that began to roll down her cheeks with quickening speed. "Oh, Daddy," she wailed softly. "I'm sorry. I'm so very sorry."

Ryan pulled her close and let her cry out all the heartache that had been growing inside her. He knew that when she finished, all the pain would be cleansed from her heart and her world, just as the approaching rain would cleanse the layer of fine grit from the world around them. That left only his world to be set aright.

Like Ginna, Ryan let himself in the back door. Facing his parents was something he couldn't cope with right now. The episode with Erin had left him drained emotionally, yet strangely satisfied. When her tears were spent, he'd sent her to start breaking up the party that was already threatened by the increasing wind and thunder. He didn't know how she would explain her tear-stained face, but knowing his daughter, she'd manage.

His talk with Kyle had been another matter altogether. A part of him wanted to beat the younger man senseless for touching Erin, yet another part of him— the part who remembered the hot blood of youth— understood the boy's unrelenting need to prove his masculinity. In the end, he had settled for a lot of swearing, a stern lecture and an even sterner warning to stay away from Erin.

He made his way slowly up the stairs, his only goal to offer Ginna the comfort she'd been denied earlier and to let her know how well things had gone with Erin. Then he had to get the two of them together to talk things out. A tired grin spread across his face. He truly believed things would be different now.

There was no light coming from under Ginna's bedroom door, but Ryan knocked anyway. Without waiting for her to acknowledge the knock, he let himself in and made his way across the dark room toward the bed.

"Ryan?" her voice quavered through the room's darkness.

"Yes."

The bed gave with his weight. He stretched out beside her, pressing his lips against her temple and holding her tightly. A remnant of her misery manifested itself in a sob that shuddered from deep within her.

"I'm sorry. I wanted to come to you, but she wouldn't let go," he whispered. His eyes closed and he swallowed hard. "And then you ran away from me again."

Behind her closed eyelids, Ginna recalled how he'd grasped Erin's arms as if to push her away. She remembered the look of pleading on his face. A pleading that, in her own need, she'd chosen to ignore. She believed him. She'd reached a lot of conclusions during the past hour or so. And most of those conclusions had to do with finding a way to reach their daughter, no matter what the cost. Like Erin had earlier, she burrowed closer into his arms.

"Shh," he murmured. "Don't cry. I'm here, and everything is going to be all right. I promise."

"E-Erin?" she hiccupped.

"We had a long talk." He smoothed the damp tendrils of hair from her hot cheeks. "I made a mistake in not doing it sooner, but I thought...oh, hell! Who knows what the right thing to do is?"

"I can't believe it, Ryan, I can't believe it. Why would she let him..." She couldn't find it within herself to put words to Erin's actions.

"Curiosity...checking out her feminine wiles...to exact some sort of revenge in her own mind. I don't know. Maybe she thinks she loves him."

"That's no excuse!"

Ryan's wry smile wasn't visible to her in the darkness. "It's the only one we had," he reminded.

"That was different!"

"Was it?"

She contemplated his question silently. "No," she said at last. "It isn't any different. Except that we really did love each other."

"That's a technicality, babe."

"I guess so," she said with a sigh. "What about Kyle?"

"I had a very serious talk with him. I told him I thought he ought to check out the girls at L.S.U.S. for a while and give Erin some time to grow up."

"What did he say?"

"He surprised me. He said he would, but that he'd be waiting for that time."

"He really does love her then?"

She felt Ryan shrug in the darkness. "Who can say? He's only nineteen. He thinks he does."

Another silence filled the room.

"It hurt so badly," Ginna said at last. "When I recognized her in the moonlight, I wanted to die."

"I know."

She sniffed. "I wanted to say so many things. And all I did was yell at her."

There was nothing Ryan could say.

"How did you feel?" she asked.

"Like someone kicked me in the gut. I was hurt and damn mad. I wanted to beat Kyle within an inch of his life and give Erin a good whipping. I guess when it's your child involved in something wrong, even if it's something you've done yourself, it's different."

"I guess so."

He pulled back to look at her in the darkness. "Are you okay now?"

She gave a shaky laugh. "I'll survive." She reached up and placed her hand against his whisker-stubbled cheek. "I'm sorry for the way I acted. I know that taking care of Erin was the most important thing at the time. I guess I was just jealous because you were giving her the attention I felt should be mine."

Ryan hugged her to him. "There's no need to be jealous. Whatever happens, I'd never put her before you in my heart."

It was the closest thing to an admission that he cared she had heard from him. But was it really caring or that innate sense of duty Lefty and Nora had instilled in all their children?

"I want you to see her—talk to her."

"Oh, Ryan, I can't! Not tonight, please. I . . . just can't face her tonight."

His chest rose and fell steadily beneath her cheek. "It won't go away, Ginna. Every time you close your eyes for a long time, you're going to remember. But we have to clear things up and go on from here."

Her fingers twisted at a button of his shirt. "I know . . . I know. But we're both so emotionally tired.

And besides being hurt, I'm still angry. I imagine she is, too.''

Ryan gauged the despair in her voice. Her body still shook with an occasional sob. He was totally wrung out himself. "Maybe you're right. Maybe tomorrow morning would be better. But I think you're going to find a big change in Erin. And I think you're going to like it."

A sharp clap of thunder shook the house, and a driving rain pelted the windowpanes. Lifting her head, Ginna glanced at the digital clock on the dresser. Three-ten and she still hadn't shut an eye. Ryan, who had refused to leave her alone, slumbered peacefully beside her, even though he was fully clothed except for his boots. Apparently all his demons had been exorcised.

Ginna's hadn't.

While his assurances that Erin saw things differently now had helped ease some of her worries over the breach in the mother/daughter relationship, she still hadn't come to terms with her own guilt. Just as Ryan had said, Kyle and Erin's actions were no different than theirs had been in the past. Or, she thought with another surge of contrition sweeping through her, their actions in the present. How could she face Erin in the morning and lecture her on the perils of sex when she and Ryan had just made love twice? Basically honest, Ginna wasn't certain she could pull off that sort of deception.

Her intellect, in an attempt to rationalize her own actions, told her that her situation was far removed from Erin's. She was an adult who was responsible for her actions. She was wiser. Savvy. And aware of what the repercussions might be. After all, she'd suffered them once before.

It isn't right without marriage. Her mother's voice spoke to her from the past. And the strange part was, Ginna believed in the premise that had been preached to her all her life. But all those teachings had flown out the window with Ryan. She had loved him so much . . .

That doesn't make it right. Her own words haunted her. If it wasn't right for Erin, it wasn't right for her. And there was no changing that, no matter how hard she tried.

Closing her lashes over eyes gritty with a bone-deep weariness, she tried again to will herself to sleep. But her mind was filled with Erin: the way she'd acted since she found the wedding certificate, the way she accepted Ryan but rejected her for an act they shared equally. In spite of Ryan's optimism, she doubted seriously that after all the futile talks she'd had with Erin, one brief conversation with him was going to bring about the change he expected.

Thunder rumbled and her heart lurched with pain as she recalled Erin seeking sanctuary in Ryan's arms instead of hers. There was no doubt she loved him, no doubt she needed him. And little doubt in Ginna's mind and heart that her daughter felt the exact opposite for her. Not for the first time, she faced the fact that she was unnecessary to her daughter's happiness. Tonight the realization was a bitter pill she found herself forced to swallow.

Inside her room, beneath the light covering of the floral sheet, Erin lay, wooing sleep. The night had passed in spells of fitful dozing that were interrupted at regular intervals by the storm raging outside the house. The storm and the dreams. Intimidated by the power and strength of storms, the thunder made her want to crawl into her mother's bed as she had since childhood. The dreams, filled with sorrow and guilt over her actions, brought the same feeling.

Lightning cracked and a drumroll of thunder bounded across the countryside. She covered her ears, trying without success to shut out the sound of the storm, trying to block out the remorse flooding her already aching heart as she stood face to face with her feelings for the first time. She hadn't intended to hurt anyone tonight. It had just happened.

She squirmed with shame. That was the source of her pain. She had come so close to doing the same thing she accused her mother of, the very thing she had convinced herself she hated her mother for, that when her parents had found her with Kyle, she wanted to throw herself into Ginna's arms and cry... to tell her how sorry she was, that she hadn't meant to hurt her. And more than that, she had wanted to tell her that she hadn't intended to let things go so far with Kyle, but that her feelings had just gone out of control. She wanted to confess that she finally understood just how easy it was to forget your upbringing. Instead, she'd stood staring up at her, rooted to the spot by an overwhelming guilt. She wasn't certain she could ever face her mother again.

If she lived through eternity, she would never forget the shock on her mother's face. That look, far more than the vicious shaking she'd received, was branded into her mind. The punishment she accepted without question; she deserved it. A quick glance at her dad, whose very calmness made him appear so much more approachable, had sent her into his arms in search of the comfort she needed.

She didn't know what it was—she hadn't heard anything—but suddenly Erin realized someone was in the room. Afraid to move, she lay curled in a fetal position and waited. Soon, legs came into view before her slitted eyes. Smooth, bare legs that could only belong to her mother. Why was she here in the middle of the night?

What am I doing here? Ginna stood looking down at her sleeping daughter without the slightest idea of why she'd come. Maybe she was looking for a moment of peace when she could look her fill at the child she'd brought into the world.

Lightning flashed, throwing the room into brief illumination and spotlighting the girl on the bed in a bright shower of light. She was so beautiful, Ginna thought when the light was gone. Even though they looked a lot alike, there was a difference in Erin. Her hair was just a bit brighter, her lashes and legs were longer and her body just a tad more curvaceous than Ginna's. The real difference, though, was that normally, Erin's personality was much more outgoing and bubbly than Ginna's could ever be.

What did I do wrong? What made her hate me so? How can I ever change it? The answer, she knew, was simple. There was nothing she could do that she hadn't already done. The next move was up to Erin. She sighed, wondering what the morning would bring. With tears in her eyes, hope in her heart and love flooding every corner of her being, she reached out a hand to touch Erin's shoulder and leaned down to press a soft kiss to her cheek.

Riddled with remorse and guilt and feeling totally unworthy of the love her mother was offering, Erin jerked away just before the kiss touched her face.

Gasping in surprise and recoiling from the obvious rejection as if she'd been slapped, Ginna's hand dropped to her side and she stood staring wide-eyed through the darkness at her daughter.

Erin's eyes filled with tears Ginna couldn't see. She felt her mother's pain as if it were her own. It must be the same as the pain squeezing her own heart. She started to say she was sorry, but just as she did, her mother whirled and ran toward the door, opening it and flying from the room.

Trembling and with new tears forming beneath her eyelids, Ginna let herself into her own room. She went into the bathroom and buried her face in a towel, crying silent, bitter tears and being very careful not to wake Ryan. She had thought that the next move should be Erin's. And it had been.

Long moments after Ginna had left the room, Erin, tears streaming down her face, rose, and with uncoordinated, jerky movements, very gently closed the door her mother had left open.

Chapter Eleven

At some time toward morning, her body temporarily devoid of any more tears, Ginna drifted into an exhausted sleep, only to be awakened at five-thirty by Ryan's kiss.

"The storm blew on through," he told her. "It's gonna be a gorgeous day."

Attempting a smile that didn't quite reach her eyes, she said, "That's good."

"I won't see you at breakfast. We're working several of the two-year-olds this morning."

She nodded. With a heavy heart, she pulled his head down and kissed him, holding him tightly to her and putting every ounce of love she could into the hungry meeting of their lips.

Pulling back, Ryan chuckled warmly against her ear. His voice wasn't quite steady as he said, "Let me get out of here while I still can and let you go back to sleep.

You look exhausted.'' With a final kiss, he left the room. She watched him go, wondering how much more could life demand of her before she was crushed beneath its weight.

At seven-thirty, dressed in slacks and a lightweight summer sweater, she went down to breakfast. She'd used a heavy hand with her makeup in an attempt to cover up the ravages of the night, but the results only looked as if she needed training in applying her makeup. As usual, she found Nora cooking and humming a current rock song under her breath.

When she looked up and saw Ginna standing in the doorway dressed in something besides her customary shorts and top, the brilliant smile she wore wavered. "Good morning. Hungry?"

Ginna's heart sank. She was afraid she knew the source of Nora's happiness. Ryan had probably told her they were getting married again. *Ryan, Ryan... why didn't you wait...* "No," she said with a tight smile. "Just coffee, thanks."

Nora's smile slipped another notch as she silently poured Ginna's coffee. "You look tired, child," she said, placing the cup of steaming brew onto a bright, appliquéd place mat and sitting down in the chair next to Ginna's.

"It was quite a night," she said obliquely. She felt she should explain, but couldn't bring herself to talk about the things that had happened, and just as unwilling to deliberately shatter Nora's happiness. She rested her chin in the palm of her hand and stared at her coffee.

"Ryan told me what happened with Erin. He thinks things will be better now."

Turning her head slightly, Ginna met Nora's troubled gaze. "I hope that after today things will be much better," she said.

"He told me the two of you had come to an understanding."

"Yes." Ginna lifted the cup to her lips and took a tentative sip. Tears sprang into her eyes. She told herself it was because the coffee scalded her lips. She blinked them away rapidly.

"I'm glad. He still loves you very much."

Oh, Ryan. She lifted limpid, glittering eyes to Nora's lined face. "I love him, too, Nora. Very much."

The confession freshened Nora's smile. She reached out and patted Ginna's hand. "I'm glad."

Then Nora rose and, as if everything was settled to her satisfaction, began to bustle around the kitchen with her usual energy, leaving Ginna alone with her depression.

Ginna was refilling her cup when she heard the kitchen door open. She heard Nora's greeting and turned to see who it was. Erin came through the door, a tired smile on her face. When she saw her mother standing near the cabinets she stopped in the middle of the room.

Her blue eyes, wide with surprise and unease, stared into her mother's. Ginna felt frozen to the spot. Her heart stopped beating. Her mind was incapable of thought. Only the hand holding the coffee cup possessed any life. It began to tremble.

Nora, who stood facing the stove, missed the entire exchange. "Two scrambled eggs, Erin?" she called over her shoulder. Her voice broke the spell binding mother and child, but the tension between them was a living thing.

Ginna watched in stunned disbelief as Erin's gaze slid from hers. "Yes, *Grandmère*. Two is fine," she said, acting as if everything was fine, behaving as if the night before had never been.

It was more than Ginna could bear. The coffee sloshed suddenly over the cup's rim. She stared at it for a moment, then set it on the cabinet. Without another word, she started toward the door. When she passed Erin, she slowed, hoping against hope she would say something. She didn't.

Nora turned from the stove just as Ginna reached the door. Speaking to her back, the older woman asked, "Where are you going?"

Blinking rapidly—where in the world were all her tears coming from lately?—Ginna looked from Nora to Erin and back again. "I...spilled coffee on me," she said in a voice shaded with desperation. "Excuse me." She turned and left the room, running toward the stairs as if all the hounds of hell were after her.

Erin watched her mother leave. The hurt inside her escalated to an almost unbearable pitch. It was her fault she'd gone. If only she could have thought of something to say that would have kept her...

Unfortunately, Erin didn't know how to deal with what was happening in her life. She couldn't find any words inside her to say that would change what had happened between them the night before. Somehow, "I'm sorry," seemed totally inadequate. So she'd done the only thing she knew to do. She'd tried to set a feeling of normalcy...tried to act as if it were any other morning. And it hadn't worked. She'd done the wrong thing again...

* * *

Ginna sat waiting for the cloud of dust that would herald Cissy's arrival. When she'd called a few minutes ago and asked her sister-in-law if she would drive her to the airport the younger woman had reluctantly agreed. Vowing that she wouldn't take a chance on another meeting with Erin, certain she couldn't take one more rejection, Ginna was sticking close to her room until time to leave.

A dust storm raced up the road toward the house. There she was! No one drove that fast on this road but Cissy. Unless, Ginna thought with a wry smile, it was Brad.

She hoisted her large suitcase from the bed and grabbed her overnight case up with the other hand, then, making a quick survey of the room, she turned and started for the stairs.

Nora, who had seen the station wagon coming up the road, was crossing the entry way to the front door, drying her hands on her apron. The look of shock on her face when she saw Ginna coming down the stairs with her suitcases would have been comical if it weren't so heartbreaking.

"You're leaving."

Ginna descended the last two steps and set her luggage on the floor. "Yes."

"Ryan said . . ."

"I know. I thought it would work, Nora, but it won't."

"But you told me you loved him." Nora's face held a defeat Ginna had never seen there before. The realization that she was the cause of it brought a cry of dismay to her lips. She put her hands on her mother-in-law's shoulders. Looking directly into her eyes, she whispered, "I do."

"Then why..."

"Because of Erin." She shook her head slowly back and forth. "Nothing's changed, Nora. I know that...especially after last night."

The older woman's forehead furrowed into a frown. "Ryan said he'd talked to her."

"He did." Ginna's hands slid from Nora's shoulders down to clasp her hands. "But I went into her room last night and—" she stopped and swallowed the emotion clotting her throat "—when I bent down to kiss her, she jerked away. She couldn't stand for me to touch her."

Nora's eyes filled with tears of sympathy. Her hands squeezed Ginna's tightly.

"The truth is, she doesn't want me in her life, and she'll never forgive me. I just can't take it any more."

"Do you think..."

Ginna shook her head. "No. I've tried. And as much as I'd like to start over with Ryan, I can't take my own happiness at the expense of messing up Erin's life...maybe irreparably."

The emotion Nora had been holding tenuously at bay broke free. Tears spilled from her eyes. Ginna's followed. Without a word, the two women went into each other's arms.

The front door burst open with such force that it banged against the wall and caused Nora and Ginna to spring apart in surprise. Erin stood in the doorway, her hair a tangle down her back, a wild look of disbelief on her face as she took in the ravages of her mother's tears. Tears that stopped abruptly and magically when she saw who was standing in the doorway.

Cissy stood just behind Erin. When Ginna's eyes questioned her, she shrugged and shook her head. Unable to face her daughter in her present condition— unable to face her at all—Ginna turned to pick up her cases.

"You're really going?" Erin asked.

"Yes," she said without looking at her daughter. *Please, Dear God, just let me get out of here with some dignity.* Turning back around with a suitcase in each hand, Ginna focused desperately on the station wagon sitting in the driveway. She started for the door, brushing past Erin without another word.

With another shrug, Cissy pulled her sunglasses from the top of her head and turned, following Ginna down the steps to the car.

Moving automatically, stiffly, Nora went to stand beside Erin, whose eyes held a bleakness and grief that was too much for any sixteen-year-old to bear. The station wagon made the circle drive and headed down the dusty road. Nora heard Erin mumble something.

"What?"

Turning to look at her grandmother, Erin said, "Daddy. Where's Daddy?"

"I don't know. The barn, I suppose. Erin? Erin? Where are you going?" The last was called to Erin's back as she raced down the steps and across the lawn. "Erin..."

Fifty minutes later, Ginna clutched the armrests of the Delta jet bound for Chicago and watched the city of Shreveport disappear from sight. But out of sight was definitely not out of mind.

Below, returning to the farm from an unexpected, but necessary trip into Shreveport Lab, Ryan sang happily along with Willie Nelson, unaware that the world he thought he'd rebuilt so carefully the night before had crumbled like so much dust.

Chicago was just the same. Humming. Hot. And with Lake Michigan so near by, it had a humidity factor that equalled or surpassed that of Louisiana. Watching the people swarming through the terminal brought an ache for the peace of Catalpa to Ginna's heart.

Even though she was expected back today, there was no one to meet her plane. She thought of going to the Petal Pusher and talking to Kay, maybe even finishing out the rest of the work day, but somehow she couldn't get enthused about starting back to work. Still, she had to start doing something. First things first. Home...

The apartment she shared with Erin nine months out of the year was located near Lincoln Park. The rent was exorbitant, but she didn't allow herself many luxuries and the pleasure Erin had received from the park was well worth the price. Silence and a faint draft of cool air greeted her as the door swung open. A prayer of thankfulness that she'd told Kay to be sure and turn on the air-conditioning before she was due home swept through her. She hurried to the thermostat and set it to a more comfortable temperature, then carried her luggage to her room. Today, even the pale rose and dusty blue of its color scheme failed to soothe her.

She began to unpack, sorting clothes and tossing the dirty ones into a pile for the laundry. Suddenly she pulled out the tank top she'd worn swimming the day before. Erin's top. Nora must have washed it and put it with her things by accident.

Ginna rubbed the soft cotton against her cheek, finally allowing thoughts of Erin into her mind. What was she doing now? Was she the least bit sorry for what had happened? And what had Ryan said when he'd come in from the barn and found her gone?

The magnitude of her spur-of-the-moment act dawned suddenly and unexpectedly on her. At the time, she had been too hurt by Erin's actions to think about anything but getting away and, she hoped, making life easier for everyone concerned. She had done the right thing, the only thing left for her to do. She had done her best to give Erin happiness, but only at the cost of the one thing that would bring her happiness of her own. A new beginning with Ryan. Depression, like a woolen cloak, settled more heavily around Ginna's heart.

You built a life without him once; you can do it again. It shouldn't be so hard this time. But somehow she knew it would be. This time her work couldn't begin to fill the void in her heart and life as it once had. She sighed. She honestly wasn't sure she had the strength to rebuild her life the second time.

For one of the few times in her adult life, she felt a need to talk to someone as she had Nora. Kay? She was working. Her own mother? A bitter smile curved her lips. Her mother wasn't exactly as approachable as her mother-in-law. She couldn't ever remember seeing Molly Cassidy bustling around the kitchen, fixing breakfast for twelve people. She would be too concerned about the antique dining table with its velvet seats to allow three sticky-fingered children to eat pancakes at it. She would never serve pancakes. A big man, Daniel Cassidy tended toward the heavy side the older he got, and her mother, too, was always concerned about adding an ounce to her well-preserved figure. Their breakfasts ran to coffee, a slice of dry toast, yogurt and a variety fruit.

Ginna didn't know why she thought Molly Cassidy—that cool lady who moved through life without letting it touch her—could offer her any comfort, but that age-old need to seek maternal reassurance surged strongly within her and refused to leave. Without stopping to analyze her feelings, she grabbed up her car keys and headed to the parking lot.

The long drive to Evanston was made in good time, though Ginna asked herself just what she hoped to gain from the visit several times during the drive. When she pulled into her parents' driveway she still hadn't reached any conclusion.

Her father's car was in the driveway. She'd forgotten he'd started taking off an afternoon in the middle of the week at his doctor's insistence ever since he'd begun suffering attacks of angina. She sighed. What on earth could she say to *both* of them? They definitely weren't as easy to talk to as Nora and Lefty. Heaving another sigh, she opened the door and got out. She'd made the trip; she might as well say hello and let them catch her up on what had been going on with the family during her two-week absence. Determinedly, she forced her footsteps up the sidewalk and her finger to the doorbell.

Molly Cassidy's surprise was evident when she opened the door and saw her daughter standing there. "Why, Ginna ... I didn't know you were back. Come in."

Hesitating just a moment, Ginna looked at her mother's classic, carefully made-up features. The flesh of her face was smooth, hardly wrinkled at all except for the tiny lines around her brown eyes. Her usual chignon was intact, defying even one dark, tinted hair to slip from its mooring. A whimsical smile curved Ginna's lips as she stepped inside. How different from Nora's pert, delightfully wrinkled face and short, curly hairstyle, she thought. But then, the two women were as different as night and day.

As was expected of her, she gave her mother a dutiful peck on the cheek. "I forgot Dad was off this afternoon, or I wouldn't have come."

"Nonsense. He's taking a nap in the study. If we go to the kitchen, we won't bother him at all," Molly said.

Ginna recognized the hospital insignia on the sleeve of the smock her mother wore. "I see today was your day at the hospital."

"Yes," Molly concurred, lifting a hand to her immaculately coiffed hair. "Excuse how I look. I haven't had time to change."

"You look fine, Mother." Ginna wondered again why her mother did volunteer work at a nearby hospital. Oh, she knew that part of it was her social standing. While her father's yearly income as owner of *Cassidy's*, the city's oldest and most prestigious family-owned department store, was extremely good, and always had been because of the length of time it had served the Chicago area, he hardly qualified as the jet set. Ginna imagined the other reason had something to do with the fact that her mother couldn't exactly be called friendly.

Charity work was socially acceptable, so Molly had chosen that over a garden or bridge club. But what on earth could she offer to sick and dying people? She had never had an ounce of sympathy for childhood cuts and bruises, telling her children to be quiet and don't cry... giving them little or no sympathy for hurt feelings and broken hearts.

"Would you like a glass of iced tea?" Molly asked, turning suddenly and interrupting Ginna's guilty thoughts.

"Is it the spiced kind with chamomile?" she asked, knowing the pride her mother took in her special tea recipe and feeling the need to compensate for the unsympathetic turn of her thoughts.

A hint of pleasure glimmered in Molly's eyes. "Yes."

"Then, yes. No one makes spiced iced tea like you, Mother." Ginna followed her mother through the tastefully appointed house and into an immaculate kitchen done in stainless steel and white. The lack of clutter on the cabinet tops lent a sterile atmosphere to the room that was only partly relieved by a lonely looking schefflera sitting near the French doors that led to the patio. Ginna couldn't help thinking how well the room suited her mother, or making the mental comparison to Nora's kitchen that was rife with plants, all sorts of kitchen gadgets and country crafts.

"How was your trip?" Molly asked, taking two frost-covered tumblers from the freezer and filling them with crushed ice and a sprig of mint.

"Okay. The flight back was better than usual."

Setting the glasses filled with clear, strong tea onto the dinette table, the older woman sat down and asked, "How is everyone?"

"They're all fine," Ginna told her, making an effort to sound cheerful, normal. "I got to know Luke's wife better. And Brad's wife is just super. They have the cutest bunch of kids." Her mouth curved into a real smile as she recalled the sticky kiss she'd received from Brad's Kristi.

"Are Lefty and Nora well?" Like most people, the Cassidys couldn't help responding to the older Le-Grands' friendliness over the years, even if their life-style wasn't to their liking.

"They're fine. Still as active as ever. Nora has a huge garden..." Ginna's voice trailed away as she remem-bered Ryan standing at the garden gate, watching her.

I see your underwear. Was it only yesterday he'd stood there so vibrantly male that he took her breath away? Was it only last night that they'd made love so beautifully, so completely?

Molly saw the look of anguish in her daughter's eyes. "And how was Ryan?" she asked quietly.

The question jerked Ginna's flighty thoughts back to Chicago. Her voice wasn't quite steady as she said, "He's fine... really... great." She looked over at her mother with tears glazing her eyes. "Oh, Mother," she said huskily. "I still love him so much."

And to her undying horror, she burst into tears.

"What the hell is going on?" Daniel's voice from the doorway brought Molly's head around.

Ginna's head snapped up, uncertainty mingling with her misery. He stood there, a frown on his once-handsome, florid face, his starched white shirt rum-pled from his nap. Hard. Critical. And as usual, showing little patience when faced with human frail-ties. Through a film of tears, she saw the emotions racing across her mother's face. Unease. Sorrow. And finally, determination.

Lifting her chin to a regal angle she had perfected throughout the years, and one that had struck terror in her offspring as children, Molly said, "Leave us alone, Dan. Ginna and I are talking."

Then, ignoring the shock on his face, she rose and moved around the table, touching Ginna's shaking shoulder with a trembling hand. Ginna froze beneath the surprising touch of her mother's hand. Her tears stopped. Lifting her lashes to reveal eyes swimming with moisture, she stared up in question at Molly, whose face held more love and compassion than she ever remembered seeing there.

"I'm sorry," Molly whispered raggedly.

The two words were more than an expression of sorrow and empathy. They were a confession of regret. A promise of better tomorrows. One slender, manicured hand reached out to touch tumbled red-gold hair. Tears—something totally irreconcilable with Ginna's image of her mother—filled Molly Cassidy's dark eyes. "I'm so very sorry," she said again.

With a strangled cry, Ginna reached out and circled her mother's slim waist, pulling her close. For a long, long time, the kitchen was filled with the sounds of their grieving. They wept for all the mistakes they had made. They wept for themselves and each other. For yesterday's failures and tomorrow's loneliness.

And when their tears were dried, they began to talk.

"I never really disliked Ryan," Molly said while she and Ginna sat sipping coffee later. "It was your father who thought he wasn't good enough. I just thought he was too old for you. Too experienced." Her gaze fell to her coffee cup. She studied the dark liquid with the intensity of a fortune-teller reading tea leaves.

Ginna, still surprised by the turn of events, waited patiently for her to continue. Finally Molly looked up, determination tilting her chin, a wary look lurking in the dark depths of her eyes. She took a deep breath and expelled it shortly. Meeting Ginna's eyes, she said, "I didn't want you making the same mistake I made."

Ginna's eyes widened at the implication of the words.

"I was fresh off the farm when I first met your dad—poor as Job's turkey and green as a gourd. I had just graduated from high school and went to Cassidy's to interview for my first job. I got it. They said I'd be an asset to the store with my looks. Of course I was flattered. Who wouldn't have been? And then, when the boss's son began to flirt with me, I couldn't believe it. Paul Cassidy's son was interested in me. He was so handsome and so popular. It didn't take me long to fall head over heels in love and he began to pressure me about . . . sex."

"Mother," Ginna began, "you don't have to tell me this."

"Oh, but I do. I've never told anyone. And there is so much that needs to be said." Her mouth wore a weary smile. "I won't bore you with the details, but I got pregnant with Kay."

Ginna's lashes fluttered down over her eyes to momentarily block out the sight of her mother's embarrassment.

"When I told Dan, he said he loved me, but he wasn't ready to settle down and that when he did, he would choose the right time to have his son. I was crushed." The tears threatened her again. "My father went to his. I don't know what they agreed on, but before I knew it, I was married. The Cassidys are really big on honor and doing the acceptable thing. There has never been a divorce in the family until yours. From what I've pieced together, I think your Grandfather

Cassidy told Daniel that he would marry me and stay married or forfeit his inheritance.'' She gave a short, humorless laugh. ''That isn't the best way to begin a marriage.''

''But to live with him all this time, and know he didn't love you...''

''Oh, I think he does. In his own funny way. He loves me as much as he's capable of. He's married to the store...his work.''

''But if he wasn't crazy about the idea of children, what about Danny and me?''

Molly's smile was genuine this time, if a bit rusty looking. ''He only wanted one son, but it took him three children to get one. And even though he didn't want children, he's always liked sex as well as the next man. These were the days before the pill, and abortion is something I would never consider. So we had all of you, and because I loved you, I did my best to keep you out of his way.''

Comprehension dawned on Ginna. ''That's why you were always sending us to our room or outside to play...why you were always telling us not to cry. Because you didn't want us to get on his nerves.''

Molly nodded. ''I loved him so much back then. My whole world revolved around him to the exclusion of giving you kids anything more than your day-to-day needs. All I thought about was what he wanted—what would make him happy.''

Ginna's heart swelled with emotion and a surge of love for the woman sitting across from her. ''Oh, Mother. You couldn't have been happy.''

Molly's smile was tender. ''No. I loved him, but I haven't been happy. And somewhere along the way that love withered from lack of nourishment.''

"Then why do you stay?"

Molly's eyes showed her surprise. "I stay because I took a vow, Ginna. And both your father and I believe in commitment. Besides, even if the love I felt for him isn't there anymore, I'm still grateful to him for giving up his freedom when he didn't want to and for giving me his name and social position. It was a big sacrifice, and I'll owe him forever. Having a baby out of wedlock was far different then than it is now. And because he did that for me, I've tried as best I can to be the kind of wife that would be good for him. I've kept this house full of his family antiques as well as any museum curator when I've been longing for years for chrome and glass. That's why I was always after you all about the furniture. It wasn't really mine. Few of the things in this house are really mine."

She tossed Ginna a half smile. "I got an education and I've kept up my appearance as well as I can, and my conduct above suspicion, even when there was a time I believe I could have found...happiness with someone else."

Ginna's mouth dropped open. She cast a cautious glance toward the door, and her voice was nothing more than a hushed whisper as she asked, "You were in love with someone else?"

Molly shook her head. "No. Not in love. But there was definite interest for both of us." She took another sip of coffee. "Nothing ever came of it. I wouldn't let myself get involved. Besides the fact that I believe in fidelity, my debt to your father was too great."

Ginna reached across the table and covered her mother's hand with her own. "Why didn't you ever tell any of us this before now?"

Molly's hand clasped Ginna's warmly. Her eyes smiled. "I don't know. Somehow it never occurred to me that when you kids grew up you could become my friends—even my confidants. Good grief, I feel guilty now for what I've told you."

"Don't, Mother. Please. I'm glad to know. Because I know now that you really did love us."

"Love you! Of course I did." Her eyes shone with moisture. "I was just so wrapped up in my own problems that it never occurred to me to tell you or show you."

Ginna's smile promised forgiveness without words.

"If I had things to do over again, I'd give more thought to how my actions affected all of you. Kids deserve some consideration when their long-term happiness is involved."

The words hit Ginna extremely hard. Wasn't that what she'd done? Hadn't she put Erin's happiness first? The fact that her mother would do the same thing seemed to reinforce her decision concerning Erin. More than ever now, Ginna felt she'd done the right thing. But that didn't make losing Ryan any easier. Even the knowledge that she had gained a mother's love wouldn't ease that ache.

"Ginna, are you all right?"

Ginna forced thoughts of Ryan to a dark corner of her mind. She could only deal with one thing at a time, and right now, the fact that she'd gained a mother and a friend should take precedence. The heaviness in her heart lifted. She smiled. "I'm fine. Better in some ways than I've ever been."

Molly smiled back, a smile tinged with a touch of chagrin. "Goodness! I've been talking so much about me I didn't let you tell me about you and Ryan."

Ryan. Ginna wanted to tell Molly what happened, but at the moment, she felt emotionally empty. Her stomach churned with nerves and growled with hunger. It was Ginna's turn to look embarrassed. "All I had for breakfast was one cup of Nora's coffee, and I didn't eat anything on the plane because I was afraid I'd be sick." She looked pleadingly at her mother. "I do want to tell you, but can we talk after dinner?"

Molly laughed, a sound Ginna didn't remember hearing very many times in her life. "Of course."

"I'll cook," Ginna announced.

"You'll cook?"

"Yes." She rose and grabbed her purse, rounding the table and pressing her mother back into the chair. "You relax. I'm going to the store."

"What for?"

Dropping a kiss to Molly's cheek, she announced grandly, "Pancake mix."

Ginna lay staring into the night with a contented smile on her face. She and her parents had gorged on the buttery, syrupy pancakes and sausage she'd fixed. Daniel Cassidy had eaten the pancakes with relish, and even Molly had devoured three, putting her figure, at least momentarily, on hold.

Surprisingly, Daniel hadn't interrupted them during their talk after dinner when Ginna had told her mother everything that had happened at Catalpa...including the events and her reasoning that led to her leaving. Molly listened to every word and, even though she couldn't offer any answers, it helped Ginna to share the misery with someone.

At ten o'clock they were about worn down, both physically and by the emotions they had expended through the afternoon and evening. Molly told Ginna it was too late to drive from Evanston to Chicago and suggested that she spend the night in her old room. Dreading the emptiness of the apartment, she agreed.

Now, snuggling beneath the cool crispness of the sheet, she thought how strange it felt to be sleeping in her parents' house after all these years. Strange and very good. She closed her eyes and smothered a yawn, wondering if Erin and Ryan were asleep yet. Wondering...

Across town, the telephone in Ginna's apartment rang at fifteen minute intervals. Becoming more angry and worried with each hour she didn't answer, Ryan slammed down the phone in his motel room, cursing roundly into the silence of the room.

By the time he'd reached Catalpa earlier in the day, Erin had worked herself into a state of near hysteria over Ginna's leaving. It had taken him at least two hours to get her side of the story. Crying, clinging to him and blaming herself for everything that had happened, she made him promise to bring her mother back.

Which was exactly what he was trying to do. Only he couldn't find her. By the time he'd landed the plane at Midway Airport, Kay had already closed the shop. He'd made a quick call to her house, only to find that Ginna hadn't so much as called to tell her she'd made it safely. No, Kay didn't have the slightest idea where her sister was, and yes, she would call him at the Holiday Inn if she heard from her. They had hung up with Kay vowing to strangle Ginna when they did find her. Her brother, Danny, wasn't at home, so it was impossible to know whether she was with him or not.

Ryan ran a weary hand through his hair. Where could she possibly be? He lit a cigarette and stretched out on the bed. Had she been in an accident? Was she with her parents? Farfetched, he thought, but possible. He shot a glance at the clock radio by the bed. Twelve-ten. Far too late to be dragging people out of bed to the phone. But first thing in the morning, he was going to call Daniel and Molly Cassidy and see if they had heard from Ginna. And when he found her he was going to...

His anger fizzled out. He smiled in the darkness. When he found her he was going to hold her close and beg her to come back to Catalpa with him. And this time he was going to hold her so tightly she couldn't ever get away.

Chapter Twelve

It was barely dawn when, still weary but unable to sleep in more than bits and snatches, Ginna rose and dressed, blaming the strange bed for her inability to sleep. Tiptoeing downstairs, she left her mother a note beside the coffee pot that promised she would call later, and let herself out of the house.

As she drove toward her apartment she couldn't help but think how different Chicago's approach to morning was from Catalpa's. Instead of a quiet stretching into the day, the city woke with clanging garbage trucks and blaring car horns. Remembering Catalpa only dampened the higher spirits she'd had on waking and knowing for the first time that she had a friend in her mother.

She struggled to keep memories of Catalpa from her mind as she readied herself to face the day and a future that stretched its long, empty arms out toward her.

After showering and grabbing a Pop Tart and a cup of instant coffee, she left for work, arriving at the Petal Pusher long before time for Kay to make an appearance.

She put on the coffee pot, then checked the supply of fresh flowers and what was on the books that had to be done for the day, hoping that if she threw herself back into the middle of a busy work day the hurt wouldn't have a chance to surface. She was looping pale pink ribbon into a large bow an hour later when the back door rattled. Ginna glanced at the clock on the wall across the workroom. About time for Kay, she thought with lifted brows and a slight smile. She'd missed her sister. It would be good to be subjected to her sometimes scathing wit again.

The door rattled louder, a sound accompanied by a no-nonsense pounding. Ahhh, Ginna thought, another, broader smile spreading across her face. Her totally together sister must have forgotten her key. She'd never let her live that down! Still holding the bow in her left hand, she crossed the room to the back door and clicked open the night bolt, turning and going back to her table without so much as a backward glance.

"Aren't you glad I came in early?" she asked as the door opened. "It would be a pity for you to have to drive back home and get the key…especially since you have such a busy day ahead."

Kay didn't answer. She was probably still angry at herself for making a mistake that was so out of character. "C'mon, Kay," Ginna said, turning around to confront her sister with a wide, teasing smile, "we all make mis—" But it wasn't Kay who stood there. It was Ryan.

The sight of him wiped the smile from her face and sent a thousand questions scurrying through her mind, the uppermost being what he was doing at the back door of her business at seven-thirty in the morning. Knowing Ryan, he wanted to talk about what had happened between her and Erin. What she couldn't figure out was why he'd come up here. Why hadn't he just called?

He looked as if he hadn't slept much, she thought, eyeing the droop of his shoulders and his rumpled appearance. Besides the mustache that looked remarkably menacing when combined with his frowning intensity, his face was covered with twenty-four hours' worth of stubble that also added to his rakishness. He hadn't shaved yet this morning, so it was likely that he hadn't slept at all. He looked, she thought a bit wildly, like one of those outlaws on the old reward posters as he stood there regarding her with that solemn expression on his face, his hands crammed into the back pockets of his Levi's and his weight thrown casually, almost insolently to one leg.

"What do you want?" she asked in a hoarse whisper. It was a stupid question and she knew it, but it was the only thing that came to mind.

"You." The answer was uncompromising. Final.

Her lashes drooped and her shoulders slumped. The unfinished bow fell to the table, sprawling in an untidy pink pile. She looked up at him. "That's impossible, Ryan, and I think deep down you know it."

"I don't know any such thing!" he told her impatiently. "And neither do you. I thought we had it all worked out. I thought we had come to an agreement we could both live with."

Ginna began an agitated pacing of the small workroom. "I thought so, too, but I can't marry you knowing Erin hates me!"

He grabbed her upper arm as she passed and jerked her so close she could count the lines fanning from his eyes. "Hates you? She loves you, dammit!"

Unable to meet his eyes, she kept her gaze focused on the pulse hammering in his tanned throat. He smelled so unbearably good, she thought, breathing deeply of the faint scent of a musky men's cologne, the aroma of tobacco and an inexplicably arousing smell that was stamped exclusively "Ryan." She wanted to put her arms around him and beg him to make love to her, to help her forget Erin—to forget everything except how she felt in his arms. But she couldn't.

She looked pointedly at his hand on her arm, then lifted her eyes to his. He released her immediately. Her voice shook with emotion as she asked, "If she loves me, why did she jerk away from me when I went in to her that night? And how could she come down to breakfast the next day and behave as if nothing happened between us?"

Ryan hooked one long leg over the corner of the work table and half sat on the edge. "Guilt."

"Guilt?"

He nodded. "She was guilty because we found her with Kyle. Guilty and sorry. She told me she knew how badly you were hurt that night."

Ginna gave a short laugh and resumed her pacing. "I imagine she was tickled pink."

"No," he said with a slow shake of his head, "she wasn't. She was sorry she'd done anything to hurt either of us."

Her brows lifted in a gesture of disbelief. "After how she's treated me I find that hard to believe."

"It's true."

"Erin would tell you anything. She loves you, but she doesn't love me or need me, Ryan. She proved that when she turned to you instead of me."

"She explained all that. Everything. She said it was the guilt over hurting us and the realization of how wrong she'd been about things."

She stopped and pivoted sharply toward him. "What do you mean, 'how wrong she'd been about things'?"

"The sex. You and I know firsthand how hard it is to keep things platonic. While she was dating Kyle, Erin was in the process of finding out."

Ginna covered her face with her hands. "I can't bear to think about them..."

Rising, Ryan went to her and pulled her hands from her face. His eyes met hers tenderly and his hand smoothed back her hair. The warmth of his breath caressed her face as he said, "Nothing happened. They both swear that it never has. What I'm trying to make you see is that this thing with Kyle—as hurtful as it was for all of us—brought Erin face to face with the same emotions we struggled with seventeen years ago. Knowing what you went through by experiencing it herself has made her realize just how hard it is to say no to something you want very badly. And knowing, she can give both of us the forgiveness she might not have been able to before."

She looked up into the handsome earnestness of his face, her eyes awash with tears. "I'd like to believe that."

"You can believe it. She's the one who sent me after you."

Her head jerked upward. "She did?"

He nodded and smiled. "She was hysterical when I got home—crying and blaming herself for your leaving. I thought I never would get her settled down enough to come after you. Then when I did get here, I couldn't find you."

Remembrances of the hellish night he had suffered refueled the anger he'd felt the night before. He grasped her shoulders and gave her a single sharp shake. "I was scared to death. I called everyone I knew. Out of sheer desperation, I finally called your mother a little while ago. She told me you spent the night there."

Reaching up, she smoothed the frown from his forehead and blinked back the tears still threatening. "Don't be mad. I can't stand it."

The frown disappeared. He cupped her cheeks with his palms. "Why on earth would you spend the night at your mother's?"

She shrugged and gazed up at him with eyes framed with wet, spiky lashes. "You know her almost as well as I do. I can't explain it. Like a child, I just needed to see my mother."

"And?"

She smiled a watery smile. "And she's really a very nice lady. We did a lot of catching up last night, but there's a lot more to do. Like Erin, I understand a lot of things now I never did before. And I think she's someone I'd like to get to know better."

"Do you want to tell me about it?"

She shook her head. "Not now. Maybe…later," she said with a quaking voice that broke completely as she forfeited her battle with her emotions and began to cry in earnest.

Ryan pulled her close. She cried slow, silent tears that cleansed the hurt from her heart. Finally she stopped, blew her nose on the handkerchief he offered, and asked, "So what do you want to do now?"

A slow smile slashed creases into his lean unshaven cheeks. "That's a mighty leading question, babe," he said, pocketing the handkerchief.

Red inched upward over her face. "Ryan..."

"Be still, Ginna LeGrand," he murmured, lowering his mouth to hers. Her breath soughed from her in a sigh of contentment. The touch of his lips erased any lingering pain, negated any stubborn doubts. Her arms went around his neck. His circled her waist. She leaned into the strength of him, allowing him to take her weight, knowing she could give him her cares. Without a doubt, the strength inside Ryan was as deep as the taproots of the Catalpa trees back home.

"Does this mean I get to buy the Petal Pusher?"

Ryan looked over the top of Ginna's head to Kay, who stood in the doorway, the sun turning the curly mop of her hair into a flaming nimbus. His lips curled into a smile. "Yeah," he answered laconically.

"Good." Kay passed through the room heading toward the shop. As she passed the couple, she winked at Ginna and held up her fingers in a victory sign. Ryan chuckled. Ginna stood in the circle of his embrace with her mouth hanging open.

"What's going on?" she asked. "I feel like there's a conspiracy going on behind my back."

He released her abruptly. She watched in amazement as he strode across the room and entered the large walk-in cooler that held the fresh flowers. When he stepped outside, he held an armful of red roses.

"Ryan, what are you doing?" she asked as he thrust the roses at her.

He smiled lopsidedly. "I planned on coming here and ordering a dozen roses just like I did before. You know—a remake of the first time I came here. I thought that I'd take it easy, woo you with some old-fashioned courting and make you see how good it could be between us again. Maybe even do some parking at Mr. Avery's place like we used to. But I've just realized I don't have time for the courtship this time, Ginna. I want us to be together too badly and we've wasted too much time as it is. Besides, I'm way too old to make out in the back seat of a car."

Ginna stared a him, hope burgeoning in her heart. "What are you trying to say, Ryan?"

"Marry me. Come back to Louisiana and be my wife. Be Erin's mother. We need you. We can have a good life together."

He didn't offer her love. He made her no promises he couldn't keep. But he wanted to share his life with her. It was an offer she couldn't refuse, even if she wanted to. "Yes," she said with a tremulous smile, placing the roses on the table and going into his arms. "Yes."

"And you won't ever run away from me again?" he asked.

She shook her head. "Never."

The following morning, Ginna sat next to Ryan in the single-engine Bonanza airplane. Already strapped in, she sat with white-knuckled intensity and a pale face while he checked out the small aircraft prior to their takeoff for Louisiana. He shot an amused glance her way, catching her in the process of chewing off her lip-stick.

"It's okay to breathe," he told her sardonically.

Breath whooshed from her lungs.

Ryan laughed. He didn't understand her terror of flying, but maybe he could help her to overcome it. Slowly, patiently, he explained what each instrument was for, taking her step-by-step through the pre-flight checklist. By the time he finished there was a touch of color in her face, even though tension still showed in the set of her jaw and unease rested in the depths of her eyes. Then he started the engine.

"Oh, Ryan, I don't know about this!" she wailed.

"It's going to be all right," he assured her as the plane taxied toward the runway.

"But it's so small..."

"Ginna, I've been doing this for years," he soothed. "You just relax. We'll be home in no time."

He waited for clearance from the tower, and soon the small aircraft was racing down the strip of asphalt. As usual, when the wheels left the tarmac, her stomach summersaulted. She swallowed and tried to think of Erin and the future the three of them would have together when they got back. She sneaked a look out the window at the ground that was growing increasingly farther away. *If* they got back, she amended dizzily.

"How long?" she asked, darting Ryan a glance and finding him perfectly at ease.

"How long what?"

"Until we get there?"

He smiled. "Good grief! You sound like Erin when she was little, asking every five minutes 'how long till we get there?'"

She didn't return his smile. "How long?'

"This plane flies about one-hundred-eighty miles an hour. You figure it out."

"How far from Chicago to Shreveport?"

"As the bird flies?" he asked with a grin. "Let's just say we'll be home before lunch."

Gradually, as the trip progressed and Ginna didn't hear any strange sounds in the engine, she began to relax, occasionally sneaking looks out the window. Different crops showed up as different hues of green, and the rich black earth of the Illinois farmland, plowed in different directions, looked like pieces of corduroy. The ground resembled a giant patchwork quilt, pieced by the hand of God and adorned with narrow ribbons of roads and highways.

Ryan pointed out things of interest and kept up a steady stream of small talk to keep her mind occupied. By the time they crossed into Missouri the events of the past few days had taken their toll on her small reserve of energy. Lulled by the monotonous hum of the engine, she fell asleep. When she woke up they were in southern Arkansas and her stomach was letting her know she hadn't eaten before she left.

"What time is it?" she asked, yawning and stretching as best she could in the confines of the cabin.

"Obviously time to land this thing and feed you if the sound your stomach has been making is anything to go by." When she threw him a dirty look, he said, "We'll be landing in a little over a half an hour."

"Do your parents know I'm coming back with you?"

"Of course they do."

She smiled. "Do you think Nora will have fried chicken for lunch?"

Ryan smiled back. "I think she mentioned it for dinner," he said. "Did I tell you I talked to the lady at Country Village?"

"No. What about?"

"Selling it to you, of course. It's fairly close and does a really great business." He grinned at the surprise on her face.

"Ryan, you didn't..."

"Oh, yes, I did. It's yours. Lock, stock and bank note."

Ginna felt those dratted tears stinging beneath her lashes again. "I don't know what to say. I love it! I don't know what to say but thank you."

He cleared his throat. "That's good enough. I've also been looking around the farm for a place to build our house."

"Our house? We're building a house?"

"Of course. I can't live with my mom and dad all my life, can I?" he teased.

She laughed. "You're right. It's high time you moved out."

The time passed faster than she expected as they talked over their plans for the future. The hills gave way to pastureland and gradually to more sophisticated vistas of houses, subdivisions and eventually the city itself, as they neared the airport.

Ginna could see the Red River that severed Bossier City from Shreveport. She sighed, happy to be nearing the journey's end. Happy to be facing a future with Ryan.

"Damn!"

"What is it?" she asked, something in his voice wiping the pleasure from her face.

He glanced at her suddenly ashen features. "The landing gear won't lower," he said, not thinking to soften the answer.

Her eyes filled with renewed terror. "B-But I thought you had it checked out?"

"I did," he said tersely. "It worked just fine when I landed at Midway. Don't panic yet, babe. I've still got the manual control."

Ginna watched as he pulled the knob that would release the lock hook. He swore under his breath.

"What is it now?"

"The gear is frozen in the up position," he explained. He swore softly. "Even though it checked out okay, I was going to let Luke have a look at it, but he wasn't back yet. When you left, I didn't even give it a thought. All I could think about was coming after you."

Ginna looked at him for long seconds, her fear freezing out every other emotion. So much for their future together. So much for plans and dreams. So much for new beginnings. "We're going to crash." It wasn't so much a question as a statement of fact.

"We aren't going to crash," Ryan consoled, reaching for the radio switch. "There's nothing the matter with the engine. I'll take it down just like I would any other time. The only difference will be that we'll slide in." He shifted his attention to the radio. "Mayday! Mayday!"

"We'll slide in and the plane will burst into flames!" Ginna cried, the panic in her voice full-grown.

"You've been watching too much television," he growled. "Mayday! Mayday! This is Bonanza 53782 calling Shreveport tower."

A calm voice came back over the wire. "We read you Bonanza 53782. Go ahead."

"We have a malfunction in the landing gear and request emergency vehicles at landing."

"Roger. Give me your present position."

Ginna's mind shut out the rest of the conversation between the air control tower and Ryan, zeroing in on one thought. They were going to die and he would never know she loved him. She looked over at him, seeing the tension etched at the corners of his mouth, the determination in the set of his jaw and the concentration in his eyes as they approached the runway. The ground rushed up at them with awesome speed.

There was a sudden roaring in Ginna's ears. The earth shifted and things began to happen in slow motion. Fear was a metallic taste in her mouth. She felt the impact as the plane hit the ground as easily as Ryan's skill allowed. The sickening sound of the metal belly scraping and screeching as it plowed its way across the surface of the runway sounded very far away.

Then she heard a soft, unintelligible sound, heard Ryan snap, "Well, now's a helluva time to tell me." She was too frightened to even wonder at the strange statement. Clutching the arm rests, she closed her eyes to block out the sight of the inevitable, sliding into a welcome darkness. Her last thought was of Ryan.

Fighting for control of the plane, Ryan let his concentration falter one split second to glance over at Ginna's still form. She'd fainted. In that one moment, the small aircraft fishtailed with a will of its own and threw him sharply to the left as it careened into a sideways slide he couldn't control.

Then, suddenly, mercifully, it slowed to a grinding standstill.

* * *

The sound of sirens and far-away, urgent-sounding voices stabbed through the shroud of darkness enveloping her. Someone was unbuttoning her shirt; the front catch of her bra gave. Hands, capable and caring, moved over her with a thoroughness that, even in her semi-conscious state, was embarrassing, yet she couldn't summon the strength to tell them to stop. Something warm covered her. It was so comfortable here. Safe. She hadn't died when the plane hit the runway...

Comprehension sent a shot of adrenaline through her. She bolted upright in spite of the hands holding her. "Ryan!" His name was torn from her very soul.

"Shh, Ginna...shh," Ryan's voice soothed. Her wild-eyed gaze slewed around. A man, obviously with the ambulance service, stood nearby. She was on a vinyl sofa and Ryan knelt beside her. The hands on her were his. He looked troubled but fine, untouched by the landing. Wonderful. The rush of adrenaline faded, leaving her in the wake of an overpowering weakness.

"Oh, Ryan!" Her clutching fingers crawled over his forearms up to his shoulders and on up to cradle his face with loving concern. "Are you all right?"

"I'm fine. What about you?"

She sniffed, trying to control the tears that had been totally out of control the past few days. "Yes."

"You scared the daylights out of me," he confessed, pulling her close and pressing a kiss to her temple. "Do you want something? A Coke...anything?"

"I want to go home."

"You really should take her by the hospital just to make sure," the paramedic who stood near the door suggested.

Her eyes flew to the stranger's then back to Ryan's. "No. I don't want to go to the hospital. I just fainted. I'm fine."

"Okay," Ryan said placating her. "I'll take you home. I can always run you into Minden if I need to." He pried her arms from around him. "Let me call home and tell everyone what happened. I have a feeling we made the twelve o'clock news."

She nodded and sank back onto the sofa. Her hands shook. She wanted to go home. She wanted to make things right with Erin. Wanted to tell her she was sorry...that she loved her. Wanted to call her mother and tell her to live the rest of her life to the fullest. Ginna willed Ryan to hurry. She had learned one thing. Life was too fragile, too easily snatched away. She didn't want to miss a moment of what was left of hers.

Forty-five minutes later, they pulled into Catalpa's circle drive. The whole family was congregated on the front porch. Ginna thought it could almost be an instant replay of the day a couple of weeks ago when she and Erin had arrived, except this time it wasn't nerves that held her back, it was the trembling in her legs that refused to hold her upright. And this time Erin was waiting instead of arriving.

Ginna waited for Ryan to round the front of the car and help her out, the cue the family must have been waiting for. She stood beside the car, bound securely to his side while they swarmed down the steps. Nora hugged her, then Lefty did, while Kristi clung to her leg and chanted, "Auntie Gin, Auntie Gin," over and over again. She was kissed and hugged by each and every member of the LeGrand family...except Erin.

When the group finally thinned, Ginna saw Erin standing near the porch watching the welcome, a longing on her face that said without words how badly she wished she could be included. Their eyes clung as Ryan led Ginna through the midst of laughing chattering LeGrands. Mere feet from her daughter, she stopped.

Wearing a tentative, unsteady smile, Ginna held out her arms. With a cry of sorrow, Erin flew into them so hard that Ginna would have staggered backward if Ryan hadn't supported her. She held her weeping daughter tightly, thankful for second chances. The family, including Ryan, disappeared into the house.

"I'm sorry, Momma, I'm sorry," Erin sobbed. "I heard about the airplane on the news. I was afraid you were going to die..." She began to cry harder.

If possible, Ginna held Erin more tightly, rocking her back and forth. Surprisingly, she didn't cry herself. Instead, she was filled with a strange contentment. "Shh," she whispered. "It's all right. Everything is going to be all right."

Ginna wasn't certain how long they stood there at the foot of the porch steps. She didn't care. They needed this time together. Eventually, Erin cried herself out. She raised her head. Mascara ran in black rivulets down her flushed cheeks. In a voice husky with emotion and laden with sorrow she said, "I've been so horrible to you."

"It doesn't matter," Ginna assured her with a tender smile as she brushed the hair away from Erin's damp cheeks. "None of it matters. I love you."

Erin's eyes filled again.

Ginna brushed the tears away. She knew she was right. None of the past mattered, except that past mistakes would serve as guidelines for the decisions they would make as they shaped their future together. "What are you doing four days from now?" she asked.

Sniffing, Erin shrugged. "I don't know. Why?"

"I thought if you didn't have any plans, I'd let you stand up with me. Your dad and I are getting married again."

Erin's mobile features expressed several emotions in the span of a few seconds. Surprise. Disbelief. A puzzled expression. And finally a glowing happiness. "Oh, wow!" she cried at last, flinging her arms around Ginna in a brief, tight hug. "Super!"

In spite of the rough beginning, it had been a fantastic day that only got better, Ginna thought, sniffing the succulent aroma of frying chicken wafting into the living room. She had called her mother to let her know that everything and everyone was all right. Molly had surprised her by saying that she and Daniel were planning a Caribbean cruise. Ginna had a feeling that everything would be all right with them, too.

Exhausted, she sat watching television with Ryan, waiting for Nora to call them to dinner. Forced by the entire family to take it easy, she had spent the day with Ryan and Erin, talking, going to look at spots to put their house and driving to look at her new business. She sighed and snuggled closer, a contented smile curving her mouth.

Ryan gave her a quick hug and leaned to nuzzle her ear with his mouth, the five-thirty news completely forgotten. She giggled girlishly.

Ryan's low laughter joined hers and caressed her soul. "You know, babe, you sure have bad timing— unlike me."

She heard the smile in his voice and pulled back to see the humor reflected in his eyes. "What do you mean?"

"I mean, I've been waiting all day to have you to myself so that I could tell you what a rotten time you picked to tell me you still love me."

Her eyes widened. Her mouth fell open then snapped shut. "I didn't."

"Oh, yes, you did."

She leaned back and put her hands on her hips. "When?"

"Just before I brought the plane down. I was worried sick about getting us on the ground safely, and I knew you were scared to death. Then out of the clear blue, you tell me you love me."

Ginna's hands knotted in her lap as she recalled all too clearly her thoughts at that moment. It was not only possible, but probable that she had spoken those thoughts aloud. Dusty rose stained her cheeks.

"Is it true?"

She nodded.

"Why did you take so long to tell me?" he asked, reaching for her and pulling her onto his lap.

The time for lies, half truths and evasion was past. Whatever future they would have together should be built on honesty and caring if nothing more. "After I wouldn't listen to you when you told me you loved me eight years ago, I wasn't sure you would want love from me. That's why I haven't said it. And as much as I still loved you, I'm willing to accept whatever it is that you want to give me now."

"Aah, Ginna, Ginna," Ryan murmured huskily, holding her tightly to him. "We're such fools."

"Why do you say that?" she queried, glancing up at him.

"Because I haven't told you I still love you for a reason that's just about as silly. Because when I tried to tell you and you wouldn't listen to me, I was hurt. I vowed that this time you would say it first." He looked down into her upturned face. "Pretty childish, huh?"

Smiling, she shook her head. "Pretty human." Her eyes dropped to the patch of crisp hair peeking from the vee of his shirt. She twisted at a button and asked, "Is it true?"

Ryan lifted her chin with his forefinger. "What?"

"That you still love me?"

"I never stopped," he confessed. "Never."

Their lips met in a feather-light kiss. Rubbing the sweep of her eyebrow with his thumb, he said, "I'm only sorry we let so much time get away from us. There's so much we've missed out on by not being together."

"I know," she said with a sigh. "But maybe we needed the time to become the people we are now. Maybe it wouldn't have worked. I don't know. But I know that we can't worry about the past and what might have been if we'd only done things differently."

"I know you're right, but—"

Ginna put her fingers against his lips. "No 'buts'. And no regrets. Agreed?"

"Dinner!" Erin bounded into the room, her eyes shining with happiness. She came skittering to a stop when she saw her mother in her father's lap.

Both Ginna and Ryan regarded the gorgeous daughter created by the hot impatience of a young love. A suspicious moisture glittered in both pairs of eyes. Ryan's look was a caress. He smiled and shook his head. "No," he said softly, but emphatically. "No regrets."

COMING NEXT MONTH

DOUBLE JEOPARDY—Brooke Hastings
Ellie came to Raven's Island to take part in a romantic mystery-adventure game but soon found herself caught in the middle of a real romance and a real adventure where murder wasn't just a game.

SHADOWS IN THE NIGHT—Linda Turner
When Samantha was kidnapped, she knew there was little hope for her unless the handsome dark-haired smuggler risked his place in the gang and his life to help her escape.

WILDCATTER'S PROMISE—Margaret Ripy
Financially, Cade was a gambler, but emotionally he was afraid to risk anything. Kate had to convince him to take that one extra step and fill the void in their lives.

JUST A KISS AWAY—Natalie Bishop
At first it was a case of mistaken identities, but Gavin soon realized that Callie was the woman he should have been searching for all along.

OUT OF A DREAM—Diana Stuart
Tara and Brian were both trying to escape, and their chance encounter on Cape Cod was perfect, the stuff out of fantasies. But could the romance last when real life intruded? They had to find out.

WHIMS OF FATE—Ruth Langan
Kirsten couldn't forget the mysterious stranger who had stolen a kiss....
He was prince of the country and heir to the throne, and Cinderella is only a fairy tale. Isn't it?

AVAILABLE NOW:

A WALK IN PARADISE
Ada Steward

EVERY MOMENT COUNTS
Martha Hix

A WILL AND A WAY
Nora Roberts

A SPECIAL MAN
Billie Green

ROSES AND REGRETS
Bay Matthews

LEGACY OF THE WOLF
Sonja Massie